STEAK THROUGH THE HEART

A JORDAN MCALLISTER MYSTERY
BOOK 7

LIZ LIPPERMAN

PUBLISHER'S NOTE: This is a work of fiction. Names, characters,
places, and incidents either are the product of the author's
imagination or are used fictitiously. Any resemblance to actual
persons, living or dead, business establishments, events, or locales is
entirely coincidental.

Copyright © Elizabeth L. Lipperman

Published by Oliver Heber Books

OLIVER HEBER BOOKS

November 2023

Published by Oliver-Heber Books

0 9 8 7 6 5 4 3 2 1

1

"Seriously! You're going to fire me if I go to Amarillo to help my brother who's in jail there?" Jordan McAllister spit the words out the minute she bypassed Jackie Frazier's desk and marched into her boss's office. Jackie was Dwayne Egan's secretary and guarded the entry into his office like a Doberman. She wasn't real happy that Jordan had waltzed right past her without a word.

Egan glanced up at her from behind wire-rimmed glasses that accentuated his big ears. "I need you here. The newspaper is starting a two-week promotion to increase the number of subscriptions. The Kitchen Kolumn is one of our most popular features, and I'm counting on you to come up with some great recipes to wow the residents of Ranchero."

"Is the paper in trouble?"

"You might say that. A lot of folks are reading the Globe online instead of actually getting a paper delivery. The owner is going all-out with several really cool, promotional giveaways to entice new subscriptions." He looked up at her. "Sorry, but that's why you can't go to Amarillo right now. You'll have to wait until after this promo, and then we can talk about it."

Jordan glared at him. She loved her job, and the last thing she wanted was to lose it, but Danny was in trouble. When her mother called yesterday to tell her that her favorite brother was booked into the Amarillo jail on a murder charge, she knew she had to get there quickly, no matter what it took, if only to offer emotional support to her family.

Standing her ground with Egan was paramount. Danny was too important to her.

Before she could respond, her boss beat her to the punch. "Come on, McAllister. You said your brother was in jail for murder. What difference will two weeks make in the scheme of things? I promise you he's not going anywhere in the next fourteen days. He's probably already out on bail and relaxing with a beer."

She narrowed her eyes, wondering how one man could be so insensitive. How could he threaten her job because of a family emergency? Although her culinary column was popular in Ranchero, two weeks without her would probably not even be noticed. In this age of digital corresponding, she could write her column from Timbuktu, and it wouldn't matter.

She shifted her weight from one leg to the other. If looks could kill, he'd be a dead man right now. But she knew she had leverage—one trump card in her hand, and although she hated having to use it, she didn't hesitate. Since she'd taken over as the culinary editor at the Globe, subscriptions had doubled. Egan had made the mistake of letting that tidbit slip out when the original culinary reporter had come back after six months and demanded her old job back. Despite the fact that the woman was the owner's niece, Jordan had ended up with the permanent position, simply because of that increase.

After several minutes of waiting to see who would

blink first, Jordan sat down in the chair across from Egan's desk. "I wonder how many subscriptions you'll lose when people find out I've been fired."

Making a veiled threat was a risk, but she was desperate. Holding her breath, she waited in silence while her boss looked away, then turned back to her.

"So, you are to write your column and deliver it to the paper on time while you're gone. Not even five minutes late. Got it?"

She tried to hide a smile. Her ploy had worked. "Absolutely, and, honestly, you have no idea what a fantastic cook my mother is. Bet her recipes alone will attract new readers." When he still hesitated, she added, "Plus Amarillo is full of really unique places that I'm sure will interest the locals, especially if they've never been there. There's even a world-famous steak house that offers free steaks to anyone who can finish off seventy ounces of ribeye. I could write a piece every day, kinda like a tourist guide—a smaller version of The Lonely Planet."

Egan leaned back in his chair without responding. Finally, he said, "You wouldn't get paid for the extra work, you know."

What a cheapskate. "I wouldn't expect it."

He breathed in and seemed to hold it for a minute before he said, "I like the way that sounds. Now get out of here and get on the road. You said you wanted to leave by noon. You're already late. Just be sure your mom's recipes are as good as you say they are." He dismissed her with a wave of his hand. "Oh, and by the way, McAllister, you're lucky I like you."

Lucky he likes me? She'd hate to see what he'd be like if he hated her.

But to be fair, he'd come a long way since the day he called her to his office and offered her a temporary position writing the culinary column after the original reporter ended up in rehab following a jet ski accident. She'd been hired three months prior to that to write the Personals—a job she despised. She'd jumped at the culinary column offer, even though her idea of a gourmet meal was a fried bologna sandwich with potato chips on it to make it crunchy.

She stood up and walked out of the office, smiling sweetly at Jackie, who reminded her of Gilda Radner with her wild, curly black hair. Jackie, who was still breathing fire because Jordan had dared to break the rules and bully her way into Egan's office.

Walking from the elevator to her desk, she couldn't help thinking back to when she was first hired at the Ranchero Globe. What she'd thought had been the worst time in her life had actually turned out to be one of her luckiest days. Since she was a teenager throwing touchdown passes to her brothers in the front yard, all she'd ever wanted to be was a sports writer, but after graduating with a journalism degree from the University of Texas, she'd put her own dreams on hold and followed her fiancé all over Texas while he pursued his. When Brett landed a once-in-a-lifetime opportunity at a Dallas TV station, she'd thought it was finally time for her to chase her own career.

But fate had other plans, and when her conniving fiancé confessed to having an affair with the petite weather girl with humongous clouds of her own, all store-bought, of course, Jordan found herself alone in a big city with no friends or family and a bank account that would barely provide a roof over her head for the next few weeks.

Feeling dejected and unloved, she'd packed up and moved as far away from Big D as she could to try to put her life back together, landing in Ranchero, a small town on the Texas/Oklahoma border. Heartbroken and as poor as a church mouse, she ended up at Empire Apartments, a dilapidated two-story building which turned out to be a godsend.

Immediately accepted by the first-floor residents as one of their own, to her surprise, not only did she survive, but she soon came to realize how foolish she'd been to put all her trust in Brett. But truth be told, she couldn't lay all the blame on him. She'd let it happen, let his career goals take precedent over hers as she'd followed him around Texas like a puppy dog. Had she married the self-centered ass, she was sure she would have become a Stepford-wife lookalike.

It had only taken a few months for her newfound friends to smother her with the love and care she needed to get on with her life. They were her family now and were there for her at a time when she'd been so close to calling her biological family in Amarillo after Brett dumped her in Dallas.

Despite the fact that she loved her parents and siblings, that would have been a disaster. As the baby and the only girl, she'd grown up with four strapping Irish brothers, who had scared off every boy who even looked sideways at her. Without a doubt, they would have all jumped in their pickups, headed to Ranchero, and forced her to go back to Amarillo with them. She knew it would have been too easy to allow that to happen—to allow them to blanket her with their love and protection—mostly overprotection. She would never have learned how to take care of herself. That's when the good Lord placed her in the hands of the Empire Apartments residents. She loved them so much and basically, owed her livelihood to them.

Writing the Personals had been the only job she

could find where she could use her journalism skills. Ha! It didn't take a college graduate to compose three or four sentences to try to make a desperate, single person seem exciting. So when Egan came to her with the offer of culinary reporter, she'd jumped at it, before the what-were-you-thinking, mind demons blindsided her.

Growing up in a big family, she'd never been introduced to gourmet food, and to this day still hated it. Her diet included fast food and bologna, and occasionally, a fried chicken salad smothered in Ranch dressing. Because of this, she had almost turned down the temporary assignment. But her newfound family had come to her rescue once again at one of their famous Friday night potluck game nights, where her friend Rosie always served mouth-watering casseroles.

Rosella LaRue, a fiftyish hippie who still wore tie-dyed T-shirts and braided her hair, loved to cook. She'd been married four times, five if you counted her fourth husband who also was her second and had somehow managed to convince her that running off to get remarried in Vegas was a good idea. That one had ended even before the wedding ring had turned her finger green. But despite her less-than-wonderful experiences with the opposite sex, Rosie had remained a romantic and could single out a good-looking man from a block away, usually finding a way to get close enough to bat her eyelashes at the unsuspecting soul.

Sitting around the table that night playing their usual Screw Your Neighbor card game, Jordan had confessed that she was going to reject Egan's offer. After pigging out on one of Rosie's awesome casseroles her friends had convinced her that it was too good of an opportunity to pass up. In the true fashion of a political war room, they'd concocted a plan to use Rosie's casseroles as recipes in Jordan's column and slap on fancy gourmet-sounding names. Calling her famous Potato Chip Chicken, Budin de Patatas Fritas con Pollo, had probably not fooled anyone, but the good people of Ranchero didn't seem to mind. Instead, the subscription rate to the newspaper doubled. Despite the fact that there was no salary bump as editor of the Kitchen Kolumn and she would still have to write the Personals, Jordan's self-confidence slowly returned.

Glancing down at her watch, she picked up speed, almost racing to her desk. Egan had been right. She was definitely late, and her friends back at the apartment were probably pacing impatiently, waiting to get the road trip on the move.

Out of breath when she finally made it to her desk, she grabbed her laptop, notepad, and pencil case that she'd had since college, and her purse from the locked drawer, and headed for the door, grateful that her friends were coming to her rescue once again. They hadn't hesitated about going with her to Amarillo when they found out her brother was in trouble. In fact, they'd insisted, which gave Jordan a little comfort, knowing she would have all that support around her in case...

Don't go there, Jordan.

But even as her brain tried to derail that line of thinking, a niggling fear of what she would find in her birth city almost made her throw up.

～

"DOES your mother know you're bringing all of us, Jordan?" Lola Van Horn asked from the front seat of the Suburban.

Lola was the matriarch of the group and owned Lola's Spiritual Readings in downtown Ranchero, where some of the most famous people visited regularly. Her puffy lips and tattooed eyeliner were a gift from one such client, a well-known plastic surgeon from Dallas who couldn't go one week without a reading.

"Yes. I've talked so much about you guys, and she's anxious to meet all of you. Matter of fact, she already has big plans for dinner tonight."

That got Victor Rodriguez's attention, and he twisted toward Jordan in the backseat. "What kind of big plans?" He chuckled. "Hope she also has big plans for a high calorie dessert. I have to get all my carbs in before Michael arrives on Wednesday and tries to get me to eat healthy."

Victor, who owned and operated Yesterday's Treasures, an antique store next to Lola's shop in downtown Ranchero, was also the owner of Empire Apartments with his partner Michael Cafferty. It had been apparent to Jordan from the first moment she'd met him that the man had no filter and sometimes said the most outrageous things that always made her laugh. Short and a little pudgy, Victor had become her best friend and partner in crime.

"She's making a huge pot of beef stew, along with her homemade jalapeño beer bread."

Victor licked his lips. "I haven't had beef stew since..." He thought for a minute. "Actually, I can't remember ever having it."

"Then you're in for a surprise, my friend." Rosie turned to Jordan. "Do you think your mother might share her recipe with me? My mom used to make beef stew all the time for me when I was a kid. I could kick myself for not getting her recipe before she got so sick."

"Oh yeah! My mom will definitely share the recipe. She says the best compliment is when somebody eats what you cooked and then asks for the recipe." Jordan glanced out the window. "Actually, my mom's recipes are how I convinced old tightwad Egan to let me go to Amarillo in the first place and still have my job when I return to Ranchero."

"You're going to print her recipes in your column?" Ray Varga asked from the driver seat. "Cool. You can call it *Boeuf Bourguignon*, French for beef stew," he continued before she had time to answer.

"That's ingenious. When we get to Amarillo, I need you to write that down for me. Along with my mom's recipes, I also promised my boss I'd write about the local attractions as kind of a touristy thing." She tapped Ray's shoulder. "Hate to ask, but I drank way too much coffee before I left. Any chance we can stop at the next gas station?"

"Anything for you, sugar." Ray was a no-nonsense retired cop who had always had a soft spot in his heart for Jordan. God help anyone who harmed her in any way. Jordan was sure that if he could have gotten his hands on the cheating Brett, her ex would be toast right now. Ray was also the father figure of the group and shared more than a cup of sugar with Lola, the love of his life.

"So, Jordan, what about dessert?" Victor asked impatiently. "You know how I need my sugar fix."

Rosie snickered. "Who doesn't know that? You'd better overdose on sweets before Michael gets here and cuts you off."

"Seriously, Rosie, you of all people should know how many times Michael has tried to get me to eat better. Somehow, I always win and can usually get him to apologize for even suggesting it." Victor tsked. "Cut me off, my butt."

"You're lucky Michael is such a good guy who hates confrontation," Jordan said before adding. "He's probably the only man on this planet who could live with you without killing you."

Everyone laughed, including Victor. "I wouldn't talk if I were you, sweet cheeks," he countered. "What that gorgeous FBI hunk sees in you is beyond me. You're so quirky, I'm probably the only one who can stand you."

She slapped his shoulder playfully. "Shut up, or I'll tell my mother that there will be absolutely no desserts this week."

Victor frowned. "You wouldn't dare—would you?" When she nodded, he threw up his hands. "Okay, I take it all back. I'm just as quirky as you are. That's why I get you." He took a breath. "So, where is that gorgeous FBI guy, anyway?"

"Alex is driving up with Michael on Wednesday. He needed to stay in town a few days to debrief." Jordan patted Ray's shoulder. "Nature is screaming at me, so unless you want a 'cleanup on aisle 2,' you'd better find a gas station soon."

"There's one up ahead. I can see the sign," Ray responded.

No one spoke again until Ray had pulled into the parking lot at Buc-ee's. "Might as well fill up while I'm here."

"I love this place," Lola said. "They always have the neatest things and the best snack foods. Come on. Let's check it out."

After fifteen minutes of browsing the huge store,

they were on the road again, each snacking from bags of goodies.

"You never did tell us what happened to Alex in Mexico, Jordan." Ray said between bites of a huge brownie.

Jordan swallowed the last of her own brownie. "Honestly, I don't know, Ray. I only had last night with him, and neither of us wanted to waste the little bit of time we had together talking about the unpleasant things that had happened to both of us."

"So he doesn't know that you almost got yourself killed at the casino in Oklahoma last weekend?" Rosie asked.

Jordan shook her head. "Not yet. Don't forget that until he walked into my apartment last night, no one had heard from him for several days. Even his handlers had lost contact. Whatever happened to him was probably way worse than what I went through."

"I know how worried you were, thinking the worst. Cartels can be vicious," Rosie said, before adding, "When he's ready to tell us what happened, he will. In the meantime, we'll give it a rest and concentrate on what's happening in Amarillo, where your brother is sitting in a jail cell right now. I know if we put our heads together, we can figure out a way to help him."

"From your lips to God's ear," Jordan said, turning away so they wouldn't notice how worried she really was about Danny. She had just gotten a brief reprise from worrying about Alex when he'd surprised her and walked into her apartment. Then her mother had called with the news about her youngest son.

So much for no more worrying.

She knew Alex well enough to understand that whatever it was that he'd been through while working undercover with the worst cartel in Mexico, it was still too painful for him to verbalize. One good thing that had come out of all this was that whatever that experience was, it had made him realize that life was too short to waste another minute on things that just don't matter.

That's when he'd dropped to one knee and asked her to spend the rest of her life with him.

She'd been dating Alex for several years and had erected too many walls to count to protect herself from ever going through another Brett experience. But despite her own history of bad relationships, she hadn't hesitated and said *yes* immediately.

She smiled to herself, remembering that the only reason she and Alex had gotten together in the first place was because he'd thought she was a diamond smuggler. Patiently, he'd broken down—no, destroyed—every last one of those walls. But before they had a chance to celebrate, she'd received the call from her mother. And now, less than twenty-four hours since she'd said *yes* to his proposal, she was in Ray's Suburban on the way to Amarillo with her gang.

And without her fiancé.

Her brother Danny was the only one in her family who'd met Alex once when he'd shown up in Ranchero on a work-related job. As an officer in TSCRA, Texas and Southwestern Cattle Raisers Association, he'd been sent to the small town to investigate a cattle-rustling ring. With the FBI's help, the mission was successful, and Danny and Alex had become fast friends.

It was hard to fathom that now, they were going to Amarillo to try to prove her brother's innocence in a murder case.

Sweet, carefree Danny. He could barely kill a

mouse, even after he'd trapped it. Was he even capable of killing a real person?

Oh God! Of course, he wasn't capable, so what made the Amarillo police think they had enough evidence to prove that he was? There had to be a reason why he'd ended up in a hotel room beside an exotic dancer with a steak knife in her chest.

But as hard as she tried, she just couldn't come up with a logical reason at the moment.

"Driving through Wichita Falls takes me back to when I was stationed at Sheppard Air Force Base," Ray said, successfully interrupting her negative thoughts. "I love this town."

"It looks so flat and dry," Victor said. "Do they really have a waterfall, or did they just name it that because it sounded good?"

"They really do have one," Ray said. "Although it's a man-made one now. The original waterfalls washed away in a flood in the 1800s. The new one was constructed in 1987 and is a multilevel cascade on the south bank of the Wichita River."

"Do we have time to go look at it?" Victor asked. "I love that kind of stuff."

Ray glanced down at his watch. "Sorry. Jordan promised her mom we'd be there before dark. We've got another four-and-a-half hours to go." When Victor pouted, Ray added, "The good news is that we'll be able to see the waterfalls when we cross the bridge on I-44."

"Promise me that if we have time on our way home, we'll swing by and have a look-see."

"That can be arranged," Ray said, turning off the radio. "After we pass the waterfalls, you all should try to get a little shut-eye before we get to Amarillo. My guess is that we're going to be up late tonight."

Jordan leaned back in the seat and tried to do just that, but her mind wouldn't let her. She kept seeing an image of her brother in jail. Danny was the brother that she was closest to, and although she knew he was incapable of murder, what would make the police so sure he was guilty and drag him off to jail?

She prayed that between Ray and Alex, they could figure out what that something was. Right now, his future, and possibly his life, depended on it.

2

Ray parked the Suburban in the McAllister driveway around 6:30, and they all piled out.

"I am literally starving," Victor said. "Your mom could be serving peanut butter and jelly sandwiches, and I'd be a happy camper right now."

"Lucky for you, she would die before serving that to guests." Jordan pushed open the front door, and the smell of something wonderful cooking in the kitchen immediately hit her.

She ushered the others in just as her mom appeared in the hallway and ran to her. After a long hug, she held Jordan out in front of her. "I can't even tell you what a sight for sore eyes you are. I'm so grateful you could come, although I knew you would never let me down." She sniffed as a few tears ran down her cheeks. "Your brothers are trying to be helpful, but they'd just as soon punch a guy in the face than reason with him. Thankfully, they've managed to stay out of jail themselves."

Jordan glanced around the living room. "Where are they? I would have thought they'd be here with you."

Sylvia McAllister pulled a tissue from her pocket

and swiped at the tears. "They were here last night, and I sent them home. They all have families and jobs, and there was really nothing more they could do since Danny's bail hearing isn't until tomorrow morning." She nailed Jordan with her eyes. "I'm counting on you to handle your brothers. The last thing we need is for one of them to let their temper get out of control. Danny's already in enough trouble as it is."

"I'll give it my best shot, but you know how they are, especially Sean. His favorite thing in life is talking smack to people he can't stand."

She took a moment to study her mother. Sylvia McAllister was a petite woman who had once been a promising dancer, and then after she got married, an instructor with her own studio. She'd never been able to get back into dancing because her kids all came soon after she'd walked down the aisle. Her hope had always been that she could turn Jordan into a ballet dancer and live vicariously through her, dreaming of watching her on stage as the principal dancer in *Swan Lake*, but that was not to be. Once her four brothers discovered that their baby sister could thread a perfect spiral between two defenders the full length of their front yard, it was a lost cause—not that Jordan was even remotely interested in putting on a tutu and dancing on her toes. She'd loved competing with her strapping brothers—loved that they all fought for her to be the quarterback of their team.

That was also the reason she'd never learned to cook. It was hard to give up time with her dad and brothers in the front yard, especially in the fall when the weather was crisp—perfect for a football game, not that the McAllister men would have allowed that.

Jordan smiled at her mom. "As anxious as I am about hearing what happened with Danny, that can wait. We have all night. Right now, let's all chill out before dinner."

Sylvia glanced toward the gang. "I hope you know how appreciative I am that you all came to support my daughter. She is so lucky to have you in her life."

"Not nearly as lucky as we are," Lola said.

"Mrs. McAllister—" Rosie addressed her before being interrupted.

"Please call me Sylvia. I think we're going to be good friends before this is all over."

"Hope so," Rosie continued. "I'm not sure if Jordan mentioned it, but I'm the cook for this motley crew. I would be honored to help you with dinner."

"Finally! I'm about to melt away from starvation," Victor said.

Several heads turned and gave him the stink-eye.

"What?" he asked of everyone glaring at him.

"You must be Victor," Sylvia said with a laugh. "Jordan has told me all about you. Actually, I've heard stories about all of you and already feel like you're part of my family."

Suddenly, Jordan remembered that this was the first time her mother was meeting her friends. "Where are my manners?" She turned to the gang standing behind her and introduced them one by one to her mother.

After acknowledging each of them, Sylvia gestured toward the kitchen. "Rosie, I appreciate your offer and will keep it in mind for the rest of the week, but tonight's dinner is ready to be served. Jordan has talked so much about your delicious casseroles, I definitely want to pick your brain about them. This German girl loves casseroles."

Rosie laughed. "Funny! I said the same thing about you and your recipes in the car."

That brought a smile to Sylvia's face. "Then let's get to it." She glanced toward Jordan. "Find out want your friends want to drink. I have strawberry sangria, peach iced tea, sodas, and coffee."

"Say no more," Jordan said. "We're all about the sangria. I'll get the glasses."

When they were all seated, Jordan helped her mother bring in the food and place it on the lazy Susan in the middle of the table. After they all had full bowls of the stew and a big piece of hot, buttered, beer bread in front of them, Ray led them in prayer, asking the good Lord to find it in his heart to be with Danny throughout his ordeal.

"Holy cow! I'd forgotten how good this was, Mom," Jordan said, after devouring her second bowl of stew. "I'll definitely need to print this in tomorrow's edition of the *Globe*." She giggled. "Ray's already dubbed it *Boeuf Bourguignon*."

"French beef stew. I like it," Sylvia said, getting up to clear the plates.

"Oh, no you don't," Lola said. "You cooked—we clean."

"Sounds like a plan," Sylvia replied. "I'll get dessert."

Victor's eyes lit up. "Did you say dessert? I'm glad I saved some room."

"I've been told that you have a gigantic sweet tooth. How does German Chocolate Poke Cake sound?"

"Like I've died and gone to sugar heaven," Victor deadpanned. He jumped up and began collecting the plates. "Come on. Let's get this cleaned up. The chocolate is calling my name, not to mention the coconut and the pecans." He winked at Sylvia. "Any more of that strawberry sangria? It was awesome."

"Absolutely," Sylvia said. "I'll bring the pitcher in with the cake."

When she was totally stuffed and unable to put another bite into her mouth, Jordan asked her mom, "Are you ready to tell us about Danny?"

"Not much to tell, really. Your brothers weren't able to get any new information from the police. What little we do know is that they found Danny naked in bed next to a stripper—also naked—in a room at the Lazy Days Motel on the outskirts of town. The woman had a knife in her chest, and according to the cops, it had Danny's prints all over it."

"I can't believe that," Jordan said, angrily. "Everyone knows that Danny wouldn't hurt a fly."

Sylvia lowered her head. "Apparently, your brother had scratch marks all over his chest. The police believe he got them while the woman was fighting for her life. That's not something a mother wants to hear about her son."

"Any other details?" Ray, who had been unusually quiet throughout the entire dinner, asked, leaning forward to make eye contact with Sylvia at the other end of the table.

"I'd forgotten you were a former policeman. Please forgive me if I've given the impression that I think the cops are the bad guys here." She shook her head. "I really don't believe that. I know they're just doing their job."

"No apologies necessary. It's not every day you're told that your son may have been involved in such a heinous crime," Ray said. "Do you have any more details about what the cops found? Were there drugs involved? Alcohol? How long had Danny known this woman?"

"Unfortunately, I don't have answers to any of

those question. I'm sure Jordan has mentioned that
her other three brothers are all hotheads, and they
wasted no time causing a ruckus at the police station.
After Sean called one of them a bloated jerk who was
full of himself, the police kicked all three of them out
and told them not to come back until they calmed
down."

"Does Danny have a lawyer?" Ray asked.

"Patrick worked in the District Attorney's office in
Lubbock for a few years before he took a position
teaching law at Texas Tech. He's going to defend his
brother."

"That's not a good idea," Ray said. "There are too
many emotions in play here. Patrick may be one heck
of a law professor, but he's Danny's brother. I'm not
sure he could put those feelings aside and stay neutral
in the courtroom while the DA paints your son as a
cold-blooded killer. Danny needs a bulldog, in-your-
face lawyer who's not afraid to use anything in his
power to get him acquitted, even if it's only because of
reasonable doubt and not a true vindication that he
didn't kill that woman."

"Ray's right, Mom. Let Patrick be at his side as a
brother and not ask him to be the one holding Danny's future in his hands. He would never get over it if
he somehow failed and Danny had to go to prison—or
worse."

Sylvia thought about it for a moment. "You're both
right." Turning to Ray, she asked, "Do you happen to
know any 'bulldog' lawyers from this area?"

"No, but I have a buddy in Amarillo who graduated with me from the Academy. Like me, he retired
many years ago. Last I heard, his youngest son was
now a lieutenant in the Amarillo Police Department.
Let me do some digging and see what I can come up

with. I feel certain he'll be able to tell us who to call. There's always that one badass—excuse my French— defense lawyer that the cops hate to face in the courtroom."

Sylvia took a deep breath and blew it out slowly. "You all have been here less than two hours, and I'm already feeling more hopeful. As much as I hated calling you, Jordan, I'm glad..." She stopped talking abruptly when her phone vibrated. After glancing down at caller ID, she was unable to hide the fear in her eyes. "It's the police station."

After two minutes of conversation, she hung up and closed her eyes for a few seconds, as if to compose herself before facing the group. The look on her face told them that whatever it was, it was not good news.

"Danny got into it with a rancher and his son in the holding cell, and the two of them apparently beat him to a pulp. He's at the hospital now awaiting surgery to stop any internal bleeding and to pin his fractured wrist. I need to get to Amarillo General *now*."

"Jordan, you go with her. We'll clean up and get settled into the bedrooms upstairs. We can always change rooms later tonight if necessary. Call us the minute you know something," Lola said.

"I will. Come on, Mom. I'll drive your car."

There was very little conversation on the twenty-minute ride to the hospital, both of them deep into their own thoughts. All Jordan could do was pray.

Please don't let him die.

~

AT THE HOSPITAL, they were directed to the emergency room, where they were told Danny was waiting to be transported to surgery. As soon as they pushed the curtain back and walked into the cubicle, tears welled up in Jordan's eyes.

"Oh my God!" Sylvia said, staring at her youngest son who was sporting two black eyes, stitches above his right eyebrow, and had his left arm in a sling.

Danny tried to smile, but failed miserably, only making Sylvia cry out. "What did they do to you?" She bent down to hug him, then backed up when he yelped in pain.

"I've got two broken ribs on that side, Mom, but if you come over to my other side, you can lay some love on me like you used to when I was a kid and Sean and Tommy would beat me up over something stupid that I did." Danny glanced up at his sister. "So, apparently it takes me nearly getting killed to get your skinny ass back to Amarillo?"

She nodded, sniffing at the same time. "I can't even trade insults with you right now. You have me at your mercy." She moved closer to the bed and grabbed his hand. "Why did they do this to you?"

He tsked. "Last year I caught old man Tucker and his kid selling contaminated meat after several of their cows came down with E-coli. Although he'd been in- structed to euthanize the remainder of his small herd, he decided that since he didn't have insurance, he didn't want to take the loss. I only found out about it after a woman in Lubbock came down with the dis- ease and nearly died after eating one of his steaks."

"And they recognized you?" Jordan asked.

"You bet they did. When I discovered what they'd done, I made certain that the county recalled all his beef. Even sent a vet to his ranch to personally put down the remaining fifty or so Longhorns." His grin disappeared. "Then I slapped him with a hefty fine that nearly bankrupted the old geezer as a warning to all the ranchers out there. Guess he never forgot about that."

"Good heavens! I worry about Sean, always running into fires on the job, but I had no idea I would have to worry about you. I thought you sat in your office at the cattle association and signed papers all day."

"If only that were true. But honestly, Mom, I'm not usually in any danger. Apparently, Tucker and his son were jailed on a drunk-and-disorderly charge on Monday afternoon, and they recognized me immediately. I asked the cop not to put them in there with me since the man had a beef with me—pun intended— and had threatened to kill me on more than one occasion. The cop just laughed and said I should've thought of that before killing somebody. The minute they left us alone, Tucker and his son attacked me, and although the police came quickly when they heard me screaming, the damage was already done." He shook his head. "Hell, both the old man and his kid are probably close to 300 pounds. I didn't stand a chance."

Just then two people in scrubs appeared and said they were ready to take him to the operating room. The taller of the two introduced himself as the anesthesiologist who would be putting Danny to sleep and gave him what he called a pre-sedative directly into the IV tubing.

"See you on the other side," Danny said, barely able to keep his eyes open as they wheeled him down the hallway.

"He'll come back to room 318 on the third floor, the surgery post-op ward," the nurse explained. "You can go up there now to wait for him. There's a vending machine outside the unit if you're hungry or want coffee."

"Thanks," Jordan said, before turning to her mother. "Wish that vending machine had some of your strawberry sangria in there. I could really use a glass of that right now."

"Me too," Sylvia said, before facing the nurse. "Do you have any idea how long my son will be in surgery?"

"He'll most likely be gone for a few hours. They're taking him for an MRI of his abdomen first to rule out any internal bleeding. If there is none, the actual repair of his wrist shouldn't take too long after that."

Jordan thanked her, then she and her mother headed down the hall to the elevators that would take them upstairs to the post-op unit. When they got to the room and opened the door, they were surprised to find two police officers already there next to a bed with handcuffs on both rails.

"You can't be in here." The older of the two stood to block their entrance.

Sylvia stepped forward. "Young man, I'm his mother, and this is his sister. I'd like to see you try and stop us."

The policeman whispered something to his partner before stepping aside and waving them into the room. Jordan had never seen her mother defy authority like that and was totally surprised by her strong response. Mentally, she high-fived her as they walked in and sat down in the chairs by the empty bed.

"Should we call my brothers?" Jordan asked.

Sylvia pointed to the cops who were now seated on chairs outside the door. "Let's wait until Danny's out of surgery. Knowing those boys like I do, I'm sure they'll rush over here and just be in the way. Probably ruffle a few feathers as well." She exhaled slowly. "We'll call them the minute we know more about his condition. Tomorrow is soon enough for them to go full-out McAllister crazy on everyone. Hopefully, by the time they get here, your friend will have a lawyer for us, and that may calm them down somewhat."

"Okay. If anyone can find us a good lawyer, it's Ray."

"I like all your friends, by the way, especially Victor. He makes me laugh."

"He cracks me up, too. He was the first one to greet me when I moved to my apartment."

"So when are we going to meet your FBI man? Or is that past tense now?"

"Gosh, with all the drama going on here I almost forgot to tell you that Alex proposed last night, right before you called about Danny. He's driving up on Wednesday with Michael, Victor's partner, and you can finally meet your future son-in-law."

When Jordan's meaning sank in, Sylvia stood and hugged her. "I'm so happy for you. Maybe now your brothers will finally cut you loose and let you live your life." She sighed. "Good heavens! I hope they don't run him off like they did with every other man who attempted to catch your eye."

Jordan laughed. "Alex doesn't scare easily."

That wasn't entirely true. Something had happened on his last assignment that had changed him, but she wasn't about to get into that with her mother. If she told her about Alex's ordeal, she would have to confess to nearly getting herself killed at the casino. It was best left unsaid, only because of the McAllister boys, who would think they still needed to protect her —especially here in Amarillo.

"That's good. I'm hoping my overbearing offspring have finally met their match," Sylvia said. "I can't wait to meet him. I only wish your father was here to meet him as well."

"I'm surprised Dad didn't hop on the first plane from Abu Dhabi the minute he heard about Danny," Jordan commented.

"You have no idea how hard it was for me to keep him from doing that. But fortunately, I was able to convince him there really wasn't anything he could do back here and the business trip was too important to postpone. What finally tipped the scales was when he heard you were on your way home. He promised to wrap things up early and be on the first plane back on Saturday."

"I'm so proud of the way you're dealing with all this, Mom." Jordan scrunched her eyebrows and stared at her mom. "I'm curious, though. What would you have done if the cops had still barred us from the room even after you challenged them?"

"My next move was to tell them we were already looking into a civil suit and offer to let them speak directly to our lawyer."

"That would have been a good bluff, Mother dear," Jordan said with a grin before turning serious again. "So back to Dad, I'll bet he's going crazy with worry and feeling helpless so far away."

"When I tell him that you brought an ex-cop and an FBI guy with you, it should ease some of his fears."

"Hope so." Jordan thought about her dad sitting in a hotel in the Middle East, trying to concentrate on business while his youngest son lay battered and bruised in the hospital.

Colin McAllister was CEO of one of the largest meatpacking companies in Hereford, a small town

about fifty miles southwest of Amarillo and affectionately dubbed the meat capital of the world. Jordan
knew his company was on the verge of a multi- million
dollar deal with the Arab Federations composing the
UAE to import Texas beef. She also knew that her
mother was smart enough to know how important
this negotiation was to her dad and his company.
Jordan vowed to do everything in her power to help
her family get through this, especially now that she
knew how much her dad counted on her.

It felt good being thought of as the adult in the
room.

She laid her head back and quickly dozed off.
Around midnight she was awakened when she heard
loud voices outside the door. At first she thought
Danny was coming back from surgery, but one of the
voices was oddly familiar, and she strained to listen.

When the door opened and she came face-to-face
with Alex, she jumped out of her chair and into his
arms, kissing his face over and over.

"Wow! If that's the reaction I get when I surprise
you, I might need to try it more often."

"I thought you weren't coming until Wednesday."

"That was the plan, but I told my boss I couldn't
debrief correctly with all this on my mind. He agreed
to wait until next week to finalize everything."

"And what about Michael? Will he have to drive up
by himself on Wednesday?"

Alex shook his head. "When he told his boss what
was going on, Wayne agreed to let him leave a day
early. Michael says the man idolizes you, probably
going way back to the cooking competition that his
radio station sponsored on the cruise ship."

"I'm lovable that way," she teased.

"No argument there." Alex looked at Sylvia, who

had awakened and walked up behind Jordan. "And you must be Jordan's mother." He held out his hand. "I've heard so much about you"

Sylvia rejected Alex's outstretched hand and gave him a hug. "From what I hear, you should probably start calling me Mom."

The grin spread across his entire face. "I can do that." He pointed to the chairs. "Now, unfortunately, I have a bit of bad news. You should probably both sit down."

Jordan inhaled and held her breath for a few seconds, not sure she or her mom were ready for more bad news.

"As soon as I got to your house, Mrs. McAllister, I dropped Michael off and rushed over here to check on Danny. How's he doing, by the way?"

"If you're not comfortable calling me Mom yet, I get it, but at least call me Sylvia. Mrs. McAllister is my husband's mother. As for Danny, he's banged up pretty good, but thankfully, his dry sense of humor is still intact. They're pinning his fractured wrist right now, and other than the possibility of internal bleeding, a couple of cracked ribs, and two shiners, the doctor says he's stable."

"Two shiners?"

"I'll tell you all about that later," Jordan said. "Now, as much as I'm dreading it, we need to hear the bad news. My head is reeling with possibilities, none of them good."

"When I first got here, I flashed my badge at the two officers outside and asked what they knew about the case," Alex started.

"I can't believe they told you anything," Sylvia interjected "We're his family, and we still don't know the details."

"I might have told them I was working with the local FBI on the case," Alex confessed sheepishly.

"Good one," Jordan said. "Now get to the news, please."

Alex studied first Sylvia and then Jordan, as if deciding how much they could handle right now. "Here's what I found out," he finally said. "The victim was a dancer at a joint called Spicy Salsa, an exotic dance hall—AKA strip joint—on the east side of town. The maid at the hotel heard Danny screaming and walked in just as he pulled the knife out of the woman's body and started chest compressions on her."

"Most of that we already knew. We heard..."

"That's not all," Alex interrupted. "Apparently, the results of the DNA found under the victim's fingernails came back about an hour ago."

"And?"

"And they're a perfect match to Danny's."

3
_____

By the time the nurse announced that Danny was on his way back from the recovery room, it was well after 2 a.m., and Jordan had dozed off.

Alex gently nudged her arm. "Your brother is out of surgery," he said, just as they wheeled Danny into the room.

Rubbing the sleep from her eyes, Jordan stood up to allow the transport team to move the gurney next to the bed before sliding Danny over. Immediately, one of the officers handcuffed him to the rails.

"It that absolutely necessary?" Alex asked. "I seriously doubt he'll try to slip past you in his condition."

"Sorry. Standard procedure," the cop said, not looking sorry at all.

"At least take the cuff off his surgically repaired arm." When the cop stared blankly at him as if he had three heads, Alex snorted. "You guys need to grow a heart. That arm is going to hurt like hell when he wakes up."

"We don't make the rules. Both cuffs stay," Jackson, the older of the two police officers, chimed in.

Alex looked first at Jordan, who was fighting to keep the tears from overflowing, then back at the officers. "Let me see if I have this correctly. You put this man in a cell this morning with two local thugs—both of whom outweighed him by over a hundred pounds each. This, after he told you there was history between them and that they had even threatened to kill him." He glared at both of the cops. "Is that about right?"

Neither cop moved, but the expression on their faces stayed defiant.

"Just wanted to make sure I got the facts straight." Alex pulled out his phone and took a picture of Danny in the bed, then walked over to the left side to get a close up of his handcuffed arm. "Pretty sure this man's lawyer will have something to say about that. I'm guessing that police brutality, when added to a running list for a civil lawsuit, will earn you a conversation with your boss, as well as the police lawyers." He put on his best poker face. "Maybe even the mayor."

The two cops turned their backs to have a whispered conversation. Finally, the younger cop reached into his pocket and pulled out the key to unlock the handcuff on Danny's left arm. "The other one stays on, no matter what you threaten."

Danny moaned and opened his eyes when the cuff was roughly pulled off his wrist. When his eyes found Jordan sitting in the chair to his left, he asked, "Is it over?"

She jumped up, rushed to the bed, and reached for his right hand. "Not yet. You're out of surgery, though. We haven't spoken..."

Just then the doctor, still in his scrubs, entered the room and addressed Sylvia. "Your son has a compound fracture of his left wrist and a couple of broken ribs on that side. We pinned the fracture, but he'll have to wear the sling for a few weeks to keep the wrist from swelling."

"When can he go home?"

"You mean back to jail," Officer Jackson said, matter-of-factly.

The surgeon ignored him and continued to address Sylvia. "The MRI showed a bruised liver but no internal bleeding. The good news is that it could have been much worse. The liver will heal on its own in time. Your brother took a vicious beating and also sustained a concussion in the process. Because of that, we'll keep him here at least another day to make sure there are no complications."

After thanking the doctor, Jordan glanced down at Danny, who had fallen back asleep. He looked so pathetic. Her sweet Danny—who had always been her strongest ally against the other three brothers—moaned softly in his sleep. Both eyes were black-and-blue, reminding her of the raccoon they'd tried unsuccessfully to catch many times when they were kids.

Sylvia walked over next to her and patted her shoulder. "In the scheme of things, this is all good news. Those two overweight hoodlums fully intended to kill him and almost succeeded. There's that to be thankful for."

Jordan nodded before turning to Alex when the cops left the room to resume their watch outside the door. "Will they really take him back to jail on Wednesday? There's no way he should be tossed in the cell while he's recovering from his injuries."

"Unfortunately, it's the law, but we do have a few cards to play before that happens."

"Like what?"

"First off, to my knowledge, no local police station has a sick bay set up for accidents that happen in the cells. Officer Jackson let that slip when I first arrived, and said that's the reason Danny's bail hearing was moved from tomorrow to Wednesday. They can't send him to the prison hospital because he hasn't been arraigned yet."

"That's good news," Sylvia said.

"Then there's the threat of a civil suit. Hopefully, by Wednesday we can find a lawyer who can use all this to Danny's benefit and get him released on his own recognizance. That's usually not an option in a murder case, but these are unusual circumstances. A good defense attorney can make the case that because of the nature of his job, a lot of people he didn't play nice with—like the two Rambo wannabes who beat the crap out of him—might be looking for payback. A jail cell is the perfect place to carry out the revenge."

"I hope you're right," Sylvia said. "Not about the revenge thing, of course. I just don't know if I can stand by and watch them taking him back to the cell."

"Alex, I forgot to tell you that Ray has an old friend, a retired Amarillo cop, whose son is an officer at the downtown station," Jordan said, suddenly remembering the earlier conversation at the house. "He's going to reach out to him tomorrow morning and see if they can come up with a good lawyer—a bulldog lawyer, as he called it."

Alex's lips curled into a smile. "That's good. I've heard it said that if you want a tough defense lawyer—or bulldog lawyer as you say—ask a cop who is their least favorite attorney to face in a courtroom, and you've got your answer."

"That's exactly what Ray said." Jordan stopped talking when the nurse entered and piggybacked a smaller IV bag to the larger one dripping into Danny's arm.

"Antibiotic," she explained. After checking his vitals, she turned to Sylvia. "Y'all have had a long night. Danny will probably sleep right through till morning, but if he wakes up hurting, I can give him a strong pain killer. You should go home and get a good night's rest. I'll have the early shift give you a call first thing in the morning with an update on his condition, but I don't anticipate any untoward effects from the anesthesia or the surgery."

"She's right, Mom," Jordan said. "We can come back as soon as we inhale a cup of coffee in the morning."

"Hold off on coming back until at least nine or so," the nurse said. "That will give us a chance to get him cleaned up and ready to face the day."

Sylvia nodded. "You have been so kind, and we appreciate it." She reached for Jordan's hand and started toward the door as Alex suddenly appeared on her other side. Glancing up at him, she asked, "Would it be okay if Jordan drives my car home? My night driving is not something I would brag about."

"Of course. You need me to stop for anything on the way? Ice? Doughnuts?"

Sylvia shook her head. "I have two large breakfast pizzas in the refrigerator that should feed everyone and then some. I also have a doughnut-like pastry called Smear Faces that will probably have Victor following me around like a puppy dog after the sugar rush."

Jordan's eyes lit up. "Where did you find Smear Faces, Mom? When Callie's bakery went out of business a few years ago, I thought I would never get to eat one of those again."

"I have my ways," Sylvia said when they reached her car. "Alex, if I haven't already said this, I need you to know how many points you've scored with me tonight. Watching you go all cop-like and dressing down those two officers, then transforming into the empathetic man that Jordan fell in love with, warmed my heart." She opened the passenger door and slid in. "Drive safely. This is the time of night when all the crazies come out of the woodwork."

EVERYONE WAS STILL awake when they returned home from the hospital.

Michael rushed over and hugged her, then fist-bumped Alex before turning to Sylvia. "You are a spitting image of your beautiful daughter," he said before hugging her as well.

Sylvia's eyes lit up with amusement. "You got the beautiful daughter part right. Spitting image—not so much. Jordan has her father's Irish red hair, blue eyes, and very little of my German ancestry."

Michael grinned sheepishly. "Caught me schmoozing, although I wouldn't discount your Western European genes." He bit his lip to hide a smile. "Hopefully, her cooking skills didn't come from you, though."

That brought a laugh from everyone, including Sylvia. "You can thank her brothers for those skills—or lack thereof. I tried so many times to get her excited about the kitchen, but all she wanted to do was tomboy stuff."

"She still only wants to do tomboy stuff," Victor said, before getting serious. "So, what about Danny? Is he all right?"

"Before we get to that, let me put on a pot of coffee," Sylvia said, heading to the kitchen.

"Any of the German Chocolate Poke Cake left?"

Victor asked, totally ignoring Michael's eyes that were now sending daggers his way.

"Of course, but I would hold off on that until you see what else I have to offer. I had planned on serving Smear Faces with breakfast tomorrow, but now's as good a time as any."

"Yowza! That's a teaser, for sure," Victor said, intrigued. "You've sold me. I'll pass on the poke cake and wait on—what did you call it?"

"Smear Faces," Jordan answered. "It's a kind of doughnut filled with enough cream to jack up your blood sugar. And I guarantee the dessert lives up to every bit of its name. One bite and you'll know exactly why it's called that."

When they were all seated around the table with a steaming cup of coffee, Sylvia emerged from the kitchen with a large tray of the cream-filled pastries.

Victor's eyes lit up. "Oh my!" He reached in and grabbed one. It only took one bite before his entire lower face was covered with the cream.

"Where did you find these, Mom?"

"I didn't find them. Nobody in Amarillo makes them, now that Callie's no longer in business. I looked everywhere, but no luck. So, I spent hours online searching for the recipe and finally had to combine a couple of them to get the right taste. These are actually called *Semlas* and are eaten during Lent in Sweden and Denmark. Are they as good as Callie's were?"

"As good or better. They're fabulous," Jordan said, after taking a huge bite.

Their stomachs full of the pastry, Jordan and Alex related the events of the night to the rest of the gang.

When they got to the part about the police returning Danny to his cell, Ray freaked out. "Not on my watch, they won't. The kid has been through enough at the hands of the police department. First thing in the morning, I'm heading down to the station myself to get a feel for things. I've already called my friend, Jack Sanders, and he's going to meet me there." He turned to Sylvia. "I promise we'll do everything in our power to keep Danny out of that jail cell while the police investigate."

"I appreciate that," Sylvia replied. She stood up and began gathering the empty cups. "Now we should all try to get whatever sleep we can before morning. I have a feeling it's gonna get chaotic."

Everyone stood to help her, and when the table was cleared and the cups stacked in the dishwasher, Lola said, "We're all settled in the upstairs bedrooms, Sylvia, but if you want us somewhere else, just say the word."

"That's perfect," Sylvia replied. "There is a spare bedroom downstairs, but I'm saving that one for when Danny comes home. With his injuries, it probably would be better if he didn't have to go up and down the steps."

"Where should I crash?" Alex asked.

Jordan held her breath, wondering if her mother would make a decision based on twenty-first-century norms and allow her fiancé to stay in a room with her.

Sylvia glanced first at Jordan, and then at Alex. "Nice try. There's a Murphy bed in Colin's office that will do just fine for you. Jordan can bunk with me."

So much for her mother joining the twenty-first century and the new sexual norms.

Alex winked at Jordan. "I'll see you in the morning."

She blew him a kiss and followed her mother to the master bedroom.

~

By the time everyone was up and about the next
morning searching for coffee, Ray had already left for
the police station. As promised, Sylvia served two
large pizzas filled with eggs, bacon, sausage, and lots
of cheese. The smell alone was enough to make Jordan's mouth water, and the actual meal itself was as
good as her mother had promised the night before.

I'm definitely using this recipe for my column.

Oh crap! She'd totally forgotten about promising
her boss she'd get her byline to the printers every day
on time. She'd have to make a special effort to find
time to do that after they left the hospital, if she
wanted to keep her job. And for sure, she'd publish
the Smear Face recipe, especially since it already had
a gourmet-sounding name like *Semlas*. The locals in
Ranchero would go nuts over it.

The gang cleaned up the kitchen, and afterwards,
Alex left to visit the local FBI office downtown to see
what he could find out. In a few minutes, Jordan and
her mother appeared, dressed and ready to go to the
hospital. Just as they were about to leave, Sylvia's
phone rang, and Jordan's heart nearly stopped.

Glancing down at the caller ID, Sylvia mouthed,
It's the hospital.

After several minutes of conversation, she hung up
and addressed the group. "That was Danny's morning
nurse. She said he had a good night and only woke up
once for pain medication. She also said he devoured
his breakfast, which means he must be feeling better.
The boy does love to eat."

Jordan smiled. "That sounds like the Danny I
know and love. Bet he would much rather have eaten
some of your breakfast pizza, though, instead of the

hospital food. He used to beg you to make that for him."

"There's some left," Rosie said. "Why don't I make a care package for him?"

"That would be awesome, Rosie. I'll bet the nurses would nuke it for him," Sylvia said, then added, "And put in a couple of Smear Faces. Danny's sweet tooth is matched only by Victor's."

A few minutes later, with food in hand, Sylvia and Jordan headed for the hospital. The first thing Jordan noticed when she and her mom approached the room was that there had been a change of guard outside the door. Two different cops blocked the entrance, and after vetting them, allowed them both to enter. Danny was in a semi-sitting position in bed talking to yet another cop. When they walked up and Jordan held up the care package, Danny smiled, and the cop turned around to face them.

Jordan took a second to size him up. Standing right under six feet tall with a buzzed haircut, the man looked vaguely familiar to her.

He held her stare. "I'm Officer Sanders. My dad asked me to come down and interrogate your son myself, but since he doesn't have a lawyer yet, I'm going to forego that for now."

Jordan narrowed her eyes, suddenly remembering why the cop looked familiar to her. "Bobby? Is that you?" When he nodded, she continued. "I knew your father was a policeman, but I didn't know you'd followed in his footsteps." She thought for a second. "Now I get it. Your dad is Jack Sanders, Ray Varga's friend, right?"

Sanders tried not to smile, but the wrinkles that appeared at the edges of his eyes gave him away. "You're just as pretty as you were in high school, Jordan." Then he got serious. "I'm sorry you're having to go through this. Danny swears he didn't kill the woman in the motel room, but unfortunately, he can't prove it since he has no memory of anything beyond drinking at the bar."

Flashbacks of her senior year at Amarillo High made her stare at him for a minute. She'd always had a crush on Bobby Sanders, and when he'd asked her out on a date, she'd been thrilled. Although his hair was a lot different, he was just as handsome then as now. She'd been confused why after that, he avoided her like the plague for the rest of their senior year. Why the change of heart?

But it didn't take a rocket scientist to figure it out. The McAllister testosterone had struck again.

She focused back on Danny. "Just because he can't remember doesn't prove that he killed her, though, right?"

"That's true. It doesn't, but I need *you* to know that just because we grew up together, it doesn't mean I'll treat this any differently than the rest of the cases I'm assigned. Whatever the outcome, know that it will be a fair and thorough investigation."

"We appreciate your coming here today, Bobby," Sylvia said. "And we trust that you will be fair."

Sanders turned to Sylvia. "I was just telling your son that Jeb Tucker and his boy have been booked for assault and attempted murder. They're headed to Huntsville to await their own trial."

"Good to know," Sylvia said. "Danny should have a lawyer by this afternoon, and I need *you* to know that he'll do everything in his power to keep Danny from returning to his cell in his condition."

A half smile spread across Sander's face. "I would

expect nothing less, but I have to remind you that the charges against Danny are serious."

Just then Ray entered with an older man who left no doubt that he was related to Bobby. "Jack Sanders," Ray said, confirming the relationship.

After nodding to his father, Bobby took his leave, and Ray introduced his friend first to Danny, and then to Jordan and her mom.

"Ray speaks highly of you," Sylvia said. "I hope you're able to help us find a defense lawyer."

"One is already on his way here," he said. "I think you'll find Simon Feldman more than capable of defending your son."

Sylvia cried out in glee. "You can't even begin to know how good that sounds to me."

Just then, two transport technicians in scrubs arrived with a gurney and explained that the doctor had ordered X-rays of Danny's wrist to make sure that it was still in alignment before they put a cast on it later that day.

After Danny was gone, Ray stepped closer to Sylvia. "Unfortunately, I also have some bad news."

Sylvia took a deep breath and then slowly released it. "What is it, Ray?"

He cleared his throat before he spoke. "The victim's toxicology report came back this morning. She had enough fentanyl in her to kill a horse. The cops are pretty sure she was dead before the steak knife pierced her heart."

"Danny has no access to fentanyl," Jordan argued.

Ray shrugged. "That's what his lawyer will contend. But the police found an empty bottle of the stuff with his prints all over it in his jeans pocket."

"Somebody must've planted it after they spiked the liquor," Jordan again argued.

Ray's voice softened, and he spoke to her like he was consoling a child who had just fallen off a bike. "Sugar, the police have confirmation that the woman bought the bottle of Scotch herself at the liquor store down the street from where the murder occurred, and the motel clerk remembers seeing her carry it to the room."

He turned his attention to Sylvia. "Plus, there was no trace of fentanyl in Danny's blood."

4

"What does that mean, Ray? Are you saying there's no other person except Danny who could have drugged that woman?" Sylvia looked to her daughter for reassurance, but Jordan was struggling herself with the implications of what Ray had just told them.

"We shouldn't jump to conclusions," Jack Sanders responded. "Nothing ever surprises me in a murder case. However, it does limit the possibilities of someone else being involved. If it were my case—"

"What he's saying," Ray interrupted, "is that it will be harder to prove that Danny didn't lace her drink. That's all. Keep in mind, though, that the prosecutor will probably base his entire case on that point. I'm sure Danny's lawyer will find alternatives to keep the jury wondering if that's the way it went down."

Jordan studied Ray's face. She'd been friends with this man long enough to know that although he was trying his best to reassure Sylvia, his expression spoke volumes. He was definitely worried. For the first time, the realization that her brother was in for the fight of his life to stay out of prison—or worse—hit her like a wrecking ball. She turned away so that her mother, who could read her like a book, wouldn't see how worried she was.

But she wasn't quick enough.

"Jordan, what are you thinking?" Sylvia asked. "Are we going to have to sit through a lengthy trial while they paint Danny as a murderer?" She lowered her head. "How could this be happening? Everyone knows he would never hurt anyone, especially not a woman. I raised him better than that."

Jordan grabbed her mother's hand. "To be honest, I think we *are* in for a rough time, but we have to believe that the truth will eventually come out. Right now, we need to stay as hopeful as we can for Danny's sake and get him headed back home to await his trial."

Just then the door opened and one of the cops let a middle-aged gentleman enter the room before speaking directly to Sylvia. "He says he's your son's attorney."

The new arrival stepped closer to Sylvia. "I'm Simon Feldman." He glanced toward Jack Sanders. "Jack called my office and asked me to come down here to see if I could be of any help to your son."

Sylvia's shoulders dropped as if a weight had just been lifted from them, and she offered her hand. "Jack mentioned that you might be willing to take this case, Mr. Feldman. Any help you can give us would be greatly appreciated." She turned to the cop who was still waiting for verification that it was okay to let this man stay in the room. "Yes, this man is Danny's attorney, and as such, must have private access to my son whenever he wants."

Without a word, the police officer walked out, leaving the door cracked a little.

Jack Sanders immediately walked over and roughly closed it before speaking directly to Feldman.

"I took the liberty of giving your law clerks the details of the homicide. As soon as Danny returns from X-Ray, he can get you up to speed on what details he remembers. In the meantime, can we assume that your presence here is a sign that you're willing to represent him?"

Feldman nodded. "I stopped by the police station and got a copy of the arrest warrant and what few details they were willing to divulge." He turned back to Sylvia and cleared his throat. "I won't lie to you. It's not going to be a slam-dunk, but I think I can persuade the jury—or at least one of them—to have reasonable doubt that someone like your son, who has a prominent position as a government employee with no record on file, could carry out such a heinous act. Before I can even ask questions, though, I will need you to officially hire me so that attorney-client privilege can be established and I'm not obligated to tell the police anything that I discover. We can discuss my retainer later, but for now, I'll need you to give me a dollar bill and sign on the dotted line to make it legal."

Sylvia reached for her purse and quickly pulled out her wallet. When she handed the dollar bill to Feldman, he gave her the file he'd brought with him and waited for her to sign.

Just then, the door opened and Danny was wheeled in. He winced in pain when they slid him over to the bed and the officer cuffed his right arm to the rail.

Carrying a tray with a syringe, the nurse walked in and quickly pushed the medicine into Danny's IV tubing before addressing the room full of people. "He's been moved around a lot today. I knew he'd be in pain. He'll sleep for the next few hours, and at some point, the orthopedic tech will take him down to the lab and apply the cast. It might be a good time for all of you to grab some lunch."

Feldman ignored her and stepped closer to the bed. "I'm Simon Feldman. Your mother has just hired me to defend you. Are you okay with that?" When Danny nodded, he continued, "They did a number on you. I know it hurts, but you can take a little comfort from it all, knowing that it may well be your get-outta-jail-free card, at least until the trial."

Danny gave him a weak smile as he struggled to keep his eyes open.

Feldman addressed the group. "I'm going to run by the crime scene on my way back to the office. I'll have the nurse call me when he's awake and has his arm in a cast. Then I'll come back and have my first sit-down with him. I'll need to be alone with him at that time and every other time we discuss the case. So, let me suggest that you all head back home and allow me do my job. I'll call you if anything breaks. You can come back tonight to tuck him in."

Sylvia bent down and kissed her son on the forehead, but he never flinched. "The wonders of morphine," she said with a smile to Feldman, before adding, "One of my other sons is a law professor at Tech. I'm sure he'd be glad to help in any way he can, if you need him."

"I'll keep that in mind." Feldman turned and headed for the door. "It was a delight to meet all of you. Hopefully, we can get your boy out of this bed and recovering at home."

After the lawyer left, Ray and Jack said their good-byes and left to meet up with a few other retired cops at a favorite bar and grill. Jordan leaned in and also kissed her brother's forehead before she and her mother headed home.

She barely heard her mother talking to her in the car. Her mind was already reeling with plans to grab Victor after lunch to check out the crime scene herself before Alex returned from his day with the local FBI officers and put a damper on the idea.

AFTER EATING ham and cheese sliders and homemade mac and cheese, Jordan asked her mother. "Can I borrow your car for a few hours this afternoon, Mom? I want to take Victor to Cadillac Ranch."

"Isn't that where Cadillac cars are shoved into the ground? I want to see that, too," Rosie said, walking closer to Jordan, who shot her with a look that very clearly said *back off*. "But I'll stay here and help Sylvia with dinner. I can see that place another time," she said, getting the message.

Jordan winked at her. "We won't be long—a couple of hours at the most."

Sylvia reached into the drawer and pulled out the keys to her car. "I didn't sleep very well last night, all things considered. It will be nice to grab a quick nap before we start dinner. My other three sons are coming over to find out what's going on with Danny's case and to see if there's something we can do as a family to help him."

"What are you cooking tonight, Sylvia?" Victor asked.

"I thought I would fix Baked Mostaccioli with a spinach salad. It makes a ton of food and will be enough to feed all of us."

"I meant what are you making for dessert?" Victor asked, impatiently. "That's what I'm interested in."

"How does Chocolate Kahlua Bundt Cake sound?"

Victor's eyes lit up. "Awesome, Sylvia. You sure know the way to a man's heart." He licked his lips, then turned to Jordan. "Let's go. I want to make sure we get back before your brothers get a look at that dessert."

"With the exception of Sean, my boys all love anything chocolate, just like you do."

"Sean doesn't like chocolate?"

"He's more of a strawberry/lemon kind of guy," Jordan said, reaching for his arm. "Let's hurry up and clean the kitchen so we can get going."

Lola put her hand on Jordan's chest, effectively stopping her from entering the kitchen. "Rosie and I are very capable of doing that ourselves. You and Victor go do *whatever* it is you're going to do," she said, with a twinkle in her eye, as if she knew exactly what Jordan had up her sleeve. "We'll see you when you get back." She turned to Sylvia. "With Victor gone and the house so quiet, now might be the perfect time for that nap you mentioned. I may even indulge in one myself."

Jordan picked up the small zippered case with her pens and pencils and a large clipboard with a yellow pad that she'd brought with her from Ranchero. Before Victor could argue with her, she turned him around and pushed him out the door.

Once they were in the car and on the way, Victor asked. "What's so great about a bunch of old Cadillacs stuck nose down in the dirt that prompted you to whisk me out of the house without the others? And why so secretive?"

"Granted, Cadillac Ranch is a fun place to visit. It originated when a bunch of art hippies decided to bury ten Cadillacs nose first into the ground and then to paint them as if they were their own personal canvas. Now everyone who visits the site spray paints their own version of art, poetry, or whatever on the cars. You're going to love it when we go there." She cleared her throat. "But today's not that day."

He faced her. "Oh, no. I should have guessed that you singled me out for a reason. You've got that let's-get-into-trouble look all over your pretty little face."

"Isn't that what you and I do so well?" she dead-panned, before explaining. "Actually, we're going to the other side of town to pay a visit to the Lazy Days Motel and have a little chat with the clerk there."

That got his attention. "And that's the reason for your journalism tools?" He pointed to the clipboard and pencil case.

She nodded. "Right now, you and I are reporters after a story."

"We're actually going to the scene of the murder?" He wiggled his eyebrows in a comical way. "Just like old times—you and me searching for clues." Then he narrowed his eyes. "You do realize that Ray's gonna kill us both, right?"

"Probably, but unless we find something juicy that will help Danny, Ray doesn't have to know that we even went there. If we do find something, though, he'll be happy we did." She paused and giggled. "Well maybe not happy, but not as mad."

Victor rubbed his hands together. "Okay, so let's play it by ear when we get there. If it looks like the dude at the front desk is into girls, unbutton the top two buttons on your blouse and take the lead. If it's boys that ring his bell, I'll use my charm to get him to tell us all he knows."

Jordan pulled into the lot and parked the car before high-fiving Victor. "Let's do it."

Back in the day, the Lazy Days Motel used to be a

favorite stopover for all the traders who came to town for the monthly cattle auctions. When the city closed down the auction house and moved it to the other side of town, business went into a slump as the traders moved with it to be closer to the actual auction. The only people who stopped there now were travelers looking for a place to sleep before heading back out in the morning.

Needless to say, with the clientele gone, the place had gone downhill in no time. Now, it was simply a cheap layover for a quick resting place for the weary travelers who didn't give a lick about anything other than catching a few Zs before facing another long day on the road. That, and probably the stomping grounds for those who needed to rent by the hour.

As soon as they walked into the office, a pimply young man dressed in a T-shirt that read FOR A GOOD TIME, PRESS THIS BUTTON with an arrow pointing to a large circle below it, looked up at them. His eyes lit up when he got his first look at Jordan. "Are you looking for a room?"

Victor discreetly pointed to her blouse and moved in front of her, allowing her to open the top button. He frowned when he saw that she had only unbuttoned one and not both of them.

"My friend and I are reporters from the Daily Star. We've come all the way from Lubbock to investigate a murder that happened here a few days ago."

Immediately, Stevie, according to his name badge, shook his head. "I'm not allowed to talk about that," he said, his eyes never leaving the top of Jordan's blouse, as if by some miracle he could unbutton the second button with his eyes.

"Oh, we won't ask you any questions," Victor fired

back. "We'd just like to have a look at the room where the murder happened."

"I can't do that, either. It's a crime scene." He sniffed, and Jordan noticed the tiny white spot under his nose.

She stepped forward, leaning over, and said in as sultry of a voice as she could come up with—which wasn't even close to being sensual, "No one would have to know, Stevie, and when I come back, I could show you how extremely grateful I am."

The clerk looked at her for a few minutes before handing her the key to Room 21. "It's the last one on the left. You can drive your car down there and park right in front of it." He lowered his voice. "And whatever you do, don't disturb the crime scene tape. Just take a quick look and get out of there."

Jordan took the key from him and rewarded him with another smile before pushing Victor toward the door. As she was leaving, she said over her shoulder. "I love your shirt, by the way. Remind me to push the button when I return the key, Stevie."

Victor nearly choked on his own spit as he followed her out the door. "You're good, girlfriend. I suspect that last remark of yours will buy us a little more time before he comes looking to kick us out."

They drove to the end of the building and parked in front of Room 21. Except for the crime tape decorating the place, it didn't look any different than the rest of the rooms. After carefully making their way under the yellow tape, Jordan reached into her purse and pulled out two pairs of gloves. Handing a pair to Victor, she said, "Put these on. I got them from my mother's stash. She uses them when she cuts up chicken. The last thing we need is our fingerprints showing up on something."

She inserted the key, but before she pushed the door open, she hesitated. "I'm almost afraid to go in. What if we find something that definitely incriminates Danny?"

"If we find something, you can bet the cops have already found it, too, so what would it matter? It might be something that will be useful to his lawyer while he figures out an alternative reason for whatever it is we might find in there."

She pushed the door open with Victor right behind her. It was a typical low-rent motel room with cheap furniture, a slightly musty odor, and carpet stained with God only knew what. She wrinkled her nose, not even wanting to go there. Walking over to the bed, she gasped when she saw her brother's watch that had apparently fallen off the nightstand and was almost completely hidden under the bed. Without a word, she pointed it out to Victor. "The cops must have missed this. Should I take it?"

"Don't you dare," Victor warned, before walking over to stand beside her. "Why isn't there more blood? You'd think a knife to the heart would have caused the victim to bleed out, or there would be at least more of a stain than this."

"Not if she was already dead from the fentanyl when she was stabbed, as the coroner's report indicated."

"Oh yeah. It's still kind of eerie, though, even without a lot of blood."

"Don't dwell on that. We've got to be quick here before sleazy Stevie gets suspicious and checks our credentials."

Even though the room had already been processed by the evidence techs and there was no longer anything of interest—like the bottle of liquor—lying around, they spent over thirty minutes walking around the entire room and bathroom without finding anything that might help Danny. When they were ready to leave, sure this little trip had been a total waste of time, they made sure that everything they'd touched was back in its original spot.

Jordan retrieved her phone from her back pocket and began taking pictures of the entire room. When she was finished, something on the ceiling over-looking the bed caught her eye. She took off her shoes and climbed onto the mattress for a better look. After staring at the ceiling for several seconds, she ex-claimed, "Oh, my God! It's a camera. The little creep out at the front desk must have planted it so that he could get his rocks off watching whatever the heck went on in this room while he snorts cocaine." She snapped a couple of close ups of the camera then grabbed Victor's arm. "Let's go have a talk with Skanky Stevie out there. As Desi would say to Lucy, the man's got some 'splaining to do."

Back at the front office, Jordan handed Stevie the key, making sure to let her fingers linger in his for a few seconds, and nearly throwing up in her mouth in the process.

"So, Stevie, how long have you been working here?" Victor asked.

"Over two years," the clerk responded. "I'm the manager now."

Jordan leaned in and gave him her sexiest look. "Congratulations." She pointed to the laptop in front of him. "Are there cameras in all the room so that no one can steal anything?"

Stevie shook his head. "That's against the law. We don't even have cameras on the outside to protect the privacy of our clients."

"How nice for them." Jordan walked around the desk and stood next to him. "Funny thing, though, I just took a picture that says differently. Unless I'm hallucinating, I saw a camera mounted above the bed in Room 21." She jabbed the button on his shirt. "Is that how you get your jollies?"

His face turned the color of a ripe strawberry. "You took a picture?" When she pulled out her phone and showed him, he inhaled and then released it slowly. "I wasn't the one who planted that camera."

"Really. You expect me to believe that?"

"I swear. I didn't —"

"Then who did?" Victor asked, coming around the desk to stand beside Jordan.

The clerk thought about that for a few seconds before answering, probably deciding how he could get out of this situation without losing his job. Finally, he looked straight at Jordan and said, "Carlita did."

"Carlita? The woman who was murdered?"

Fear grabbed Jordan's heart when he nodded. If there was footage of that night, it meant that the police probably had it in their possession—that it might prove to be damning evidence against Danny.

"And did the police take the video?" Jordan asked, her eyes filling with tears, anticipating Stevie's answer.

"No."

"No? Why not?" He had her undivided attention now.

Stevie sniffed, before reaching for a tissue and blowing his nose. "Carlita didn't turn on the camera that night like she always does."

5

As soon as they climbed into the car and were headed home, Victor turned to Jordan. "So why do you think Carlita had a camera over the bed? Do you think she wanted proof in case one of her 'boyfriends' got a little too aggressive?"

Jordan thought about that for a minute, then shook her head. "Although that may have been part of her reasoning, my guess is that she was using the videos to blackmail the men she entertained in that room."

Victor squinted in thought. "You've probably just hit the nail on the head. If she hooked up with some out-of-town man at one of the bars she frequented and then brought the poor sucker back to her little 'studio,' she could make a small fortune when she threatened to send the video to the man's wife. That could prove to be a very lucrative business plan—not to mention dangerous."

"Bingo," Jordan said. "Sleazy Stevie knew about the camera when we asked. Wonder if he was in cahoots with her?"

"My money's on *yes*. Did you see his face when you

told him you had a picture of the camera above the bed?" Victor laughed. "I wouldn't be surprised if the guy needed an underwear change after we left."

"A well-deserved consequence if that did happen," Jordan said, before she got serious. "So if she brought Danny back to the motel to blackmail him, why didn't she turn on the camera?"

Victor shrugged. "Maybe whatever happened to her happened before she had time to do that. Or maybe she liked Danny and had no intentions of blackmailing him—just wanted to have a little fun with him."

"Maybe," Jordan replied. "As much as I could kill my brother sometimes, he is lovable and the life of every party, keeping everyone in stitches with his impressions and antics. To a female, especially a wasted one, he's like catnip to a big old kitty. Most women will gravitate toward someone who makes them laugh."

"I guess our next stop should be to the honky-tonk where Carlita and Danny both got snookered."

"That's a good idea, but first we have to talk to him about this. Although he says he can't remember anything after leaving the bar, maybe we can jog his memory and he'll think of something that may prove to be useful to the investigation."

"Good idea," Victor said. "In the meantime, should we tell Ray or Alex about what we discovered at the murder scene?"

"Oh, Lord, no. Do you have any idea how much trouble we'll be in if they find out we were snooping around?" She narrowed her eyes. "We don't even know yet if the camera had anything to do with Danny. All it proves is that Carlita was probably using it as a source of income. I say we talk to my brother first, then we can all sit down and figure out if it's something that we should discuss with his lawyer."

"Sounds like a plan," Victor said. "Now, tell me about your brothers so I can be prepared for the onslaught."

"An onslaught, for sure. They can be a force of nature if they gang up on you."

"Yeah, but are they hot?"

Jordan slapped his shoulder. "No way should you even be thinking about that. You'd be in big trouble, mister, if I told Michael."

"You wouldn't do that to me, would you?"

She grinned. "You never know, but it would behoove you to be nice to me for the rest of our time here." Then she added, "And yes, if I have to say so myself, my brothers are all handsome. They always had girls making fools of themselves just to get their attention."

"Which one is your favorite?"

Without hesitating, Jordan responded. "Danny has always been my best friend. The others picked on him just as much as they picked on me. But of the other three, I would have to say that I am closest to Sean. He's a fireman and lives on the other side of town with his wife and a baby in the oven."

"And the others?"

"Patrick's the oldest. He's the law professor my mom keeps talking about. He lives in Lubbock with his wife, who's the head buyer at Lindy's. They have two teenage girls, who are giving them fits, according to my mom. Tommy's the second-born and lives in Canyon, which is about twenty minutes away. He's a bigwig at Canyon Independent Bank and Trust, and he and his wife divorced about a year ago. They share joint custody of their two kids."

"Are they gonna like me?"

"As long as you don't drag me off in a car and take me to Inspiration Point, you should be fine."

"As cute as you are, sweet cheeks, there's no chance in hell of that happening. I'm presuming that Inspiration Point is where everyone goes to make out?"

Jordan nodded. "You would be correct. On the few instances that I was there, I had to sneak out the window so my brothers wouldn't chase us down and shoot my date on sight. Word spread quickly that I had four crazy brothers, and needless to say, I didn't make it to Inspiration Point very often."

"Sounds like your brothers were the protectors of their innocent sister. You should be glad they had your back."

"Oh, they were protectors, all right—protectors of my virginity." She giggled. "The thought of their little sister doing the things they did with all their girl-friends freaked them out. They were my very own four-way chastity belt."

"I find it hard to believe that you emerged from your childhood without some kind of psychological damage," Victor quipped. "Oh wait! You *are* pretty messed up."

"Shut up! What part of you having to be nice to me so I won't tell Michael what you said earlier did you not get?"

"*Mea culpa.* Consider me warned," he fired back. "So when I knew we were all coming to Amarillo, I did a little research. Did you know they call Amarillo the Yellow Rose of Texas?"

"Of course I do, you dufus. I grew up here. But you should have connected the dots since *amarillo* means yellow in Spanish, your native language. In your defense, though, you might not have known that it was actually named for the yellow soil along the creek banks and the yellow wildflowers growing on the plains and not because of the rose."

She pulled into the garage at her mother's house. "Looks like Sean and Tommy are already here."

"Just to be sure before we meet the chastity belt brothers and come face-to-face with Ray and Alex, we're really not going to mention our little chat with Skanky Stevie and the camera in Room 21?"

"Not if you want to have a nice evening. Like I said, let's talk to Danny, hopefully tomorrow after his bail hearing, and decide if any of what we found out is important to his case. Then if we decide that the camera has significance, we can sit down with everyone and tell them what we discovered in that room.

"So, lips sealed for now?"

"Yes, and God help us when they're unsealed. Trust me when I tell you that no matter when we finally do 'fess up, we're in for a long lecture."

She reached for her clipboard. "Gotta hide the evidence before one of our smart friends put two and two together and figure out that we were up to our old tricks." Twisting around to look into the back seat, she exclaimed, "Dang it! I must have left my stuff on the counter at the motel. I've carried my pencils and pens in that zippered bag since I graduated from high school. I call it my journalism bag."

"Quit whining. I'll buy you another one. Lucky for you Stevie isn't smart enough to put two and two together and figure out that the blank yellow pad you left behind means that our reporter story was bogus." He giggled. "That's probably the last thing on his mind right now. My guess is that he's shoving more of that white stuff up his nose and fantasizing about you opening the second button on your blouse."

THE NIGHT TURNED out to be more enjoyable than Jordan could have imagined. Introducing her fiancé to her brothers was a little hairy at first, but it didn't take Alex long to enchant the men with some of his undercover stories.

With an ugly scene avoided, Jordan breathed a sigh of relief, sank back in her chair, and watched as Alex kept them mesmerized. The fact that he didn't say a word about his latest undercover assignment in Mexico spoke volumes.

"Jordan, I asked you a question," Sean said from across the table.

She looked up, embarrassed to be caught day-dreaming. "Oh, sorry. I was thinking about Danny's bail hearing tomorrow. What did you ask me?"

"I asked what everybody else around the table is wondering. Alex wisely deferred to you for the answer. When's the wedding?"

She glanced toward Alex, and he cocked his eyebrows. "Take a breath, you guys. We literally just got engaged two days ago. Mom called right after Alex proposed to tell me about Danny, and we headed to Amarillo the next day. So, no date yet, because we haven't even had a chance to discuss it."

"Well, I think I speak for the entire family when I say we're glad to know that you've chosen someone who's one-hundred percent capable of keeping you out of trouble. Not like that pansy you followed all over Texas after you graduated," Tommy said.

"Jordan is perfectly capable of taking care of herself," Alex said, turning to face Sylvia's second-born. "Truth is, she was capable back then as well but chose to follow her heart. Sometimes love leads you in the wrong direction, as *we* all know."

"*Touché,*" Tommy said. "And my divorce proves that. So enough about Jordan. We need to talk about Danny's case."

Patrick took the lead. "I talked with Feldman before I came here tonight. He's cautiously optimistic and can argue that Amarillo jail cells have no medical facilities that can provide the post op care that Danny will need for his injuries. He's also going to argue that the possibility of infection, coupled with the chance that those broken ribs might puncture Danny's lungs, is too big of a risk."

"Honey, can that really happen? Can he end up with a punctured lung?" Sylvia asked, as she and Rosie caught the end of the conversation when they carried in the Kahlua Cake and ice cream, setting them in the middle of the table with plates and forks. "Jordan, can you dish this up?"

Patrick shrugged as Jordan nodded and stood to cut the cake. "Anything can happen when you're dealing with injuries, Mom, but Feldman is prepared for Plan B, if by chance his first option doesn't work."

"Plan B? And what's that?" Ray asked, unusually silent up to this point.

"Anyone heard of Jackson Kramer?" When they all shook their heads, Patrick continued. "He's probably the best civil litigator in all of Potter County. Just mentioning his name will almost bring a cop to tears when that officer is involved in a lawsuit with Kramer as council for the defendant. The man's nearly one-hundred percent win-ratio speaks for itself."

"Why are you bringing up another lawyer, son?" Sylvia asked.

"Because, Mom, Kramer has agreed to help Feldman tomorrow, should it come down to that. Although he's heavily booked and really picky about his cases, hearing about what happened to Danny at the hands of those two thugs struck a nerve with him. Certainly, it's a case he feels he can win, and he's agreed to act on Danny's behalf if the family decides to sue." A half-smile crossed Patrick's face. "Believe me when I tell you that the judge will not be happy to see him show up in his courtroom tomorrow with Feldman and me."

"Are you saying that Danny is definitely going to sue the Amarillo police department?" Ray asked. "In my experience, that can backfire and turn public opinion against a person."

"No, I'm not saying that. Feldman merely wants to be prepared in case the hearing doesn't go as hoped. He's pulling out all the stops, and both Danny's orthopedic surgeon and his liver specialist will also be in the courtroom tomorrow. They're ready to argue that sending him back to a germ-filled cell might prove to be disastrous with a fresh surgical incision. Knowing that he would be on record as going against medical advice, the judge will be less inclined to send our boy back to jail."

Tears welled up in Sylvia's eyes. "And the doctors agreed to do that for Danny despite their busy schedules?"

"Feldman said neither of them hesitated when he asked." Patrick stopped talking to take a bite of his dessert. "And if all this fails, Kramer will announce that he will be filing a million-dollar lawsuit against the county if Danny comes down with so much as a cold in the cell."

"Oh, thank you, Lord!" Sylvia exclaimed. "Can we all go to the bail hearing tomorrow?"

"Technically, yes, but Feldman thinks it would be best if we leave it to the doctors and the civil litigator to do the intimidating." Patrick grinned. "Apparently there's a rumor going around associating the McAllister name with uncontrollable emotions and anger that usually leads to someone getting hurt." He pointed to his brothers. "He's afraid that one of you will cause a commotion in the courtroom and hurt Danny's chances of coming home to recuperate."

"That's bullshit," Sean said, slapping the table.

"I do believe you just proved his point, bro," Jordan said with a smirk.

"She's right, Sean. You and I both know we all have short fuses. I'm the lawyer here, and I'll be the only one representing our family tomorrow. The bail hearing is set for 9 a.m., and I promise I'll let *you* know as soon as *I* know something."

"What exactly do they consider in a bail hearing?" Jordan asked.

"Danny's work record, community ties, family ties, length of residing in the county, prior criminal history, conformity with any prior bonds, and the existence of any outstanding bond period." Patrick stopped talking and spoke directly to his sister. "Danny has all that in his favor, but unfortunately, the severity of the crime takes precedence over all of those considerations."

When Sylvia sniffed back tears, Patrick continued, "We can't lose hope, Mom. Danny's not a flight risk, and given the extent of his injuries, he won't be seen as a risk to society. Feldman will argue hard for bail and fully expects the judge to agree. He's already negotiated with a bail bondsman located downtown, who will also be at the hearing and ready to write a check when that happens."

"Sounds like you picked the right lawyer, Sylvia," Ray said. "Let's hope this judge has a soft spot in his heart and will let Danny come home under house arrest."

Sylvia rewarded him with one of her gorgeous smiles before turning to her eldest son again. "As much as we want to be there tomorrow just for Danny, I will see to it that we all abide by Feldman's wishes to stay put and just pray."

"Perfect, Mom," Patrick said. "If we're gonna pay the big bucks for a lawyer like Feldman, we'd be foolish not to take his advice." He paused before adding, "Oh, and I almost forgot to tell y'all what Feldman found out at the police station tonight."

Everyone stopped eating and leaned closer into the table as Patrick swallowed the last bite of his Kahlua Cake, then chased it down with a big gulp of beer.

"The cops found a camera mounted over the bed in the room where the killing... where Danny and the woman were found."

Jordan nearly choked on her dessert. "What was on the tape?" she asked, closing her eyes as if to block out what his answer might be.

"Nothing. The camera was turned off, and the tape was blank."

"It's been my experience that a camera in a motel room usually means some kind of extortion," Ray said.

"That's exactly what the cops think. They're doing a deep dive into Carlita's financials and executing another search warrant at her house to see if they missed finding any additional tapes."

"Do you think maybe there might be something on the tape, and the cops are not telling Feldman?" Sean asked.

Patrick shook his head. "By law, if they had evidence like that, they'd have to disclose it or risk prosecutorial misconduct if they didn't." He rubbed his chin in deep thought. "The question is why was it there in the first place? And why was it blank?"

6

Jordan glanced toward Victor, anticipating how he would react to Patrick's declaration that the police had found a camera in the motel room.

She was right.

Victor's mouth hung wide open, and his eyes were as big as saucers. Catching his attention, she shook her head slightly, and thankfully, he got the message and seemed to relax a little.

Or at least, he closed his mouth.

Now was not the time to reveal that she and her partner in crime had already known about the camera. She decided that after her brothers left tonight and her mom and the others were tucked into their beds, she and Victor would sit down with Alex and Ray and tell them everything. She didn't think it would make a difference, though, since they all knew about the camera now. Still, she hated keeping secrets from her fiancé.

The last couple of days had been stressful for her family, and between the drinking and the captive audiences as they took turns telling stories about both Jordan and Danny growing up, the McAllister brothers were on a roll, and it seemed like they would never go home. Jordan kept glancing at her watch and even fake-yawned a couple of times, but the gesture went right over their heads. They were having too much fun, and for the first time, her mother was laughing.

Plus, Alex was bonding with her brothers and was also laughing at some of the stories about her. Despite the fact that her entire childhood was being played out as comic relief in front of her, it warmed her heart to see Alex enjoying her family.

That had to be good for both him and her mom.

'Fessing up to Ray and Alex could wait. It probably was inconsequential and would shed no light on Danny's case, anyway, so why get everyone freaked out, since the police already knew about the camera and the blank tape?

So she sat back in the chair and even joined in with a few stories of her own about her brothers. Finally, at midnight, she—along with everyone else—was yawning for real. Sylvia stood and announced that she was going to bed because, as she said, "Tomorrow is a big day for all of us."

Alex singled out Patrick. "Since you live in Lubbock, why don't you stay with your mom tonight and sleep on the Murphy bed in your dad's office? I'll take the couch."

Patrick stared at him for a second before responding, "As much as I appreciate the offer, I've already made arrangements to stay downtown. Matter of fact, I left my car in the parking lot of the hotel and took an Uber here. I wanted to be closer to the courthouse and hopefully be able to talk to Danny before the arraignment tomorrow."

"Okay, then. I'll drive you to the hotel."

"Thanks, Alex, but I've already called Uber for my-self and my two brothers, who wouldn't dare leave this house in their own cars after drinking with a retired cop and an FBI agent." A half-smile formed on his face before he became serious again. "We're all coming back tomorrow night with our families, and we can pick up our cars then."

Sylvia stood on her tiptoes to kiss his cheek. "Now I can go to sleep without worrying about you three. God knows I'm going to have a hard enough time as it is, thinking about Danny in front of the judge tomor-row." She turned to Rosie. "There are two casseroles of Blueberry French Toast in the refrigerator. If you wake up before me, could you put them on the counter to bring them to room temperature? I'm leaving the recipe next to the stove, so that if by some miracle I'm still not awake by then, I'd appreciate if you'd put them in the oven according to the directions."

"Of course, I will," Rosie said. "Now you go and try to get some rest. As you said, tomorrow will be a big day."

When her brothers left and everyone had gone to their own bedrooms, Jordan waited until she was sure her mother was asleep before sneaking into her dad's office.

Alex was sitting up in the bed reading some kind of report, and his eyes lit up when he saw her. "Do you have any idea how many times I looked at you from across the table tonight, wishing we were alone and watching you be a good sport while your brothers en-tertained all of us at your expense?"

"I do, because I was thinking the same thing." She climbed into the bed and snuggled against him. "I hope you weren't too overwhelmed by my obnoxious brothers."

He grinned. "Are you kidding? I loved hearing about you growing up. Loved hearing how they chased off all your boyfriends. But most of all, I loved finding out that you played football better than they did. You must have been a real Tom Brady back then."

"Still am," she bragged. "That's the real reason they tolerated me, although deep down, I know they do love me. I am their only baby sister, after all."

"That love was obvious in their eyes every time they mentioned you." Alex put down the report. "I've enjoyed myself more tonight than I have in a long time."

"My family adores you," Jordan said. "I'm so glad my brothers didn't try to intimidate you like they've done to every other male who's shown an interest in me."

"The truth of the matter is, I think they're glad to have help with you, knowing how you manage to get yourself into trouble." He squeezed her shoulder affectionately.

There it was—the perfect opening for confessing to her snooping. She opened her mouth, but he stopped her with a kiss that seemed to go on forever.

Finally, he pulled away. "You'd better get back to your mother's bedroom, or I'm not sure I'll be able to let you go. We have to respect that this is your parents' house, not to mention that I think I scored some points with your brothers tonight. I'd hate to be the subject of the McAllister wrath if they found out we were sneaking around in the very house where they grew up."

Hesitating for just a minute, Jordan realized he was right and climbed out of bed. Heading to the door, she turned around just enough to blow him a kiss before exiting and shutting the door very softly so as not to wake the others.

Surprisingly, she slept pretty well, despite the fact that the next twenty-four hours were going to be very stressful waiting to hear about the bail hearing. She smiled to herself, thinking that the long, sensual kiss from Alex was probably the reason why she didn't lie awake all night worrying about tomorrow, but although she could still taste his lips on hers, common sense told her that her mother's melatonin probably had more to do with it.

Everyone was already up and sitting around the table when she walked into the dining room. As soon as she sat down, Ray placed a steaming cup of coffee in front of her.

Geez! I love these people so much. They were all looking at her, knowing how stressed out she and her mom would be until they heard something and trying desperately to find a way to put them at ease. She didn't even have to say a word. They just knew.

Several minutes later, Rosie and Lola brought in the two casserole dishes with her mother's Blueberry French Toast.

Sylvia stood to help but Lola shook her head. "You cooked. We'll serve."

"I'm learning so much from you," Rosie said to Sylvia, as she placed the dishes in the center of the table, along with blueberry pancake syrup.

"I'm glad someone is," Sylvia joked. "Because Jordan is surely not interested. I can rest easy thinking that my recipes will not go to the grave with me."

"Mother!" Jordan exclaimed. "Quit talking like that. Maybe one day after I get married and have kids,"—she winked at Alex across from her—"I'll spend a week or two with you to pick your brain about cooking."

"Yeah! That'll be the day," Alex teased. "If I didn't do all the cooking in our relationship, the menu would only include fast food and fried bologna sandwiches. Despite the fact that those sandwiches are pretty good, if I might say so myself, our poor kids would starve or get scurvy."

That brought a laugh from everyone as they enjoyed their breakfast.

They spent the next hour around the table, sipping their coffee and making small talk to pass the time. When the grandfather clock in the hallway chimed nine times, there was a hush.

Sylvia blew out a slow breath and reached for Jordan's hand. "It's in God's hands now."

Jordan could only nod, afraid if she spoke, her mother would see how scared she really was.

After an hour had passed with all of them chit-chatting about nothing in particular, Sylvia glanced down at her watch and cried out. "This waiting is killing me. Why doesn't Patrick call and give us an update?"

"He will when he can, Mom. There are probably a lot of reasons why he hasn't called yet, none of which may have anything to do with Danny," Jordan said, hoping her face wouldn't give her away. She had no idea how these hearings went and was making it up as she went. Seeing the terror in her mother's face was way worse than her spouting off things she had no idea about.

"Jordan is right, Sylvia. It's not unusual for hearings to get delayed for reasons like the lawyers being late or the hearing ahead of them simply lasting longer than expected."

"I hear you, Ray, but I wish I could have been with..." She stopped talking when the phone rang. "It's Patrick," she said after looking at caller ID.

"Please tell me you have good news," she said, without even saying hello.

"He's coming home."

"That's wonderful news. Our prayers have been answered," she exclaimed. "When?"

She put her cell phone on speaker as Patrick explained that it would take several hours to complete the paperwork before Danny could come home. The judge had apparently decided that it was too risky for the county to allow the prisoner to go back to the cold jail cell to recover from his injuries. According to Patrick, the fact that Danny had two lawyers sitting beside him, two of his physicians, and the well-known civil litigator sitting behind them had to have been a little intimidating.

The sight of the bail bondsman standing in the back didn't hurt, either.

If all went without a hitch, Danny would be home by dinner time, and Patrick mentioned that his brother had asked for the famous McAllister brothers Beer Marinated Pork Steaks for his first dinner as a semi-free man.

"Beer Marinated Pork Steaks? That sounds yummy," Rosie said. "I will definitely be watching and writing everything down."

"It's something the boys always made with their dad. We usually have baked potatoes and a big salad with that, but my friend Gina just gave me her recipe to make a loaded baked-potato casserole. That will make it much easier to feed a crowd."

"And for dessert?"

Sylvia hugged Victor. "I love that you have such a

sweet tooth since making desserts is one of my favorite things to do."

"So?" It was obvious that Victor was not blessed with the patience gene at birth.

"One of Danny's favorites is my Layered Lemon Delight."

"Yum! Nice way to get in my daily fruit requirements," Victor exclaimed. "Now, what about lunch?"

"Victor, you just ate breakfast," Michael admonished him.

"Can't a guy think ahead? You know how I am, Michael. I hate surprises."

"Mom, I was thinking that lunch should be takeout since we'll all be getting ready for Danny's homecoming tonight. What about if I run over to Buddy's for burgers and fries?"

"I hate not cooking for your friends," she argued.

"Nonsense!" Lola said. "But instead of burgers, Jordan, do you think you could get Mexican food? You probably know where all the local hole-in-the-wall restaurants are. I don't know about the rest of you, but I could sure use a Mexican fix. Some tacos and fajitas would be awesome." She looked around. "Everyone okay with that?"

"Sounds terrific to me," Alex said. "I have to run down to the FBI office for a few hours to powwow with them about a case they asked me to look into. I could pick something up on my way back here."

A light bulb went off in Jordan's head. Her favorite Mexican restaurant, La Casita, was right down the road from the Lazy Days Motel. "No, honey, I'll do it. I know where all the good places to eat in Amarillo are located. Victor and I will run out around noon and grab the food. That way, if your meeting runs over, you won't have to rush out. Fajitas are easy to reheat."

"Are you sure?"

Jordan stole a glance toward Victor before anyone else could pick up on it. They could stop at the motel on their way to the restaurant and pick up her note pad and pencil case. "Positive. Then when you get home, Mom can make a list, and you and I will run out and do a little grocery shopping."

"Sounds good." He hugged her, then kissed her forehead. "More to come tonight when everyone is asleep," he whispered in her ear.

"You, sir, are tempting fate with all my brothers coming again tonight. They can sniff out a horny guy from a mile away."

That made him laugh, and when everyone looked at him like he was crazy, he said," Just thought of something one of the FBI guys said yesterday." Before anyone could comment, he walked to the door. "See you all at lunch. My mouth is already watering for those fajitas."

The morning crept by painfully slowly, with no further news about Danny, but as Patrick had warned, he and Feldman would be busy negotiating the terms of his home release.

When noon finally rolled around, Jordan grabbed her mom's car keys, and she and Victor walked out and climbed into the car.

"Is this another Jordan and Victor secret spy mission?"

"Absolutely. We're about to pay Stevie boy another visit. Maybe if he hasn't just shoved powder up his nose, we might be able to get some useful information out of him."

STEVIE SQUIRMED in his seat behind the desk, staring at the newcomer and hoping that he would be a rich man soon. He already had big plans to blow this crappy job and get on the next plane to Aruba, where he could picture life on the beach with a couple of bikini-clad babes.

"So you lied to me when you said there were no copies of the tape except the one in the recorder?"

Stevie nodded. "The camera is connected to my phone so that if Carlita ever tried to cut me out of her little schemes, I had insurance."

"Where's your phone now?"

"I'll tell you after we agree to what we spoke about earlier this morning. If you give me ten grand right now, I'll give you the burner phone I used with a copy of the recording from Carlita's room."

"Do you really think that's the way this is going to play out today, Stevie? Do I look like the type to let a scumbag druggie like you extort me?"

Just then the door opened and two people walked in. Although Stevie didn't know either of them by name, he recognized the shorter one from the tape. He caught his breath, and his heart raced.

He was staring right into the eyes of the killer who had shoved the knife into Carlita's chest.

"Look, dirt bag, trust me when I say that you don't want to be playing games with me.

Threatening me would be utterly stupid, although I'm pretty sure your IQ doesn't even come close to double digits."

Stevie lowered his eyes. Three against one didn't give him much of a chance. He decided to play nice and give them what they wanted. Maybe he could persuade them to take the phone and walk away without inflicting any pain.

"It's hidden in my room next door. Follow me, and you can have it."

He led them to the room next to the office where the owner of the motel allowed him to live so that he could be on call twenty-four hours a day. As soon as the door closed behind them, they heard a car pull up. The younger man, who up to this point hadn't said a word, walked over and peeked through the curtains.

"It's a woman and a man, probably looking to rent a room for a quickie at this piece of crap No-Tell Motel," the man said, before he opened the curtain a little more.

Carlita's killer joined him by the window and stared at the newcomer before exclaiming, "Damn! That woman looks familiar."

JORDAN AND VICTOR walked into the motel office ready to interrogate Stevie once again, but he was nowhere in sight.

"Hello? Stevie, are you here?"

When there was no answer, Victor said, "Do you think he could be showing someone a room?"

"Do you honestly believe this is the kind of motel where you are shown a room before you pay and get a key? I'll bet the people staying here don't even have to show ID."

"You're probably right." He leaned over the desk for a peek. "His laptop's not here. Maybe he had to answer nature's call and was afraid someone might swipe it."

"Maybe. Let's just wait a few minutes to see if he returns. Surely, he wouldn't leave his post for very long."

Jordan glanced around the small office area, looking for her notebook, but it wasn't on the desk where she'd left it. When they were about to leave for the restaurant, she spied the edge of her red pencil case sticking out of a wooden desk tray labeled LOST AND FOUND.

"There it is." She scrambled around the desk and claimed her belongings. "No need to wait any longer for Stevie now. He probably won't tell us anything new anyway, and I got what I came for. Let's head to the restaurant. Our order should be ready."

As they walked to the car, out of the corner of her eye, she noticed that the drapes in the room next to the office were slightly opened. When she stopped to get a better look, they closed.

"That jerk Stevie knew we were here and hid in his room. What kind of loser motel clerk does that?"

"One who probably knows more that he told us yesterday would be my guess."

"You're right. The little weasel is probably high on that white snow he sniffs and most likely wouldn't have come clean with us, anyway."

She slid into the driver's seat and turned on the ignition, but before she drove away, she noticed a burnt orange F-150 Ford pickup parked in the lot a little farther down. Then she noticed the University of Texas sticker on the window and was about to comment that someone occupying one of the rooms was probably a UT grad, just like she was.

But before she could mention that to Victor, he whistled. "Geez! Would you look at the size of those wheels? How a normal person climbs into the front seat without a ladder is beyond me."

"I know." She looked back toward the motel office one last time. By the time they made it to the highway, she had the distinct feeling that something wasn't right.

She remembered that Stevie had come across as a little weird, but where was he?

And why was he hiding from them?

7

After a trip to the grocery store, Jordan and Alex spent the entire afternoon with her mother and the gang, decorating the living room with streamers and balloons. Lola placed the flowers Jordan had picked up on the way home in a vase and carried them to the spare bedroom. They wanted to make sure Danny felt welcomed and that he knew how glad they were that he was finally home.

The festivities began around 2 o'clock when Sean and Tommy showed up to grill the pork steaks before simmering them in a mixture of BBQ sauce and beer. Truth be told, between her brothers and her friends, there was way more beer consumed than was used for the pork steaks. Fortunately, knowing her brothers the way she did, she'd bought more than enough at the grocery store or else she would have been asked to do a beer run, even before Danny got home.

With Rosie following her around and recording everything, Sylvia prepared the Layered Lemon Delight. Between the pork steaks and the lemon dessert in the oven, the smells that filled the house were enough to make them all hungry, despite the fact that they had consumed every last bite of the Mexican food from La Casita just a few hours before.

Finally, a little after five, Patrick arrived with Danny, and they all congregated in the kitchen, the heart of Sylvia's home.

Getting her first look at the younger McAllister caused Lola to gasp, while the others stared in disbelief. To Jordan, he looked better, but despite the smile, she could see the fear in his eyes. Although his arm was in a sling and his black-and-blue eyes were now turning yellow as they healed, it was great to see him out of handcuffs and not chained to a hospital bed.

Danny made the rounds hugging everyone, and all were careful not to squeeze too hard because of his broken ribs.

"You look like you fought with a bear and lost, bro," Sean said, giving his brother a second hug.

"You should see the bear," Danny joked, then sniffed. "Is that what I think it is?"

Sylvia nodded. "A little birdie told me that you specifically asked for the famous McAllister pork steaks on your first night home."

"Oh, man! You have no idea how much hospital food sucks. That may have been the worst thing about my stay, even more so than the pain from my broken wrist." He lifted the lid of the Dutch oven and bent down for another smell. "So when can we eat this?"

"It'll be ready around seven. That gives you about ninety minutes to get settled in the spare bedroom down the hall. It has a bathroom attached and will be perfect for you until you recover enough to climb the steps to your own bedroom." Sylvia smiled up at her son. "While we're waiting for the pork steaks, I made Aunt Lilly's Churro Chips and Dip, just for you."

"Thanks, Mom. You're the best." He gave her a

quick kiss on the cheek then pushed up his jeans to show them the monitor on his right leg. "My new ankle bracelet, compliments of the Amarillo Police Department. I'm only allowed to travel as far as 150 feet, and I have to alert them when I have a doctor's appointment. Otherwise, an alarm goes off in their monitoring center, and I'm back in jail."

"You gotta admit, a little leg bling is better than sitting in that cell with those two thugs who beat you up." Jordan moved closer to him. "Are you ready to tell us about the hearing, or do you want to wait?"

"Nothing much to tell. You should have seen the look on the judge's face when Feldman marched into the courtroom with his army of pro-Danny soldiers. If I hadn't been so scared, I might've even laughed." He stopped talking and swallowed.

"If this is too hard for you, Son, we can get all the details later."

He took a deep breath. "I'm okay, Mom. It's just that when the judge asked me for my plea, I realized for the first time how much trouble I really am in. I pleaded not guilty, of course, after which the prosecutor asked for a $500,000 bail. Feldman put up a good argument and got that reduced to 50K. He definitely came prepared and even had a bail bondsman standing in the back of the room, ready to pay up." Danny looked around. "Y'all have no idea how great it is to be home. I will never complain about anything ever again."

"At least not for a day or two," Patrick teased, before facing the group. "Danny's trial is set to begin in five months. That should give us more than enough time to prove his innocence."

"Hopefully," Danny said. "I'm not a cop, but even I

think the evidence makes me look guilty, especially since I can't even remember anything after the bar."

"What *do* you remember, honey?" Sylvia asked.

Danny shrugged. "Not much. I stopped at Cowboy's for a drink before heading home after a particularly frustrating day. Mary Alice came over and sat beside me shortly after I sat down at the bar. She—"

"Mary Alice?" Jordan interrupted. "Don't you mean Carlita?"

"Her real name is Mary Alice Winters. She lived over on Trimble Street and went to Amarillo High School. She was a few years ahead of you and me. Do you remember her?"

Jordan shook her head before Tommy said, "I do. Mary Alice was every adolescent boy's wet dream, always wearing sexy clothes that showed off a great figure. I think she even got sent home a few times because of those outfits."

"She still has a great figure," Danny said. "I didn't realize that she had graduated with you, Tommy."

"She didn't graduate. One day she just quit coming to school. Rumor had it that she got knocked up, and her mother sent her off to live with her aunt somewhere."

"I didn't remember her at all," Danny said, "Until she reminded me that we knew each other from school. Like I said, she sat down next to me soon after I arrived, even bought me a beer while we talked. She seemed to know a lot about me and my job. It felt so good to be relaxing with a woman who looked like her after the day I'd had, that apparently, I didn't hear the alarm bells that must have been going off in my head."

"Weird that she knew you. Makes me think you were targeted," Ray commented.

"The more I think about it, the more I agree with

you, Ray. At any rate we talked for about an hour before I got a phone call from someone who said there were four cows in the middle of the road on the outskirts of town, and they were worried that one of the speeding cars would hit one of them. I went outside, because I couldn't hear the guy over the blaring music. After I called the officers on call to let them know about the cows, I went back into the bar." He shook his head. "I guess I had a couple more drinks and then, unfortunately, I'm drawing a blank about what happened after that."

"That's probably when she slipped a mickey into your drink," Jordan said.

"What makes you think she would do that?" Danny asked, grimacing when he made a sudden move to face his sister.

"Because the cops found a camera mounted above the bed at the motel. She was probably planning to blackmail you with the pictures," Patrick said.

Danny laughed. "Have you looked at my bank account lately? Last month, my ten-year-old pickup died, and I had to get a new one." He whistled. "I had no idea how much auto prices had sky-rocketed." Narrowing his eyes, he continued, "And also, there's the fact that I have a reputation as a ladies' man around town, so no one would blink an eye at pictures of me in a bed with a pretty woman."

"Ha! Ladies' man? You gotta be kidding me." Sean punched his brother's shoulder playfully.

"If you don't believe me, just ask the ladies," Danny fired back, before turning to all of them again. "What I'm saying is that if Mary... *Carlita* was planning to blackmail me with a sex tape, she would have been sorely disappointed." He addressed Patrick. "If there was a tape, do the police have it now? Did it show me pushing the knife into Carlita's chest?"

"Apparently, the woman hadn't turned on the camera that night," Patrick said. "The tape was blank."

"Maybe that's a good thing," Danny said, his eyes glassing over. "I'm not sure I could handle knowing that I killed her like that."

"No way you killed her," Jordan said. "And we're going to prove it. Now go to your room and freshen up. Take a pain pill while you're at it. I can see how hard you're trying to tough it out."

"I never could put anything past you. I won't argue with you like I always do." He leaned over and kissed her cheek before addressing his mom. "Forgot to tell you. I talked to Dad on the way home. Apparently, the negotiations aren't going as fast as he'd anticipated. He said he would leave the final talks to his assistant and see me on Saturday. I assured him that now that I was home, there was no reason to rush his departure. I talked him into staying until next Tuesday."

"That's good, honey," Sylvia said. "I know how important this trip was to his company, and finding out that you're home and that he can stay and complete the deal must have taken a weight off his shoulders."

"Hope so. Now, I really need a nap."

"We'll wake you when dinner's ready," Rosie said." And before I forget, have I mentioned how good it is to see you, battered and all? And I might add that we really enjoyed you when you came to Ranchero a few years back on business."

"Thanks, Rosie." He waved his left hand, then turned and headed for the bedroom.

With Rosie, Sylvia, and her brothers all crowded into the kitchen preparing the food, Ray and Lola sneaking in an afternoon nap, and Victor and Michael sightseeing with a map they'd bought at the 7-11, Jordan found herself finally alone with Alex. She grabbed his arm and pulled him toward the back porch where she sat down on the swing, then patted the seat next to her.

It was a gorgeous Texas day, and although the afternoon temperature was in the high eighties, there was a nice breeze that made the heat bearable. She took a deep breath, enjoying the sweet fragrance coming from the honeysuckle vines blooming on the trellis behind them.

When he sat down next to her, she scooted closer and grabbed his hand. "What a relief to have Danny finally here, although we all know that he's got a long road ahead. It will be stressful for the entire family." She got choked up and paused. "I'm not sure you know how much I appreciate that you drove all the way to Amarillo to support me so soon after you returned from your own stressful ordeal."

He stared into her eyes, then bent down to kiss her —not the passionate kiss like the one the night before. More like a comfortable-in-love gesture that still sent chills up her back.

"My boss called," he said suddenly. "I need to go back to Ranchero and finish debriefing, so that he can file his reports." He lifted up her chin with his hand. "I'm thinking about leaving Saturday morning. Are you all right with that?"

"Honestly, I may leave then, too. Lola and Victor have businesses to run, and Michael needs to go home as well. If Danny's trial isn't even going to start for five months, I see no reason for any of us to stay. There's nothing we can do to help him, plus my Dad will be home on Tuesday to take over."

He nodded. "I hate that I'll miss meeting your dad,

but as much as I wish there was something we could do, you're right. The hard work will fall on Feldman's shoulders. It's up to him to find indisputable evidence that Danny is innocent..." He paused.

"Or something that causes reasonable doubt in at least one of the jurors," Jordan finished for him. "Oh gosh! Even though I know there's no way he could have killed that woman, so far, the evidence overwhelmingly points to him." She swiped at a tear that had spilled over and was making its way down her cheek.

"We just have to pray, love."

"I know." She used her sleeve to wipe away another tear that had escaped. "Enough about Danny. I want to know about you. You mentioned you were helping the local FBI agents on something. Can you talk about it?"

"Some of it, yes," he replied. "Apparently there's been six overdose deaths at Texas Tech in the past month. Phil Norris, the lead investigator on the case, said that during that same time frame, they'd also noticed an increase in the number of homeless people dying from an overdose, as well."

"That's awful. Was it fentanyl? I read somewhere that fentanyl is now the number one killer of our kids."

"True, but we're talking about fentanyl with a twist. The lab analyzed the blood samples from all of the deceased, and found traces of an animal tranquilizer—dubbed Tranq on the

Street—in every one of the bodies. The working theory is that the combination gives a longer and better high, and because of this, gives the user more bang for his buck." He stopped to take a deep breath and blew it out slowly. "Unfortunately, it also kills them. Xylazine—that's the tranquilizer—is used to anesthetize animals, but unlike fentanyl, it doesn't respond to Narcan."

"Oh no! So there's not an antidote for this new drug?"

"There is one, but unfortunately, it's kept at the veterinary clinics and not routinely carried around by the police or the medical people the way Narcan is."

"That's terrible." She snuggled closer. "So how are you helping the Feebs downtown?"

He looked away for a second, probably trying to decide how much he could tell her without compromising the case. "You know I was undercover with the Terrazes cartel, right?" When she nodded, he continued, "After Norris related the stories about the increased number of overdoses, I remembered a conversation I'd heard between two high-level soldiers while I was being held prisoner. They were discussing how they were able to get the fentanyl across the border in Juarez. They said their gang members here in the States could then add the other drugs, including the animal tranquilizer, to the pills to make them more addictive and more expensive. When he heard that story, he asked if I would look over the information they had gathered on the cases so far, to see if there was anything I might add that could help them. Of course, I agreed."

"Was that the file you were reading when I paid you a hospitality visit last night?"

"So that's what we're calling it now? You sneaking into my bed—hospitality?" He wiggled his eyebrows in a comical way. "And yes, that was the file, and because of you, I didn't have a chance to finish reading it." He gave her another eyebrow wiggle. "But I'm not complaining, mind you."

"Shh! One of my brothers might hear you," she joked, before staring into his eyes, wondering if she should proceed. She decided he could tell her *no* if he didn't want to talk about it. "You never did tell me what really happened to you in Mexico when even your handler couldn't make contact with you."

Alex lowered his eyes. "I'm not ready to go there yet, but when I am, you will definitely be the first person I tell. Suffice it to say, I truly believed that I was going to die without ever seeing your beautiful face again."

"However long it takes for you to come to grips with your emotions, I can wait." She stood up. "Now, let's go inside and see if we can help my mom get dinner on the table. My mouth is already watering for those pork steaks."

He stood up and walked with her to the door. "Mine, too, but before we go in, there's something I want to say to you."

She looked away, afraid of what he was about to tell her. Was this where he confessed that he had only proposed because he believed he was going to die? Was it the near-death experience that pushed him to do something he wasn't ready to do?

"I can see your busy little mind working overtime. Hear me when I say that no matter what happened in Mexico, my decision to ask for your hand in marriage was not in any way connected. Truthfully, I've been thinking about it for months, just waiting for the right moment. When you agreed to spend the rest of your life with me, it made me the happiest man on the planet. Sure, my priorities have changed, but you have to know how crazy in love with you I am—how thinking about returning home to you was the only thing that kept me alive in that jungle."

"That's pretty impressive, Moreland," she replied, trying to lighten the mood before realizing it probably wasn't the time to make a joke. "Now might be as good a time as any to tell you that as much as you love me, I love you that much and more." She opened the door. "Now let's go pig out on pork steaks. I know that you adore anything lemon, and my mother's Lemon Delight is gonna water your eyes."

HE WALKED into his apartment and went straight to the bedroom, intending to sneak in a nap before his meeting. He'd been surprised when he'd gotten the call that the boss needed to talk to him. He searched his brain for a reason.

Had he somehow screwed up and was about to get fired—or worse?

He decided that since he had no control over whatever was going to happen, he wasn't going to worry about it. He had enough on his plate as it was, without trying to speculate on why the sudden meeting.

Lying down on the mattress, fully clothed, his eyes strayed to the corkboard on the wall above his desk. At least a dozen pictures of the stripper covered the entire area. Looking at her caused an array of emotions, none of which even resembled sorrow.

Then, just like every other time when he looked at her, he got angry. He had to let it go. She'd paid the ultimate price for her sins. Maybe now he could get on with his life.

But the more he looked at her pictures, the angrier he got.

He jumped out of bed, ran to the kitchen to retrieve a paring knife, then returned to his bedroom and stood in front of the pictures. Taking a deep breath, he closed his eyes and shoved the knife into the heart of the woman who had ruined his life.

He stared at it for several seconds, imagining blood running down the picture frame, wondering how she must've felt when she realized she was dying. He thought he would feel a little sadness, but there was nothing.

The woman had learned the hard way that Karma was a beotch with a capital B.

8

A fabulous dinner plus watching her family having a good time made it a perfect evening for Jordan. At one point, Danny had to ask them to quit telling funny stories, because every time he laughed, he yelped and grabbed his ribs. As expected, Alex charmed the pants off of her family, especially Patrick's teenage daughters, who crowded around him with doe-like eyes and hung onto his every word, like he was Superman.

Jordan giggled to herself. Her nieces had the right idea. The man *was* Superman, at least to her.

She caught her fiancé's attention and pointed to her finger where she would one day wear a diamond ring if they ever found time to check out a jewelry store. "Remember, you're engaged," she mouthed playfully.

He rewarded her with one of his big smiles, then went right on with the story he'd been telling.

Since there was no news in Danny's case, the small talk around the table continued as everyone devoured the lemon dessert. Jordan caught a glimpse of Alex licking a little whipped cream off his lips, and for a split second, she fantasized about being alone with him. Quickly, the grin she knew must be spreading across her face changed to a scowl when she noticed the hard look Sean was sending her way. It was almost as if he could read the X-rated fantasies running rampant in her head.

Patrick's wife and daughters left soon after the dessert plates were rinsed and stacked in the dishwasher. Renee, who was the senior buyer at Lindy's World Market had to be at work early the next morning for a meeting, and it was a school night for the girls. Since Patrick was still staying at the hotel in downtown Amarillo, he'd driven his own car to the house. When his mother had asked why he hadn't gone back to Lubbock, now that Danny was home, he'd explained that the first week of any criminal investigation was usually the most productive, and he felt it was still necessary to be close to Feldman's office so he could keep up with the investigation.

After listening to his two teenage daughters jibber-jabbering all night and arguing with their mother about everything, Jordan would bet money that the real reason her oldest brother didn't want to go home right now had little to do with being close to Danny's lawyer. In today's world, technology had made it easier to conduct businesses from long distances, even as far away as another country. A simple conference call between him and Feldman seemed like more than enough at this stage, while Danny's lawyer and his own investigators searched for clues.

There was no doubt in Jordan's mind that the downtown hotel offered peace and quiet and a respite from raising not one, but two teenage girls with all their raging hormonal moods. Jordan wondered if she had been that moody in her teenage years, then decided she had been—and probably more so.

Her eyes strayed to her mother, the matriarch of the family in her father's absence, and decided that any woman who had raised four rowdy boys and one fiercely independent daughter deserved a medal.

Around 9 o'clock, Patrick's phone rang. After glancing at caller ID, he excused himself and disappeared into his father's office.

The silence that followed contrasted with the loud, boisterous scene from just minutes before when everyone was talking at once. Now, they all sat quietly while they waited for Patrick's return. Jordan said a quick prayer that it was only Renee calling about something she'd forgotten at the house.

Finally after fifteen minutes, Patrick emerged from the office and walked over to the table. Although he attempted to smile, he wasn't able to hide the worried look on his face as he moved over to stand behind Danny.

Sylvia picked up on it immediately. "What's wrong, Son? Who was that on the phone?"

"It was Feldman, Mom. They just delivered some discovery documents from the DA's office, and something caught his attention right away. He wants me to talk with Danny about it." He motioned for his brother to follow him back to their father's office.

Danny didn't budge. "I consider everyone around this table as family. What you have to say to me can be said in front of all of them."

Patrick blew out a breath before addressing his youngest brother. "Three things, really. After hearing your story, it's obvious you were drugged. Unfortunately, that will be hard to prove since the bottle of liquor in the room had no trace of any drugs in it. Matter of fact, the only drug the police did find was a dusting of fentanyl around the rim of the glass Carlita used for her Scotch-on-the-rocks. That tiny amount is enough to kill an adult—and did."

"What about my glass?" Danny asked. "Did it have fentanyl on it as well?"

"Fortunately, there was only one glass in the room. You were probably semi-conscious at that point. Otherwise, you would have died right beside that woman. More bad news is that rohypnol, the date rape drug, usually the culprit in cases where the victim loses his or her memory, wasn't detected in your blood."

"Wait a minute. I happen to know that rohypnol is detectable in the blood and urine for up to seventy-two hours," Alex said. "Are they sure Danny's blood was negative?"

Patrick nodded. "The tox screen didn't show anything other than the drugs they administered at the hospital."

Alex eyes widened. "Are you saying that they didn't get a blood sample from him until he was in the hospital? That should have happened immediately after they booked him at the police station."

"Keywords here being *should have*. After transferring him from the motel to the jail, Danny was printed and his mug shot taken, then they put him in the cell to await the arrival of the lab tech to draw the blood." Patrick shook his head. "Apparently, someone dropped the ball and never followed up on the fact that the lab tech never showed up. Turns out the desk sergeant forgot to make the call. In the meantime, old man Tucker and his delinquent son, who were booked on a drunk and disorderly charge after they shot up their neighbor's parked car, were put in Danny's cell and proceeded to pound the crap out of him."

"I tried to tell them that those two were nut jobs,

and that they'd follow through on their threat to kill me if they put them in the cell with me," Danny said.

"The more I think about it, the more I'm convinced that you ought to consider a lawsuit once this ordeal is over. Kramer, the civil litigator who was at your bail hearing this morning, said you had an excellent case against the city, and he was ready to go after them if you decided to pursue it," Patrick said.

"I'm really not interested in that since most of the cops in the precinct are my drinking buddies. Hell, I went to school with half of them."

"Yeah, right. Did your buddies have your back when they put the Tuckers in the cell with you, bro?" Sean asked sarcastically.

"Those were two young guys who probably just got out of the academy. The older cops rarely work the cell block."

"All I'm saying is that you have that trump card to play if things don't go your way. It might make the judge a little less inclined to throw the book at you if there's the threat of a multi-million-dollar lawsuit hanging over the city." Patrick shifted in the chair. "But back to my original story about why your blood wasn't drawn at the police station. After those two thugs were put in the cell with you and the cops heard you screaming, they rushed in and called for an ambulance to transport you to the Amarillo General, where they immediately scheduled you for emergency surgery. They finally drew your blood while you were waiting in the X-Ray Department for the MRI."

"I had an MRI?" Danny looked confused.

Ray leaned across the table to speak directly to him. "Just curious. What time did you find the woman dead?"

"I don't know. Is that important?" Danny thought

for a minute. "I'd say it was around ten or eleven Sunday morning."

"Could be important. What time do you think you left the club?" Ray continued.

"Not sure, but I know it was after midnight because the bell goes off every night at that time. Traditionally, every Saturday night when the bar is packed, the dude closest to the bartender when it does ring has to either buy everyone in the place a drink or wear a Cinderella T-shirt and do the Cotton-Eyed Joe in the middle of the dance floor all by himself."

"Been there—done that," Sean said. "Trust me, once it happens to you, you make a special effort to keep your eye on the clock and be as far away from the bar as you can get when midnight rolls around."

"Happened once to me, too, along with most of the regulars at the bar. Like you, we know better now. Unfortunately, Jimmy Ackerman was too snookered to remember about the tradition and was pounding on the bar demanding another Corona when the bell sounded. Believe me, he was not a happy camper having to pay for a round of drinks for all of us there, so he elected to go the cheap way." Danny's eyes lit up with amusement. "You should have seen him out there dancing like the fool he is. He must have fallen two or three times, but to his credit, he stayed out there shaking his booty the entire time. He was so entertaining that the bartender rewarded him with a drink on the house. That made him forget that he had just made a complete idiot of himself."

"And your surgery was around seven on Monday night?" Ray pressed on. "So, if you were drugged sometime after midnight, even if they didn't draw your blood until Monday in the hospital, the rohypnol should have shown up on your toxicology screen. Like

Alex said, it can be detected up to seventy-two hours after ingestion." He paused, then said, "Unless another tranquilizer was used, and I have a feeling that if that's the case, I might know what that other drug could be."

Everyone stared at him, hanging onto his every word, while he took a sip of his beer before turning to Alex. "You and I talked about this very thing not so long ago. Remember?"

Alex nodded. "I see where you're going with this. Yes, there is another drug that would totally erase any memories Danny would have had after taking it. I was telling Ray about a case last year when we investigated a pediatric anesthesiologist who was dosing his six-year-old child so he could spend a few hours at a singles bar. The kid would still be asleep when the guy returned with a woman he'd picked up at the bar, and he'd wake up with no memory of anything the next morning. Apparently, the good doctor had been doing this for some time without consequences. His luck ran out, though, when one of his one-night stands ended up beaten to death in an apparent rough-sex orgy. We were called in by the local police to help after the cops arrived on the scene and couldn't wake the kid. He was rushed to the emergency room, where they discovered he'd been drugged."

"What was that drug, Alex?" Sylvia asked.

"Midazolam. It's used with other drugs for what they call a twilight sleep during quick procedures like endoscopic surgery and other less invasive ones that don't require general anesthesia."

"I had a personal experience with that one," Ray said. "Last year when I had a colonoscopy, I was complaining to the nurses because of the long wait. They laughed and said my procedure was already over and they were getting ready to discharge me. The miracle of midazolam, they called it."

"That's the one," Alex said. "It's usually administered intravenously, but in children, it's given in a syrup before they start an IV and do all the pre-surgical preparations. I'm thinking there's a really good possibility that Carlita slipped you midazolam, Danny."

Patrick scrolled down on his phone. "I'm looking at the tox screen right now, and midazolam is one of the drugs they tested for." He looked up at his brother. "It's positive."

"Does that prove that Carlita drugged me and that I didn't kill her?" Danny asked, hope filling his eyes.

"Not necessarily," Alex said. "Midazolam is also used before surgery as a pre-op sedative to calm a patient. I'm wondering if you were given that injection, Danny."

"He was." Jordan looked toward Danny. "Right before they transported you to

X-Ray for the MRI before surgery, the anesthesiologist came in and pushed a syringe full of medicine directly into your IV. Said it would help with your nerves."

"The fact that you can't remember having an MRI makes me believe it was midazolam the anesthesiologist gave you before they transported you." Alex turned around to face Patrick. "If Feldman can get a warrant for copies of Danny's medical records, we'll know for sure. The bad news is that the DA will argue the reason Danny's blood tested positive was because of the pre-op injection and not because Carlita drugged him with it."

"And you think she slipped this drug into my drink at the bar?"

"That's the only thing that makes sense, since no drugs were found in the motel room." Alex shook his head. "What's puzzling to me, though, is that midazolam syrup is bitter tasting. When they give it to kids, they put it in a mixture with salt and a lot of sugary dilution. You would have noticed that and probably not finished the drink. It's that bitter."

Danny sat back in his chair, deep in thought. "We were doing tequila shooters with a lot of salt around the rim. I kinda remember it being a little weird tasting, but tequila is already bitter on its own. That's why you have to lick, shoot, and suck. Lick the salt off your hand first, drink the shot quickly, and finish by sucking a lime after chugging it."

"Like I said, salt cuts some of the bitter taste. How many shooters did you do?" Alex asked.

"Only that one. Carlita ordered them, then dared me to chug mine before she did. It went down fast, but I do remember thinking it had a bitter after-taste. I went back to beer after that."

"One drink was probably all it took to sedate you in your already semi-inebriated state." Alex turned to Patrick. "Midazolam is not a drug that the average person can get with a prescription. It's only available to the medical community. We need to find out where Carlita might have gotten it, assuming it's the drug that knocked Danny out."

"I'll have Feldman's law clerks check all the local pharmacies to see if anything suspicious turns up. I'll also have them check the hospitals and clinics where they might use the drug and find out if more than usual was purchased."

"That's a start." Alex turned to Ray. "We only have one more day until we head back to Ranchero. What do you say to you and me paying a little visit tomorrow night to the strip club where Carlita worked? Are you in?"

"I haven't been to a strip club in years," Ray said, a grin spreading across his face. "It's a tough job, but I guess someone has to do it."

Lola slapped him playfully on the shoulder. "Listen up, old man. When you're looking at all those young, sexy, half-naked women, you'd better remember that I talk to the spirits. I'd hate to have them come after you."

"Point taken, dear. I'll definitely close my eyes."

"Yeah, right."

"Patrick, you said there were three things that Feldman wanted you to tell me. What was the third thing?" Danny asked.

"He only mentioned it in passing, but he wanted you to be updated about everything involving your case. Apparently, there was an attempted robbery at the 7-11 around the corner from the motel around three that morning. On the surveillance video, police noticed a stocky man wearing a baseball cap hanging around an SUV parked on the side. The guy was there for over fifteen minutes and then left. They were able to find the guy from the license plates on his own car at the pumps."

"And this is important why?" Danny asked, interested now.

"It could have been. The guy was an operating room technician who had been called in late that night for emergency surgery on a car accident victim. On the way home, he stopped at the gas station to fill up and to grab a gallon of milk for his kids' cereal the next morning. While he was pumping the gas, he noticed the SUV, which he said had SPECIALTY CAKES on one of those magnetic signs on the passenger door.

According to him, he went over to see about ordering an Italian Cream Cake, his wife's favorite, for her birthday the following week." He paused. "The cops looked into it, and his story checked out."

"I still don't see how this is important," Danny said impatiently. "Now if you told me that the guy had a steak knife or a scalpel in his hand, you would definitely get my attention."

Patrick grinned. "You never could make it to the end of a story, even when you were a kid and reading a book. You'd go to the last page to see what happened after one or two chapters. If you didn't like the way it ended, you'd quit reading it."

"I can't tell you how many times I fussed at him about that," Sylvia said, before flipping her hand Patrick's way. "So, get on with this story. Like Danny, I want to know how it ends."

He sat down in his chair and continued, "Anyway, the medical guy assumed that whoever owned the car had gone into the store for a late-night snack or a restroom break. After waiting there for over fifteen minutes with no sign of anyone he went inside for the milk, but he was the only customer in there. He figured maybe someone had a little too much to drink and left the SUV there, rather than risk a DUI."

"Patrick, why does Feldman think this is important?" Alex asked.

"He doesn't, really, but he wanted Danny to know that the police were following all leads in the investigation. When they interviewed the owner of the SUV, he told them that he'd run to the 7-11 for some late-night snacks on Saturday, and when he got back to his vehicle, he noticed that one of his hubcaps was missing. Said he spent about thirty minutes backtracking and finally found it on the road about a mile back."

"What about any other leads, Patrick?" Sylvia asked.

"Unfortunately, Mom, just like this lead, none of the others tips they received panned out, either."

"So, I'm their one and only suspect?"

"Right now, yes, but don't lose hope, bro. It's been less than a week since this all happened. All of us are working to find new information that might clear you." Patrick looked down at his smart watch when it dinged. "It's a news alert. Turn on the TV. Something's going down at the Lazy Days Motel."

Sean got up and walked to the television. As soon as he turned it on, a picture of the sign outside the motel flashed and a BREAKING NEWS banner crawled across the screen. Quickly, he turned up the volume so that everyone could hear, as the screen changed to the pool area of the motel.

"The police discovered the body of Steve Hudson this evening in the swimming pool of the Lazy Days Motel, where he lived. It was believed that Hudson, the motel manager, had overdosed and fallen into the pool after several bags of cocaine and a small bag of fentanyl pills were discovered in his room. As of now, the police are treating this as an accident, pending an autopsy and the toxicology results."

"My goodness!" Sylvia exclaimed. "I've never heard of the Lazy Days Motel until this week, and now we find out there have two deaths there in less than seven days."

The others began chattering about the news report, but Jordan had tuned them all out. Stevie was dead. Could it be a coincidence? Was he floating in the pool the entire time she and Victor were standing in his office waiting for him? She glanced toward Victor who was staring daggers at her.

She couldn't wait any longer to admit that she and Victor had been to the motel not once, but twice, and had actually talked to the dead man. She braced herself for the fallout they would get, especially from Alex, for putting themselves in harm's way.

She cleared her throat and said, "I have something to tell you all."

9

"Let me get this straight. You went to the Lazy Days Motel and talked to the guy they later found floating in the motel pool?" Alex's eyes flashed anger. "Why would you do such a thing? For all you knew, that man could have been the killer."

"Alex is right, Jordan," Ray chimed in. "Besides the danger involved, there's the little issue of the police. Technically, they could arrest you for obstruction of justice just for crossing the crime scene tape, not to mention that you actually went inside the room that's still considered a murder scene. There's a reason the crime scene tape is still there, you know."

Jordan lowered her eyes. "I know. I screwed up. We —I had this bonehead idea that if there was something the police missed, maybe I could find it. It was one of my worst 'hold my beer' moments." She nodded toward Victor. "Don't blame him. I coerced him into going with me."

"A person who is with someone in the commission of a crime is just as guilty as the one who actually commits it," Ray admonished, before his voice softened. "Okay. Enough beating up on Jordan over this. What's done is done. Let's hope that Steve Hudson didn't have a chance to talk to the cops and tell them about you two before he overdosed and fell into the pool."

"I'm curious, Jordan, how did you convince the office manager to give you a key to the room in the first place?" Alex asked.

Jordan glanced toward Victor again, and for a short second, she saw a flash of amusement in his eyes. There was no way she was gonna fess up to unbuttoning her blouse to get that key. Alex would kill her, and he'd have a pretty good reason for doing it.

What had she been thinking?

"I slipped him a twenty-dollar bill," Victor said, rescuing her. "The kid had traces of white powder under his nose and was already high on drugs when we arrived. I knew he was probably anticipating his next fix and would jump at the sight of cold hard cash to pay for it."

After listening to his lie, Jordan didn't dare look his way, knowing she might blurt out the truth and take full blame if she did. She decided that her lame attempt at being sexy to get the information she wanted from a druggie would not go over well with all the people around the table, except maybe Rosie, who would probably high-five her.

"He was only too happy to hand over the key," she said. "He knew what he was doing, cautioned us not to disturb anything in the room, even though the evidence guys had already checked it out."

"You and I will need to have a discussion about this later," Alex said. "For now, you might as well tell us what you saw in the room."

"Nothing really, except that the bed was not very bloody."

"That's because Carlita was already dead when she

was stabbed," Ray said. "You're a reporter, Jordan, and you have good investigative instincts. Did you see anything out of the ordinary—something the police might have missed?"

Jordan grabbed her phone from the table and scrolled through the pictures. She handed it to Ray. "We found a camera mounted above the bed."

"And you didn't think that was important enough to tell us?" Patrick asked, slamming his fist on the table.

"We did, Patrick, but when we asked Stevie about it, he said that there was no

tape in the recorder—that Carlita must have forgotten to turn it on. You said yourself that the police had found the camera, but they knew there wasn't a tape. We didn't think it was an issue any longer since they already had that information."

"So, did your friend Stevie say anything else that might help Danny's case? Did he maybe see anything unusual that night?" Patrick asked, a little calmer now. "Since there definitely was a camera mounted above the bed, he must've known about it."

"He did, but he said he only found an empty recorder. When Victor and I went back the second time, he wasn't even in the office. We waited a few minutes for him to return, but he never did."

Patrick's face turned beet red, and Jordan worried that he was about to have a stroke or something. "Why in God's name would you go back a second time, Jordan?" He shook his head. "I can only pray that we don't see your pretty little face in a jail cell next to Danny."

"She left her case with all her pens and pencils there," Victor said. When Patrick looked confused, he continued, "The first time we went there, we pretended to be reporters from Lubbock. She brought along a yellow pad and her pencil case as props. It wasn't until we were in the car on our way home that she realized she'd left it on the counter in the office."

"Dad gave me that case when I went off to college. It's been my good-luck charm ever since. That's why we had to go back to get it," Jordan said, her eyes pleading with her brother before turning defiant. "I'm sorry, Patrick, but I had to at least try to help Danny, and I didn't think about the consequences of my actions."

Alex stood and walked around the table and put his arms around her from behind. "Nobody can fault you for that, love. But promise me that in the future you'll leave the dangerous stuff to Ray and me? We've been trained for that, you know."

She took a deep breath for courage. Now that she was no longer Enemy Number One in the room, she might as well tell them the rest. "There's something else I forgot to mention. When Victor and I left the motel, I noticed one of the drapes moving in the room next to the office. According to the news last night, Stevie lives—lived— at the motel. I just figured he was hiding out there snorting more coke."

"He probably was. You and Victor might well have been the last ones to see the man alive." Ray got up from the table. "Okay, so now that we have that out of the way, my lady and I need to call it a night." He turned to Alex. "What time tomorrow do you want to check out the strip club where Carlita worked?"

"They probably won't open the doors before seven or eight. We can head over there after dinner, which by the way, I have a great suggestion for all of us. How about if I treat everyone at that steakhouse I've heard so much about—the one where you get a free steak if you can eat half of a cow?"

That brought a laugh from everyone and lightened the mood.

"Count me out," Sean said. "I'm on shift at the firehouse tomorrow."

"And I've got the kids overnight," Tommy said. "Enjoy the steak, though."

Patrick looked down at his watch. "I'm afraid I'm out as well. Tomorrow I'm going to work with Feldman most of the day to process what little evidence we have so far. Then, unless he needs me to stay on, I'll be heading back to Lubbock tomorrow night. Seems Renee is pulling her hair out dealing with our two hormonal daughters by herself, along with one of her migraines that came on suddenly. Right now, though, I need to get back to the hotel to examine the discovery documents that Feldman sent over."

"You know I can't go, either," Danny said, pointing to the monitor on his leg. "You can make it up to me, though, by bringing me a big helping of dessert."

"You always talked about the Hot Fudge Cake at Yellow Rose Steakhouse, Danny. Would a big slice of that do it for you?" Jordan said.

Danny laughed. "You know it would, Sis, but if Alex has his heart set on seeing the 'eat a cow' steakhouse, any old dessert would do."

"I couldn't care less about seeing people gorge themselves on a piece of beef," Alex responded. "And I've never had a piece of cake with both chocolate and hot fudge in its name. I could be easily persuaded to go there instead."

Victor's eyes lit up. "Sounds yummy! I've never had it, either. Please, please, Alex, can we go to the Yellow Rose Steak House?"

"Oh yeah! That cake there is the best," Danny said. "And if you do go to the Yellow Rose, Jordan, say hello to Abby Rivera for me. She's the manager there."

"I haven't seen her since high school," Jordan said. "Is she still as pretty as she was when she had all the pimply-faced boys fighting to carry her books from one classroom to another?"

"Maybe even prettier. We dated a few times last month, but we discovered we were better friends than lovers."

"Oh dear, you got the old 'friend zone' speech from her?" Rosie asked.

Danny laughed. "Nothing like that, Rosie. Actually the break-up was mutual. She rarely gets a day off, so it was kinda hard trying to build a relationship. Like I said, we're only friends now."

"Mom, are you gonna go with us?" Jordan asked. "You could use a break from the kitchen."

"Nonsense! I love to cook. So I'll stay home and keep Danny company. You all have a good time at one of Amarillo's famous landmarks," she said before adding, "I could sure use a big helping of that dessert as well. They say chocolate elevates your endorphins and makes you feel better."

"You've been hanging out with Victor too long," Michael joked.

~

THE NEXT MORNING, the sun drifted in through the window in Sylvia's bedroom, hinting at what would be a beautiful spring day in Amarillo. The weather forecast had called for a high of eighty-five, which was unusual for the month of May. Jordan sat up in bed, noticing that her mother was already 'up and at 'em,' probably fixing the crowd a big breakfast.

Before everyone had retired to their own beds last night, Jordan managed to sneak in a few minutes alone with Alex. She thought he would still be mad at her, but if he was, he had a funny way of showing it. The kiss he sent her to bed with had kept her awake half the night, dreaming of what might have followed that kiss if they'd been back home now. Despite the verbal whipping she'd taken from both Ray and her brother Patrick, she knew telling everyone about visiting the Lazy Days Motel had been the right thing to do.

And now that she had, it felt like a weight had been lifted off her shoulders.

After breakfast, Alex made his apologies and left for downtown Amarillo. Apparently, the FBI had received a break in the case involving the fentanyl laced with Xylazine, the animal tranquilizer. Since Narcan had no effect on the tranquilizer, the combination had proven to be more deadly than fentanyl by itself, which was killing far too many young people as it was.

The local FBI guys had called Alex late last night to tell him they'd discovered a veterinarian on the outskirts of town who had been ordering an unusually large amount of Xylazine. They were planning to pay a visit to the clinic with a search warrant in hand and asked Alex to go with them, since he had worked undercover for so long and was knowledgeable about drug trafficking.

Alex made sure that Jordan was okay with him being gone most of the day, which she was. He promised to be home in time to go with them to the Yellow Rose Steak House, especially since he'd opened his big mouth and offered to spring for everyone's meal.

Jordan wanted to spend the time showing off her hometown to her friends, including the world-renowned Route 66, which ran from downtown Chicago to the Santa Monica Pier in California, passing right through the center of Amarillo. The plan included a trip to Cadillac Ranch, followed by a quick walk through downtown Amarillo to do a little souvenir shopping, and then a drive through Palo Duro Canyon State Park, where they planned to picnic with a bucket of fried chicken.

Sylvia and Danny were just gonna chill at home until Danny's appointment later that afternoon with his orthopedic surgeon to make sure that his wrist was still in alignment.

The gang all piled into Ray's Suburban, and with Jordan as their tour guide, they set off on their afternoon adventure. The first stop was Cadillac Ranch, just off Interstate 40.

"Holy cow! Look at all those Caddies nose down in the dirt," Victor exclaimed, practically falling all over Jordan to get a better look.

Rosie narrowed her eyes in his direction. "Thought you saw this the other day with Jordan."

Victor's face colored a little, and he looked toward Jordan for help. "We didn't make it there."

"We were going to," Jordan said, rescuing him. "But I talked him into doing some detective work with me instead. That's when we went to the Lazy Days Motel to snoop around."

Victor rewarded her with a big smile. "And she promised we would check out this place before we left Amarillo." He turned to Michael. "Did you know that all those Cadillacs are covered in graffiti?"

"I did know that. A couple of years ago, I interviewed a hippie artist on my radio show who bragged that some of his best work was displayed on the cars."

"Pretty awesome, really," Jordan said. "There are always half-empty cans of spray paint lying around for anyone who wants to take a shot at becoming graffiti artists themselves."

"Cool," Lola said. "I used to be pretty good with a canvas and a paint brush in my day. This will give me a chance to show off my talents."

"One of your many talents, I might add, my dear," Ray said, before winking at her.

"Criminy! Get a room, you two," Victor said. "Oh, wait! You have a room at Jordan's house. Hope you're not christening Sylvia's guest bedroom."

Lola playfully slapped his shoulder. "Wouldn't you like to know?"

"TMI," Victor exclaimed, covering his ears.

"Victor might not want to know," Rosie said. "But I do. With my social life, or lack thereof, I live vicariously through you two lovebirds."

"Some things are better kept secret," Ray said, as he parked the SUV.

Like promised, Cadillac Ranch was amazing, and they spent a good hour designing their own creations. Lola painted an image of a horse's head that had them all singing her praises. It was so pleasant being there that they decided to kiss off the visit to the state park. Instead, they sent Lola and Ray out to get a bucket of chicken, spread out the blankets Jordan had brought on the ground, and enjoyed lunch while they admired their handiwork on the cars.

After leaving Cadillac Ranch, they drove to downtown Amarillo, where Jordan had promised they'd find really neat niche shops where they could get souvenirs to take back to Ranchero.

They had barely stepped out of the car on their way toward the shops when Victor began to complain about the wind, which had definitely picked up since they'd left their last destination.

"Wow! I didn't realize that Amarillo got this windy." Ray was out of breath after successfully chasing down his Texas Ranger hat that had blown off his head and floated down the street.

"The Texas Panhandle is probably one of the windiest regions in the US, especially in April and apparently spilling over to May," Jordan explained. "The westerly winds come in over the Rocky Mountains and can be as fierce as sixty-five miles per hour on the high plains."

"I have to admit that with warm weather like today, the breeze feels pretty good right now," Michael said. "Is it always this hot in May?"

"It's a little warmer today than the average temperature here in Amarillo at this time of year, when the highs are usually in the seventies. Like I said, the winds are common, and occasionally, a tornado rips through here. Fortunately, it's usually an F1 or F2 and not the more destructive kind, although Amarillo has had a few of those F4s and F5s in the past as well," Jordan explained.

Rosie stopped walking abruptly. "Is that a gourmet shop I see up ahead?"

"Like you cook gourmet food," Victor teased.

"Shut up! I might just want to expand my cooking skills," she fired back, before adding, "And you should talk, mister. You wouldn't know gourmet food if it bit you on your cute little tushy."

Jordan tried unsuccessfully to stifle a grin. "First of all, his tushy is neither cute nor little."

"Ha, ha, Jordan. I could go on and on about your skinny little butt."

"Please don't. I surrender." She turned to Rosie. "And I for one, hope you never learn to cook that way. I hate everything about gourmet food and love—love—*love* your casseroles."

"Thanks, dear." Rosie slowed down in front of the gourmet shop. "I'm still gonna check it out, but I know that none of you are interested in going there with me. Why don't we all do our own thing and meet back at the car in an hour?"

"Lola and I are just going to sit on that bench over there and people-watch, as we enjoy this gorgeous Texas day," Ray said.

"Sounds enticing," Michael agreed. "I love to watch people and try to figure out what they do for a living, but I see an electronics store across the street that's calling my name."

"Boring," Victor blurted. "I think I'll stay with Jordan. She likes to look at the goofy things that I like."

"Suit yourself." Michael pointed to his watch. "We need to meet back at the car at two. Agreed?"

They all agreed and went their separate ways. Jordan and Victor's first stop was an antique store, where Victor proclaimed in his outside voice that his own antique store in Ranchero offered a much nicer selection and lower prices. As the store owner walked toward them, probably to kick them out, Jordan grabbed Victor's arm and shoved him out the door.

As they headed down the street, they walked past Golden's Jewelers, and Jordan couldn't resist staring into the window, where a variety of diamond rings were displayed.

When Victor caught her looking, he grabbed her hand and guided her into the store. "Come on. Let's go pick out a ring for you, since you and Alex haven't found the time to do it yourselves."

Jordan opened her mouth to protest, but actually, the idea intrigued her. Not because she wanted to buy a ring in Amarillo, but because she could get an idea about what style she liked when she and Alex did find time to go ring shopping in Ranchero. She was curious about the price of diamonds as well.

As soon as they entered the shop, a middle-aged man dressed in a navy-blue suit and a matching shirt and tie approached them. His name tag identified him as Martin Grover. "May I help you?" he asked. "Are you two looking for wedding rings?"

Victor giggled, then recovered enough to nod. "Yes, please show us what you have to offer."

For the next twenty minutes, Jordan tried on at least fifteen different rings. "I like the emerald cut diamonds the best," she said, holding her hand in the air to stare at the ring on her finger, marveling at the way it sparkled.

"That one's a beauty. It's a flawless, one carat, and lists for $9,500." When both Jordan and Victor frowned, Grover lowered his voice. "This one has already been reduced from $12,000, and I can't offer any further reductions. I'm sorry."

"Money is no object for us. I want my sweetheart here to have the very best."

Jordan coughed to cover up her laugh as she kicked him in the shin.

"Ouch!" he cried out, before turning back to the salesman. "My fiancée and I will talk about this one over dinner tonight, and if we decide that she can't live without it, we'll be back tomorrow," he lied.

Grover stared at them for second, and as they turned to leave, he said. "Wait! If money isn't an issue with you, there's a ring in my office that you have to see."

He hurried into the back room and returned with another ring box, which was pretty awesome-looking all by itself. When he opened it, Jordan knew she was looking at the most gorgeous diamond she'd even seen. Nestled in a rich, black-velvet bed, the round-cut diamond was so brilliant, it almost hurt her eyes to stare directly at it. The diamond had to be at least four or five carats and was surrounded by a multitude of smaller diamonds, equally brilliant.

"Wow! That's gorgeous, but I'm afraid my fiancé exaggerated just a little. There's no way we can afford something like this, but just in case we decide that our budget can handle it, how much does a ring like this cost?"

"Seventy-five grand. I know you prefer the emerald-cut diamonds, but I have to tell you that the round brilliant—which is what this one is—is by far the most popular with its fifty-seven perfectly aligned facets. Total internal reflection is the key here as light travels through the stone, giving it optimum sparkle and scintillation. This one is set in a combination of eighteen and twenty-four-carat gold and has a total of six carats of flawless diamonds."

Jordan couldn't stop staring at the ring. "It is gorgeous, but definitely out of our price range." She grabbed Victor's arm and headed toward the door. "We'll talk about the other ring you showed us and get back to you sometime tomorrow," she said over her shoulder.

"Wait." Grover called out again. When they turned and faced him, he continued, "I can't discount that emerald-cut ring, but I can give you a great deal on this one."

"I'm afraid that won't make much difference," Jordan said. "It's still way too expensive for us."

The salesman motioned for them to come back to the counter, and when they did, he leaned over and whispered. "What if I knock off fifty percent?"

Jordan glanced down at the ring. It was way too gaudy for her taste, but her curiosity got the best of her. "You would do that?"

He straightened up. "I personally designed this for a woman who paid me twenty grand up front," he said, glancing around the room to make sure the other customers and salespeople were not within hearing distance.

"I remember that she and the guy with her insisted that I use eighteen and twenty-four carat gold and only flawless diamonds. When I quoted them a price, neither of them even flinched. That's why I was so surprised that she hadn't come back to pick up the ring. Thought she'd stiffed me."

"Why didn't she pick it up?" Victor asked. "If I'd put out that kind of money up front for something, I'd sure as heck make certain to come back for it."

"I'm afraid she can't do that."

"Why not?" Jordan asked, really interested now.

"Because she was murdered on Saturday night."

Jordan's mouth dropped open. Finally, she recovered and asked, "What was this woman's name?"

Again, Grover made sure that no one else could hear before he responded. "Carlita Fontaine. Honestly, after I heard what happened to her, I half-expected the guy to return for it, since they had put so much money down, but he never showed back up here, either."

Jordan grabbed Victor's hand and practically pushed him out the door, leaving a very surprised salesclerk behind. Once outside she blew out a slow, noisy breath. "How in the world could a stripper afford a $75,000 ring?" she asked, as they hurried away from the jewelry store.

"She was blackmailing the men she slept with. Remember? Wonder who the guy was that came with her?"

"No clue, but blackmail or not, that's still a lot of money to put out for a ring." Jordan closed her eyes for a second, thinking about what they had just heard, before she opened them and stared right at Victor. "Ten bucks says that Carlita Fontaine was involved in more than just blackmailing out-of-town johns."

10

"And you say that Carlita paid this jeweler twenty grand for a diamond ring?" Rosie shrugged. "I don't get what the big deal is. Diamonds aren't cheap. I have a friend whose physician hubby just surprised her with a ring that expensive for their twenty-fifth wedding anniversary."

"The twenty grand was just the down payment," Victor explained, waving his hand in the air for emphasis. "Weren't you listening? The six-carat ring cost more than three times that amount."

"Oh my! I guess I wasn't listening," Rosie said. "Where in the world would a woman who takes her clothes off for a living get that kind of money?"

"I guess it's possible that her blackmailing scheme was pulling in way more cash than we suspected, but Jordan doesn't buy that. She thinks Carlita was probably involved in something more lucrative—more than likely, something illegal."

"I agree with Jordan," Ray said. "I'll have my friend Jack nose around down at the police station and see if he can find out what they discovered when they subpoenaed Carlita's financials." He pulled into the driveway at the McAllister house. "Let's keep this to ourselves, at least until Jack can get that report from his son, Bobby, and we have a chance to talk this over with Alex. It could be something important, but then again, it could turn out to be something as innocent as the woman inheriting money from a relative. If Carlita *was* blackmailing a lot of men, it's not beyond the realm of possibilities that one of them may have grown tired of forking over the cash every month and decided to off her."

"That was my thought, too, Ray," Jordan said. "I agree that we shouldn't tell my mother or Danny just yet. It would be really hard on my brother if he got his hopes up only to have them dashed by some little thing that we might be missing about Carlita. Who knows? Maybe strippers do make way more money than we think they do."

"Doubtful," Ray said. "But the good news is that it's been my experience when the victim is blackmailing as many men as she probably was, it's enough to cause reasonable doubt at a trial."

They exited the car and went inside, where Sylvia and Danny were sitting at the dining room table playing cards.

"Well, did you get to see all the totally awesome sites that Amarillo has to offer?" Sylvia asked, greeting them with a smile.

"We did," Lola said. "I even got to show off the artistic side of me at the Cadillac Ranch."

"Wonderful! I'll have to check that out," Sylvia said, "But the fact that you're talented doesn't surprise me, because all of you are so gifted. I thank God every day that Jordan found you all in her moment of despair."

"I know, Mom," Jordan said before turning to her brother. "How'd your doctor's appointment go?"

Danny wiggled the three fingers sticking out of his cast. "Everything was perfect. Doc said I should be totally healed in about six weeks and can get out of this annoying cast then, which won't be a minute too soon. It's already starting to itch under there."

"That's terrific news." Jordan sat down beside him. "Whatcha playing?"

"Spades," he replied. "Anyone want to join us?"

"Spades isn't a game we all can play together." Rosie flopped down in the chair beside Sylvia. "Have either of you ever played Screw Your Neighbor?"

Sylvia looked up at her. "No, but I've actually thought about doing that to one of my neighbors for real." She tsked. "The man always walks his dog across my yard and never pooper scoops. I wear myself out trying to get him to stop doing that."

"When Alex gets home, we'll have a little talk with that jerk," Ray said. "I can't wait to see the look on his face when Alex flashes his FBI badge."

Sylvia laughed. "I would be forever grateful. The dog is a German shepherd and eats a lot, if you get my drift." She handed the deck of cards to Rosie. "So, are you ready to teach Danny and me how to play Screw Your Neighbor?"

～

ALEX PARKED across the street from the Amarillo FBI field office and headed toward the entrance. He was excited to be able to help his fellow agents with their fentanyl case. He'd worked undercover for so long that it would be nice to be involved in a regular investigation where he didn't have to pretend to be the bad guy.

"Agent Norris is waiting for you in his office," the woman manning the front desk said, as soon as Alex entered. "It's the third door on the left, in case you forgot."

"Thanks." Alex headed that way, and when he reached the door with SPECIAL AGENT IN CHARGE PHILLIP NORRIS painted on it, he knocked.

An attractive young woman opened the door and led him to the back room, where the man who had asked him for help with his investigation stood and shook his hand.

"Agent Moreland, I'm glad you agreed to break away from your other commitments in Amarillo and help us out on this case. Your experience with the many Mexican drug cartels is impressive, and right now, we could use some of that expertise."

"First of all, call me Alex. If we're going to be to-gether all day, it will get tedious using my title every time you address me."

"I will, if you'll call me Phil. Have a seat, Alex." He directed him to the chair opposite his desk. He wasted no time explaining to him where they were in the in-vestigation. "We think one of the cartels is behind the drug trafficking in the area."

"Why do you suspect the cartel is involved?" Alex asked. "Last time I checked, Amarillo was pretty far from the border, so if the cartel is behind this, there would have to be a lot of middle men involved."

"That's what I'm thinking. I'm hoping that's some-thing you can help me figure out. Although our sources do suggest some kind of cartel presence, we just don't know how deep it goes."

"So, what about this veterinarian we're going to see today? How do you think he figures into all this?"

Norris reached for the cup of coffee his secretary brought in and offered the other one to Alex.

"No thanks. I've already had my one cup for the day. Any more than that, and I get jittery."

"I should probably limit myself as well, but coffee gets me through the day." Norris leaned back in his chair. "Like I mentioned on the phone, when the lab identified Xylazine as one of the drugs found in the deceased kids, DEA asked us to join in their investigation, as they believe the fentanyl is coming from Mexico. We're working with them to see if we can track down the origination of the drugs so they can swoop in and arrest the local dealers. We did a deep dive into all the medical facilities in a hundred-mile radius to see it there were any unusual amounts of the drug being shipped to Amarillo." He shoved a picture across the desk for Alex to see. "You're looking at Doctor Barry Rollins."

Alex studied the image for a second before looking up. "And this is the guy you suspect is supplying the cartels with the tranquilizer?" He looked down at the photo again, at a man who could easily have been anyone's brother. Middle-aged with a receding hairline and a slightly protruding belly, the veterinarian was probably the last person you might suspect in a drug operation like this one.

He put the photo down and looked directly at Norris. "What's your plan?"

"Were going to pay a visit to Dr. Barry Rollins this morning and see what he has to say about all this. I'm waiting on the judge to sign warrants for both his veterinary clinic and his residence. We've already got his financial records, and although it's not enough to arrest him, there are several entries that Rollins will have to explain."

"How can I help you?" Alex asked, scanning the

veterinarian's financials after Norris handed them to him.

"Tell me all you know about the Mexican cartels."

"First and foremost, they're ruthless," Alex began, taking a deep breath before continuing. He'd just been through the worst two weeks of his life with one of the most savage cartels in the Mexican jungle and had seen up front and personally just how vicious they could be. "If the cartel *is* involved, I can almost guarantee that your veterinarian won't tell us anything. I'm sure that it was made clear to him in no uncertain terms what would happen to him and his family if he talks to the police."

Norris stood. "If we find what I think we're going to find with these warrants, he won't need to tell us his story. The evidence will speak for itself." He glanced down at his watch. "The clinic opens at nine. I want to be right there to surprise him when he opens the doors."

"And you think I'll be able to help you in some way?"

"Absolutely. I've already cleared it with your Dallas supervisors so that you could be on loan to us while you're in Amarillo. If nothing else, you're someone who can sit down with me and bounce around ideas about the case."

Alex stood and followed Norris to the door. Once outside he was surprised to see twenty or more agents crowding the lobby and apparently waiting for instructions on their next move.

"We asked the Lubbock field office for backup, and they didn't hesitate to send us the extra manpower," Norris said when he noticed the look on Alex's face. "They're just as anxious to clear this up as we are because of the Tech students who overdosed and died the past month from the Xylazine."

The men piled into eight black Escalades and headed to the north side of Amarillo to Rollins's Veterinary Clinic. Despite the fact that it was not yet nine, there were several people with dogs, waiting outside for the doors to open. Norris instructed them to get back into their cars and leave the premises. After banging on the door and identifying himself as FBI, he waited until a young woman in scrubs opened the door to let them in.

"Can I help you?"

"Where's Doctor Rollins?" Norris asked.

"Today is our surgery day. He's in the back getting ready for his first case. The room is a sterile environment, so you can't go back there."

"This paper says I can, and if you try to stop me, I'll arrest you for interfering with a federal officer." Norris handed her the warrant. "And here's a couple of things I'll need you to bring to us."

She opened her mouth to say something, then thought better of it and reached for his list. "Follow me."

She led them to the surgical suite in the back where they came face-to-face with the man who might very well be responsible for all the fentanyl-related deaths in the county.

Dr. Barry Rollins was a short man, probably no taller than five-six, with balding hair and a paunch straining his scrubs. Nobody would have pegged him as a drug smuggler. He placed the surgical instrument in his hand on a tray next to the operating table and looked up. Confusion spread across his face when he saw the barrage of men in uniform rush into the room.

"Special Agent Philip Norris of the Amarillo FBI

office and Special Agent Alex Moreland of the Dallas office. We have a warrant to search both your office and your house. My agents are at your residence right now, Dr. Rollins."

The expression on the doctor's face changed from confusion to sheer panic. "What in the world could you possibly be looking for?"

"Our records show there's been an unusually high amount of Xylazine shipped to your facility over the past two months."

"That's true," Rollins said. "I do a lot of surgeries, and Xylazine is something I use to tranquilize the animals. This is a veterinary clinic, you know. We also use that drug when we euthanize an animal." He paused and stared at Norris. "Why are you asking me all these questions about my surgical drugs?"

The receptionist entered the room and handed a stack of papers to Alex.

"Unless you've been locked away in a cave somewhere, you have to have seen the news that a lot of our young adults are overdosing and dying because of tainted fentanyl and—"

"What's that got to do with me?"

"The toxicology reports on the deceased children are showing that they had Xylazine in their systems. The medical examiner confirms that the amount of the drug isolated was more than enough to stop their breathing. Since Narcan doesn't overturn the effects of Xylazine and the EMTs don't routinely carry the antidote necessary to counteract the tranquilizer, they haven't been able to save these victims."

"While that's a truly sad story, what does any of it have to do with me?" Rollins asked.

"Since Xylazine is only available to veterinary clinics, we've been checking every clinic to see if there's been an uptick in the drug orders for the tranquilizer." Norris narrowed his eyes and glared at the doctor. "And you, sir, definitely have been ordering a large amount of the drug."

"I know nothing about that," Rollins interrupted. "My assistant is the one who does all the inventory and ordering. You might want to check with her."

"We already have," Alex said, waving one of the papers the young girl had delivered in front of the man. "And she said she only orders supplies and not actual drugs. She said you do that yourself."

Rollins blew out a slow breath. "Xylazine isn't normally something used as a recreational drug on the street, is it?"

"It's being cut in as a filler with fentanyl to increase the quantity," Norris answered before he pressed on with his questions. "Since you use it to sedate the animals during surgery, I'm assuming it's given intravenously. Is that correct?"

"Yes, although it can be given intramuscularly or orally—even can be inhaled in some instances," the vet explained. "Again, I have to ask where you're going with this line of questioning, Agent Norris."

Norris handed him a sheet from the file he was holding. "This is a list of all the drugs you've ordered in the past two months. As you can see, Xylazine is definitely on here, but what's curious to me is why the amount of Xylazine pills on this receipt is nearly five times the amount of intravenous or intramuscular Xylazine. Don't you find that a little odd?"

Rollins's face turned white before he responded. "Like I said, I use the oral route to sedate the animals before putting them down. It takes the edge off for them, and then I can start an IV."

"So, is this higher amount of the oral Xylazine

something that you usually order every month?" Alex jumped in and asked. Without waiting for the doctor to respond, he continued, "And before you answer that question, you need to know that we've already executed warrants on all the major drug companies that deal with veterinary clinics." Norris handed him a read out, and he held it up for Rollins to see. "If you're dumb enough to lie to us, which is a felony, by the way, let me assure you that we already know the answer to our question."

The sweat beads were already beginning to form on the doctor's forehead, and his breathing sped up. "I would have to check my books to find out exactly how many animals I've euthanized this month before I can give you an accurate answer for why I needed an increased amount of the oral drugs."

"Don't bother." Alex held up another printed paper. "Your receptionist was kind enough to give us that information as you can see. According to your own records, in the past two months, you've euthanized eleven dogs and six cats," Alex said. "So, my question to you, is how can you justify ordering that much Xylazine?"

"I must've made an error this month when I ordered supplies," Rollins explained.

"And you made that same error last month, as well?" Alex probed. "One mistake I might buy, but no way you can convince me that it happened twice."

Tears formed in Rollins's eyes and threatened to overflow. "I didn't have a choice," he said, unable to make eye contact with Alex. "I'm being blackmailed, and I was told if I didn't cooperate fully, I'd be disgraced, and my family would suffer dire consequences."

"And why exactly were you being blackmailed and by whom?" Norris asked, moving closer to the doctor.

The vet walked over to the desk in the corner of the operating suite, unlocked a drawer, and pulled out a picture. He showed it to the agents. "This is the woman blackmailing me."

Norris looked down at the photo then handed it to Alex. He immediately recognized the woman caught on camera in the course of a sexual act with Rollins, who was either sleeping or drugged. He'd seen that face splashed across every newspaper and TV station in Amarillo the past few days.

Finally getting his emotions in check after realizing who the woman was, he asked, "How long has Carlita Fontaine been blackmailing you?"

"About three months. I got really drunk at Cowboys one night and ended up in some seedy motel across town. When I woke up, I was naked and alone. My money was gone, but nothing else was stolen from me. Since I couldn't remember ever going to the motel with that woman, I chalked it up to one stupid night on the town and forgot about it. A week later, this photo arrived in the mail, and two days after that, she came to my office and told me that I had a choice. I could either get the Xylazine pills for her, or she'd go to my wife and send this photo to all the news outlets in Amarillo."

"And you didn't find it strange that all she wanted was Xylazine and not opioids or something more street-friendly?"

Rollins choked up. "I thought she was just a druggie and would use the pills for her own private parties. I was at my wit's end and knew this couldn't go on. I was about to go to the police and tell them everything when I heard that she was dead." He sniffed back tears. "God help me. I cried tears of joy, thinking that my problems had been solved. You have to believe me when I tell you that I had no idea she was using the drugs to kill people."

Norris motioned to one of his agents before announcing to the veterinarian, "Regardless of your reasons, you are an accessory to murder, Doctor Rollins, and I am placing you under arrest for supplying the drugs that killed several people over the past month. You have the right to remain silent..."

Alex blocked out the rest of the Miranda rights being recited as his mind raced with the implications of what they had just discovered. There was no doubt that Doctor Barry Rollins would spend a lot of years in jail for his part in all this, but something didn't feel right. Why would a stripper demand Xylazine when her usual scam was simply drugging and blackmailing men she'd met at the bars for cash? From what Jordan's brothers had said at dinner the night before, Mary Alice Winters, AKA Carlita Fontaine, had never even finished high school—had gotten pregnant and left Amarillo. They had no idea when she'd returned to her hometown.

Was Carlita smart enough to run a drug trafficking ring in Amarillo—one that potentially could turn out to be one of the biggest drug operations in the Texas Panhandle?

He struggled with the possibility that it could be true, but he had a hard time believing it. He walked over to the veterinarian, who was now cuffed and being led out of the room. "Doctor Rollins, are you absolutely positive that you never gave Carlita Fontaine any money, only the drugs?"

"Other than what she stole out of my wallet that night, no money was involved, although I always thought she was probably going to start demanding cash as well as the drugs."

"What about the liquid midazolam I saw on your drug order? Did you also give Carlita that one as well?"

"Yes. I believe that's what she drugged me with," Rollins said.

Alex's mind raced with possible scenarios. The fact that Carlita had access to the amnesiac drug would also explain Danny's loss of memory the night of the murder. The woman had to be associated in some way with the cartel, but how deep was that relationship?

Either she was simply a soldier for them, or she was the female version of "El Chapo."

And he was staring at a man who had more than enough reasons to see her dead. He stopped the officers from taking him away.

"One last question, Rollins. Do you have an alibi for the night Carlita Fontaine was murdered?"

11

The Yellow Rose Steakhouse was on the southwest side of Amarillo, nestled between Amarillo National Bank and the Comedy Club. Alex and Ray drove to the restaurant in Ray's Suburban so they could go straight to the strip club after dinner to see if anyone had any information about Carlita. Jordan drove the rest of them in Alex's Range Rover.

Jordan had never been to this restaurant since it had only opened three years before, but both her mom and Danny had said they had great food. Her first impression when they drove up to the door was that the restaurant was bigger than she'd imagined. The valet rushed over to them and began opening their car doors, while a man in a tuxedo held the massive front door open for them. Jordan decided that if this attentive service was any indication of the quality of the food, then they were in for a treat. She couldn't remember any other restaurants in Amarillo with this kind of service.

"High class," she muttered to Rosie, as they were led to a table with a view of Amarillo City Lake.

As soon as they were seated, a waiter appeared and introduced himself as Jamie. Dressed in a white shirt and black pants, he was about five-ten or eleven with dirty blond hair that fell just below his ears and a five-o'clock shadow that made her think of Don Johnson in the TV show, *Miami Vice*, which Rosie made her watch with her on the rerun channel. Jamie was definitely what she would describe as a hottie. She reminded herself that her fiancé was sitting across from her and watching how she responded to the man's flirty smile. She looked away and kicked Victor under the table to remind him that his partner was also watching his reaction to the good-looking waiter from across the table.

"What's the best cut of steak here, Jamie?" Alex asked, now glaring at the man, who continued to eyeball Jordan. "I'm treating my *fiancée* here and her friends to celebrate our engagement, and I want only the best."

Jordan bit her lip to keep from losing it. She had never seen Alex jealous before, and truth be told, she kinda liked it.

Jamie's smile deepened. "That certainly calls for our best steak, which I believe is the ribeye. It's shipped directly from Hereford and has excellent marbling throughout, which makes it both flavorful and tender. It comes with baked sweet potato wedges, asparagus with Hollandaise sauce, and a house salad."

"That sounds yummy," Rosie said. "Do we even want to know the price?"

Alex held his hand up to stop the waiter from answering. "Don't worry your pretty little head about that, Rosie. There's not a whole lot of shopping that goes on in the jungles of Mexico, so I have money to spare."

"Well then, shall we start with appetizers?" Victor asked, excited now. Everyone at the table knew that free food brightened his spirits better than anything else. "Which ones do you suggest, Jamie?"

"Definitely the Wisconsin Cheese Bites and then maybe the Warm Spinach and Artichoke Dip."

Victor's eyes lit up. "Sold. How about one of each for the table to share?"

"Make that two each," Alex chimed in. "We're all starving."

"Let me take your drink orders, and then I'll get those appetizers going," the young waiter said, smiling only at Jordan, making her feel a little uncomfortable.

When he walked away, Alex rolled his eyes. "Am I going to have to fight for my lady tonight?"

"Geez, Alex, did you get a look at him? I could probably be his mother."

Jamie came back with the drinks then, cutting off any further discussion about him.

Everyone ordered the ribeye except Jordan, who had a definite aversion to steak, going back to when she was a teenager and her dad forced her to take a bite of his rare steak. To this day she was sure she heard the cow moo when she put that one piece of red meat into her mouth before promptly spitting it out in the napkin. She'd never touched steak again after that. Lucky for her they had chicken tenders on the menu, and with a large order of fries and fried okra on the side, she wouldn't have to go home hungry.

When they were finished with the meal, they decided to get dessert to go. That way, when Alex and Ray got home from the strip club, they could all sit around the table with a cup of coffee and enjoy the Hot Fudge Cake with Danny and her mom since they didn't get to come to the restaurant with them.

While they were waiting for Jamie to come back and take their dessert order, a young woman approached the table. She looked to be in her late twenties or early thirties and was dressed in a stunning lime-green dress that empathized her dark eyes and creamy olive complexion. No doubt she turned a few heads wherever she went. Jordan snuck a peek in Alex's direction to see how he was reacting to the new arrival. Like the good fiancé that he was, he didn't even look impressed.

A light bulb went off in Jordan's head as she realized who the woman was. "Abby?"

The woman smiled. "I wondered if you'd remember me. You haven't changed a bit since high school, still as pretty as ever."

"I was just thinking the same thing about you," Jordan said. "Where's my manners?"

She turned to the gang, who were all mesmerized by the woman as if she were a celebrity. "Abby, this is my fiancé, Alex, and the rest of these folks are my closest friends from Ranchero where we all live. Guys, this is my high school friend, Abby..." She paused. "Is it still Rivera?"

"Afraid so. I've been working so hard building my career for as long as I can remember, and somewhere along the way, I forgot I was supposed to have a social life."

"Take it from me, honey," Rosie said. "You never want to forget the fun part of life, no matter how hard you're working at a job. You know what they say. All work and no play makes for a dull girl."

Abby laughed out loud. "Boy, do I know that." She turned back to Jordan. "I heard about what happened to Danny. Is that why y'all are in town?"

"Yes, we came to see if we could help him somehow. There's no way my brother could ever murder someone, and we're trying to find a way to prove that."

"I agree that your brother wouldn't hurt a fly," Abby said. "So, are the police looking at anyone else for the crime, or are they concentrating just on Danny?"

"Unfortunately, Danny is all they have right now, but we're all working hard to find something that might make them look in another direction."

"Hope you're successful. Your brother is a doll baby with an incredible sense of humor. He can make me laugh, even when I don't want to." She paused. "You know we dated for a few weeks, right?"

"Yeah. He said you were better at being just friends."

"As much as I hate to hear that, I know it's true. Neither one of us had time for a relationship."

"So, Danny tells me you're the manager here," Jordan said.

"I am. I started out as a waitress on the weekends while I was working on an accounting degree at Tech. I fell in love with the whole idea of running a restaurant and quickly changed my major to restaurant management. When Johnny DeLuca—the owner—retired to spend more time with his grandchildren, he trusted me enough to put me in charge."

"Fantastic," Jordan said, just as Jamie appeared and asked if they were interested in desserts.

"We definitely are. We'll take nine orders of your famous Hot Fudge Cake, but we want them to go," she said, and when Abby looked confused, she explained. "Danny couldn't come with us for obvious reasons, so we're bringing dessert to him and my mom."

A smile crossed the woman's face. "In that case, dessert is on the house."

"Wow! Thanks. It was so nice seeing you tonight," "Jordan said. "Wish I had more time to catch up."

"Me too." Just then a man walked up behind her, tapped her on the shoulder, and whispered something into her ear. She pointed to the guy. "Jordan, do you remember my brother, Marco? He was in your class, but he dropped out when my mom got sick. He runs the bar here."

"Of course I remember him. Hey, Marco."

He waved at her, then turned and walked away.

"He never was a big talker," Abby said with a shrug, before adding, "Well, as much as I'd like to keep shooting the breeze with you all, there are apparently some fires that need putting out at the bar." She turned to go, then said over her shoulder, "Be sure to tell Danny that I'm praying for him, and that I'm confident things will work out in his favor."

"He'll be glad to know we were able to touch base," Jordan said. "And I'm sure he'll appreciate the prayers."

"What a classy lady," Lola said. "It's too bad that she and Danny didn't hit it off. She would have been a nice catch."

"There's still hope," Victor said. "Especially after we tell him that she sprung for the desserts because of him."

"Maybe we could play Cupid," Lola said with a wink.

"Don't even go there," Jordan said. "This is Danny you're talking about. He likes the single life too much right now to even think about settling down."

They got up and walked to the door, where they asked the valet to bring up their cars. While they waited, Jordan stood on tiptoes and kissed Alex's cheek and wished him luck on the information-finding adventure at the strip club.

"You do understand that Ray will tell me if you

even dare to *look* at one of those half-naked women, right?"

"Now, why would I want to eat hamburger when I have steak waiting for me at home?"

She swatted his shoulder playfully. "Good answer, and appropriate after that gigantic steak you just devoured in there, I might add. Now go find something that will keep my brother out of jail."

As they drove away from the restaurant, Jordan noticed a pickup parked in the lot on the side. It was the same burnt orange F-150 with the UT sticker on the bumper, the one she'd seen in front of one of the motel rooms at the Lazy Days Motel when they went back to retrieve her yellow pad and pencil case.

She looked toward Victor, who was sitting next to her in the front set to see if he noticed the truck, but he was so busy sticking his fingers into one of the dessert containers trying to get a sneak taste that he hadn't even looked up.

The man was incorrigible, which is why she loved him so much.

She scolded him and slapped his hand away, then decided not to mention the truck. It was probably just some weird coincidence, anyway. She wasn't the morality police. It was none of her business if someone was at the motel for an afternoon delight.

On the twenty-minute ride to her mother's house, they made small talk, mostly about the gratis desserts and how sweet and easy on the eyes Abby had been. Jordan would bet money that more than one of them was going to mention to Danny what an opportunity he was missing.

Her mom and brother were sitting in the living room watching a rerun of *The Closer* on TV. When they looked up, Victor held up the bag of desserts.

"These smell wonderful," he said. "I'm not sure I can wait for Ray and Alex to get back before we dig in."

"You can, and you will." Jordan grabbed the bag from him and headed into the kitchen.

She was anxious for the two guys to return from Spicy Salsa herself, not only so that they could devour the yummy desserts, which would probably jack them up with a sugar high all night, but also to hear if they had found something useful that might help Danny's case.

It would sure make the chocolate cake taste even better if it was served with a dash of renewed hope for her brother.

~

RAY PULLED into the completely full parking lot at Spicy Salsa and had to drive around for several minutes before a spot finally opened up. After grabbing it just as the car coming toward them was speeding up to claim it, he parked, and they walked to the door where the bouncer—who must've weighed over 300 pounds—greeted them and took their twenty-five-dollar entry fee.

Alex squinted as soon as they entered the darkened room, but his eyes quickly adjusted, and he glanced up at the runway where two young girls were doing their thing on the poles.

He whistled under his breath. They didn't call it Spicy Salsa for nothing. He wondered why women who looked like those two would prefer dancing half naked in front of a room full of mostly older men, all of whom were probably a little tipsy, some downright inebriated, over other careers. Both of them were attractive enough to be models, in his opinion. He decided to put his judgmental hat away for the time being and concentrate on why he and Ray had come to this joint in the first place. Besides, from the looks of all the money stuffed into their bikini panties as they gyrated around the pole, they probably made more in tips in one night than he made in a single week working for the government.

"Over there." Ray pointed to a small table with four chairs in the corner of the room. It was far enough away from the runway to observe without actually being part of the mob of horny gentlemen who were acting like they had just been released from prison and hadn't seen a girl in years.

As soon as they sat down, a waitress appeared to take their drink orders. Although she was considerably older than the two performers on stage, there was no denying that she had probably been just as sexy— or more so—in her younger years.

"What are you gentlemen drinking tonight?" she asked.

Alex took a minute to size her up. Almost five-eight with flaming red hair that fell in ringlets around her slightly weathered face, he wondered if she'd ever danced around a pole herself.

After she had the drink order, the woman leaned in. "I'm Destiny, by the way. Although I don't dance on stage anymore, I can still do a fabulous lap dance for the two of you, if the price is right."

"We'll keep that in mind, Destiny," Ray said. "When you get back with our drinks, we'll talk about it."

"I promise I won't disappoint. It's not often I get to party with men who look like you two and whose eyes go farther up than my boobs." She straightened up. "I'll be back in a flash."

When she was no longer within hearing distance, Ray whispered to Alex. "How much cash do you have on you right now?"

Alex looked surprised. "Surely, you're not thinking about getting a lap dance, are you?"

Ray shook his head. "To quote you, why would I get hamburger when I have steak at home?"

Alex grinned. "I guess we're just two old guys, crazy in love with our ladies and trying to pretend that we might still be in the hunt." He pulled out his wallet and counted the bills. "I have a little over a hundred and fifty in cash."

"Good. I have about that much as well. Now we just have to convince Destiny to sit down and chat with us for the time it takes for her to do a lap dance, just in case her boss is watching." He looked up. "Here she comes. Follow my lead."

"There you go." Destiny set two beers on the table. "So what about that lap dance?"

"Darling, as gorgeous as you are, we'll take a pass for right now. What we really want is to talk to you about one of the employees here," Ray said.

"You cops?"

Both of them shook their heads. Technically, that was true. Ray was retired, and Alex was an FBI agent.

"I can talk to you, but time is money, you know."

"How much would you charge for a fifteen-minute conversation?"

Destiny eyed them both. "Two hundred each."

"That's too bad because all we have is two hundred between us," Alex said.

"I can take a credit card," she fired back.

"No can do, sweetheart," Ray said. "We're in town

on business, and we leave tomorrow. As much as we'd like to have that conversation with you, if our wives spot a charge to a strip club on our credit cards, we'll both be sleeping on the couch for a long time."

"It doesn't show up as a charge from the club. It would list the money as payment to a fake investment firm."

"Pretty clever," Alex said. "Still, we can't take any chances. We're in town to sell farm equipment to the ranchers in the area. No way would our wives ever believe we used the services of an investment company. I have a very suspicious wife who wouldn't rest until she found out what the money was for." He turned to Ray. "Maybe one of the other waitresses will take the two-hundred just for talking to us."

"Hold on a minute," Destiny said, sitting down in the empty chair opposite them. She held out her hand. "Money first—talk later."

After they squared up with her, she leaned back in the chair. "So who do you want to talk about?"

"Carlita Fontaine," they said in unison.

The smile on her face turned into a hard cold stare. "Why do you want to talk about her? She's dead, you know, and I can't stop myself from saying that it couldn't have happened to a more deserving person."

Alex's interest jumped off the charts. "Why would you say that, Destiny? What did Carlita do to you?"

Destiny tsked. "The better question is, what *didn't* she do?"

Alex was on the edge of his seat, waiting for her answer while she stopped and looked around before lowering her voice.

"Carlita Fontaine was a big fraud, always parading around here acting like she owned the joint and treating the rest of us like we were beneath her." She shook her head. "The witch was nasty to so many people, I'm surprised that she lived as long as she did."

"Are you one of those people?" Ray asked, leaning across the table.

"Hell, yeah. Me and every other female in this place. The only one she treated with any respect was the owner."

"Was she having an affair with him?" Alex asked.

"No way. Jonathon Harris is *my* man. I asked him several times why he treated her like a queen, knowing how she abused the rest of us. All he would say was that they had a business arrangement and he couldn't fire her. Besides, Carlita had a boyfriend. She kept bragging to everyone that he'd already bought her a really expensive engagement ring."

Alex glanced around the room, thinking that if what Destiny had just said was true about the way everyone resented Carlita, he was probably staring at a roomful of suspects, all with motive to kill her. Plus, this was the first time he'd heard about a boyfriend. A jealous man who may have followed his woman to a motel with another guy had a pretty good motive for murder.

But as curious as he was about that aspect, he was more interested in the supposed business agreement between Carlita and the owner of the club. Had she been blackmailing him, along with the veterinarian that he and his newfound FBI friend had arrested earlier that day, or was it something else?

"Do you have any idea what kind of business arrangement Carlita had with your boss?" he asked.

Destiny shook her head. "All I know is that Jonathan once let it slip that Carlita brought in more money by herself than all the girls combined." She looked down at her watch. "Time's up, boys, unless you cough up more money."

"Just one more question," Alex said. He nailed her with an icy glare. "Where were you last Saturday night around midnight?"

12

He opened the door, then pointed to the chair by the desk. "Sit," he commanded.

After taking a seat behind the desk, he took several deep breaths before he spoke, almost as if he were trying to formulate the right words to say. "You said there wouldn't be a problem, and if there was one, you'd take care of it."

"It's only a slight glitch, and I've got it under control."

"Then maybe you can explain what the Feds want with Barry Rollins?"

"What do you mean? Why would they want him? The Feds don't usually get involved in homicides or drug cases unless it involves terrorism or crimes that cross state lines. We were very careful not to connect anything back to Rollins."

"Really? If that were true, you might want to explain to me why I saw the police taking him out of his clinic in handcuffs."

"What? When?"

"This morning. I was sitting outside the clinic in my car waiting for it to open. I'd heard a rumor that the FBI had Rollins on their radar, and I was hoping to have a little chat with him before they did. I wanted to make sure that he understood why it would be a tragic mistake if he cooperated with them. Before I had a chance to do that, a bunch of Caddies pulled up to the door, and a boatload of FBI agents, all with assault rifles, along with several local police officers rushed the building just as the clinic opened."

"Do you think they know about the tranquilizers?"

"Like you said, unless the man is embezzling or transporting kidnapped victims across state lines, the Feds normally wouldn't be involved. So, yes, I think they know."

"Whatever they have on him can't be good for us."

"Hell no, it isn't. I need to understand how this could happen if you had safeguards in place like you say you did. And more importantly, how do you plan to take care of this mess?"

"I'm not sure yet, but I'll figure it out. Have I ever let you down?"

"No, and I hope this won't be the first, or I can promise that you won't like the consequences."

"Stop worrying. The cops will take Rollins back to the Amarillo jail to await his arraignment. I'm sure they'll offer him a deal to get him to talk. I have a local cop on my payroll, and he's indicated that he has a friend who is interested in coming aboard as well. Apparently, there's been a shake-up in the police department, and neither of them are happy with the change of guard. I'll have my guy find out why they arrested Rollins. If it was because of the tranquilizers, rest assured that I've covered my tracks and made absolutely sure that the paper trail goes directly through Carlita Fontaine and not me."

"It doesn't matter why they arrested him. He's definitely a huge liability now." He looked out at the view of downtown Amarillo from the hotel window. "You're sure that stripper didn't drink too much and tell the vet about our operation? From what I understand, she didn't meet a bottle of booze she didn't like."

"To my knowledge, the answer is no. She had just as much to lose as we do. Regardless, as soon as I talk to my inside man, I'll have him snoop around to find out what Rollins actually does know."

The man pulled out a bottle of liquor and a cocktail glass from the drawer. He poured the whiskey all the way to the top of the glass, then lifted it to his lips and chugged it before speaking again. "And if Rollins does know more then he should and decides to sing in return for a sweet deal?"

"Trust me. I pay my snitch enough money to do what has to be done, but I have a backup plan just in case."

"And that would be what?"

"To make sure the songbird is silenced."

"That's good." He leaned back in his chair. "And sooner or later, we're gonna have to deal with our other problem."

"I know. I told you I'll handle that one, too. Just give me a few days."

He sniffed. "You really don't want to see my reaction if you don't."

~

THE HOT FUDGE CAKE was as good as Danny had promised. When they finished, they pushed their plates aside, totally stuffed from all the food they'd consumed at the restaurant and now at home. With Rosie and Lola's help, Sylvia brought in a pot of freshly brewed coffee and nine cups. Before anyone spoke about the events of the night, they all filled their cups.

It was the perfect way to end a fantastic food day.

"So, are you two gonna tell us if you found out anything at Spicy Salsa?" Jordan asked, unable to hide the impatience in her voice.

Ray and Alex exchanged glances before Ray began to speak. "At the risk of having Lola's evil spirits hunting me down, let me start by saying that the girls on stage were way younger than we imagined. Watching them convinced Alex and me that Carlita probably didn't dance anymore and worked there only in some kind of administrative position."

"You promised me you'd close your eyes," Lola said, shaking her finger at him.

"I did," Ray responded before grinning. "Is my nose growing?"

"You old fool. It's a wonder you didn't have a coronary, watching those girls on the poles," she scolded. "Good thing you don't have heart issues."

"First of all, my dear, the two girls performing there could have been my granddaughters." He bit his lip to hide a smile. "No one over thirty would be able to move the way they did around those poles."

"Okay, okay," Jordan said. "We get the picture. Were you able to talk to either of them?"

Alex shook his head. "Not them. They were on stage the entire time we were there."

"So your little visit to the strip club was a bust," Victor said, shaking his head,

"Alex never said that, Victor," Ray chimed in. "Actually, it turned out to be very informative."

"Get on with the story, you two. We're dying to know," Rosie said.

"We could have slipped the bouncer a couple of

twenties for a seat around the stage, but we declined and were led to a table in the back of the room. A scantily-dressed woman, who introduced herself as Destiny, came over to take our drink orders." He chuckled. "She was older and probably a pole-dancing reject herself."

"Enough about pole dancing already," Lola said. "Did you get to talk to the waitress?"

"We paid her the equivalent of a lap dance," Alex said before raising his arms in the air. "Hold on. We needed her to sit down and talk to us, and that was the only way she'd do it. Her exact words were— and I quote—'*time is money*.'"

"Now you're getting somewhere," Jordan said. "So did this Destiny woman tell you anything interesting?"

"Matter of fact, she did," Alex said, after taking a sip of hot coffee. "Once she started talking, there was no shutting her up—not that we wanted to. Anyway, she blurted out that Carlita was hated by every girl there because she was so arrogant and condescending to all of them."

"Ah ha! Now we have a roomful of potential suspects," Michael said. "That's good to know. We should call Patrick and tell him this little tidbit. They can call Destiny to the stand at Danny's trial where she can tell that to a jury."

"I'll call him tomorrow," Danny said, locking eyes with Alex. "Did this Destiny person say anything else that might be useful?"

"Several things." Alex said, after taking another sip of his coffee. "First of all, she let it slip that she and Jonathan Harris, the club's owner, were in a relationship. When I suggested that Carlita might be a third wheel in that triangle, she laughed. Said there was no way, even though she never fully understood why her boyfriend treated Carlita almost with kid gloves, despite the fact that he knew all the others hated her."

"Sounds like we can add Destiny to our growing list of possible suspects," Jordan said. "And maybe even Jonathon Harris."

Alex nodded. "Destiny also said that her boss had some kind of business arrangement with Carlita, and more than once he explained to her that he couldn't fire the woman because she brought in more money than all the others combined. She figured that was the reason Carlita got special treatment."

Danny's eyes lit up. "Do you think the club owner was in on Carlita's blackmailing scheme?"

"That's the confusing part, Danny," Alex said. "I find it hard to believe that Carlita could make the kind of money she did by nickel-and-dimeing the men she videotaped at the motel. Remember, Harris said she brought in more money than all the girls combined. In my head, that's probably a lot of cash."

"So, what are you thinking?" Victor looked at Jordan before continuing, "We forgot to mention that while we were killing time in downtown Amarillo this afternoon, Jordan and I went into a jewelry store and discovered that Carlita had ordered a specially designed diamond ring, handed over twenty grand as a down payment, and then was killed before she could pick up the $75,000 piece of jewelry. One has to wonder where she got that money as well."

Alex caught Jordan's eyes and held them captive. "And what were you two doing in a jewelry store, love?"

Jordan swallowed hard. How could she tell her fiancé that she'd been shopping for an engagement ring with her best friend and not with him?

"I saw this really cool watch in the window, and I

dragged Jordan in there to check it out. Turns out the guy wanted almost fifteen hundred for it," Victor said, rescuing her once again. "While we were pretending to be high rollers, the clerk couldn't help himself and had to brag about Carlita's ring. Said the woman and her boyfriend commissioned him to design it for her. Since she never returned to pick it up, he offered us a fifty-percent discount on it."

"Can he do that? Wouldn't that ring become part of Carlita's estate?" Rosie asked.

"Not sure how that works," Sylvia said. "But I would imagine that whoever is listed as the heir in Carlita's will could claim the ring. Am I correct, Ray?"

"Technically, the ring belongs to the jeweler until the full balance is paid, but assuming that whoever the heir is would pay off the balance due on the ring, then yes, I believe you are correct. If no one claims the ring or pays the difference, since the jeweler shelled out the cash for the diamonds in the first place, he can do as he pleases with the piece." Ray turned to Alex. "All this has got me thinking. Do we know if Carlita left a will or if she has any living relatives?"

"I don't know. That's a good question to ask Patrick tomorrow. The answer might point to another potential suspect, which leads me to one more thing that Destiny mentioned. Apparently, Carlita told everyone at the club that she was engaged and her fiancé had already bought her a very expensive diamond ring. That's got to be the ring you and Jordan saw, Victor."

"The jeweler did tell us that some dude was with Carlita when she ordered the ring. Bet he was the boyfriend," Victor said, his voice escalating with each word.

Alex leaned back in the chair and blew out a long breath. "That's definitely food for thought. We need to be sure to add that to the list of things to tell Patrick in the morning. He can get Feldman to pull the footage from the jewelry shop. It wouldn't be a reach to think that a jealous boyfriend could have followed Carlita and Danny to the motel and did her in himself."

"Be careful, y'all. You're starting to get my hopes up," Danny said.

"That's okay. We have a lot more to go on than we did just a few days ago. There's also something else I found out this morning when I went with Agent Norris of the local FBI to execute a search warrant on a local veterinary clinic."

"Why in the world would you be involved in something like that, Alex? And why would a veterinarian clinic fall under the watchful eye of the Feds?" Ray asked, obviously intrigued with the story.

Alex was quiet for a moment. "Okay, what I'm about to tell you has to stay in this room. I'll call Patrick myself tomorrow and give him the details so he can use the information for Danny's defense if he thinks it will help."

After everyone agreed, Alex continued, "The FBI has been working with the local DEA agents on a drug case that they believe is run by the cartel. They know about my latest undercover mission and thought I might be able to offer some insight into the inner workings of a Mexican cartel."

"That makes sense," Ray said. "You certainly saw up close exactly how ruthless they can be."

"I did, which is why I agreed to help. Lately, there's been an increase in the fentanyl deaths in both Amarillo and Lubbock. We're not talking about the usual deadly fentanyl. Like I told you all earlier, they found the presence of Xylazine, an animal tranquilizer, in the overdosed kids, and they believe someone locally is lacing regular fentanyl with the more deadly Xylazine. What makes this new product especially lethal is that the tranquilizer can't be reversed with Narcan the way fentanyl can be. Consequently, by the time the 911 call comes through and the paramedics race to the scene, more than likely, the user is already gone."

"Oh, my heavens!" Lola said. "And they think this animal clinic is providing that tranquilizer?"

Alex nodded. "Norris subpoenaed all the major drug suppliers in the area and the records showed that the clinic has been receiving a much larger shipment of Xylazine over the past two months. Coincidently, that's about the same time the fentanyl/Xylazine combination began showing up in the tox screens of the dead kids."

"Did you arrest him?" Rosie asked.

"We did, but what we found out when he finally decided to admit to the crime surprised all of us, especially me."

"Moreland, you're killing me," Victor said. "If you don't hurry up and tell us the entire story, I think I'm gonna have to dose you with that tranquilizer myself."

"You are such a drama queen, Victor," Jordan said, before turning to Alex. "Despite his impatience, I agree with him. If you don't hurry up and tell us what the guy said, I'll have to help him do you in."

"Although patience is a virtue, it's never been a strong point for either of you." Alex winked at her before speaking again. "Okay, so when we finally got the veterinarian to admit to purchasing such a large amount of the tranquilizer, he confessed that he was being blackmailed. He showed us a very compromising photo of him with a woman at the Lazy Days Motel."

Victor jumped out of his chair. "Please tell me that

woman was Carlita. It would definitely give Danny's case a boost in the right direction."

"Without a doubt, it was Carlita," Alex said. "The weird thing, though, was that the vet told us that Carlita wasn't blackmailing him for money. She only wanted Xylazine and threatened to expose him to all the news outlets and to his family if he didn't provide her with the tranquilizer."

"Holy cow! Talk about burying the lead," Danny said with a laugh. "And you think Carlita is involved in all the fentanyl/Xylazine deaths?"

"Not only do I think that Carlita was involved, but I'm also beginning to lean toward her being at the top of the food chain." He paused. "The vet was also supplying Carlita with liquid midazolam, the drug we think she used to sedate you, Danny."

Danny smiled up at him. "You two did good. I can't wait to hear what Feldman has to say about that."

While everyone began talking at once, Sylvia stood and yawned, "Well, I don't know about you, but I'm exhausted by all this new information." She glanced down at her watch. "No wonder. It's after one. Why don't we all head to our bedrooms and try to get whatever sleep we can for the rest of the night? Tomorrow is soon enough to start making calls to Patrick and figuring out what our next move should be."

After all the cups were in the dishwasher, Jordan turned out the kitchen light and followed her mother to the bedroom to settle down for the night. But as hard as she tried, she had a hard time getting to sleep. Her brain was on overload after all the news they'd heard. She prayed that at least some of it would help vindicate her brother.

The next day was their last in Amarillo, and the plan was to just chill at the house, ordering take-out all day, and spending time with Danny and her mother. Jordan was awakened by Rosie shouting to everyone to come to the living room. She and Danny had been the first ones up and were enjoying their first cup of coffee while they watched the local news.

Jordan grabbed her robe and high-tailed it out there to see what the excitement was all about. After they were all seated around the TV, Danny turned to the local news channel that he had taped only moments before. A trailer crawled across the bottom with a Breaking News alert.

Jordan gasped when an image of the neon sign in front of the Lazy Days Motel filled the screen.

"Turn it up, sweetheart," Sylvia said when the picture changed to one of the pool at the motel. "This may be about your case."

They were all silent as they listened to the news reporter speaking.

"An autopsy was conducted on the body of Steven Hudson, the manager at the Lazy Days Motel in southwest Amarillo. Mr. Hudson was found in the pool at the motel yesterday afternoon by one of the occupants who called 911. Initially, the death was ruled an accidental overdose after which the deceased tumbled into the pool. Today our sources tell us that the police have reversed that finding and are now investigating Hudson's death as a possible homicide. No further details were given. We will stay on this story and report any new information as it comes in."

Jordan's eyes widened. "Stevie was murdered?"

Ray grabbed his phone. "Let me put in a call to Jack's boy down at the police station and see if I can get him to tell me why they now think the man's death wasn't accidental."

After several minutes of conversation, Ray hung

up and addressed the group. "Apparently, the medical examiner didn't find foam in Hudson's lungs."

"Foam? What does that have to do with anything, Ray?" Lola asked.

"Bobby, Jack's son, explained that when someone drowns, the water mixes with the mucus in the lungs, and when the victim gasps for air, it causes the water-mucus mixture to churn, creating a foam." He looked at Alex. "Stevie didn't have foam in his lungs, which led them to believe that he was already dead when he went into the pool."

"Why would they jump to homicide over that? They've already confirmed that the toxicology showed a lethal dose of fentanyl in Steve's blood. Wouldn't it make sense to think that he might have already been in the pool when he overdosed or that he dropped dead into the pool?" Michael asked.

"That would certainly be one explanation," Ray said.

"Then why do they think he was murdered?"

"Since Hudson's shoes were scuffed, his jeans torn, and both knees were scraped and bruised, and they found traces of his blood imbedded in the concrete by the pool, they've concluded that someone had dragged his body over to the pool and then shoved him in."

"Oh gosh!" Jordan exclaimed. "Somebody actually killed Stevie and then threw him into the pool?"

"That's what the cops think."

Jordan tuned out the rest of the conversation happening around the table, unable to stop a niggling fear that was racing across her brain.

Why was the orange-and-white pickup truck at the scene around the time the police estimated that Stevie was killed? When she'd noticed that same truck parked at the Yellow Rose Steak House the night before, she should have taken a few minutes to go back in and scan the place to see if anyone looked familiar to her.

The easy way to find out who owned the F-150 would be to get the license plate and then ask Ray to get his friend to run it. But if the truck's owner was simply eating at the steakhouse the night before, she might never see it again. She decided she'd have to invent a reason to go out on her own after lunch and go back to the Yellow Rose and see if Abby might know who owned the truck.

Her gut told her that whoever it was could be a potential witness to Stevie's murder.

She decided to take Alex with her instead of going alone, just in case the truck's owner turned out to be the killer himself.

13

"Ray, I've decided to stay a few more days here to spend more time with my mom and Danny." Jordan sat down at the table with her morning coffee. "Alex has cleared it with his boss to stick around with me and to help the DEA with their case against the doctor they arrested yesterday. We'll head back to Ranchero sometime Sunday afternoon."

Ray turned toward the others who had all stopped talking and were listening intently to every word out of Jordan's mouth. "Sugar, do you want to be alone with your family this weekend, or would you like us all to stay with you?" He shrugged. "It's not like any of us have to be back in Ranchero any time soon. We've enjoyed being with your family, and I think they've enjoyed us, as well. Now that some of the pressure has been taken off Danny, it might be fun showing them how the Empire Apartment gang does potluck game night."

"We definitely have enjoyed all of you," Sylvia said. "And I would love spending the extra time with you. I have just the potluck recipe that I want to try, plus I could use the company, now that Colin won't get home until Tuesday."

Ray surveyed the group. "Anyone here opposed to staying until Sunday afternoon?"

"Not me," Victor said. "I've been surfing the internet. I can't believe all the amazing things to see and do in Amarillo. I'd love to check out Palo Duro Canyon."

Lola ignored him and turned to Sylvia. "And you're sure it's okay with you? Don't you want a little peace and quiet with your kids?"

"That's the last thing I need. You've met my boys." Sylvia chuckled. "Until this trial is over, they're probably going to drive me crazy. Having you all here has kept me from losing my mind worrying about Danny. I know he'd love for you to stay longer, too."

"Then it's settled," Rosie said. "But only on one condition. It's my turn to cook. You can show me that recipe, and then sit back and relax while I make it."

"I can live with that." Sylvia flopped down on the couch. "So, what's on the agenda for today?"

"I need to go back to Yellow Rose Steakhouse," Jordan announced. "I want to see if I can talk Abby into giving me the recipe for that fabulous dessert."

"Good luck with that. Do you honestly think she's just gonna hand it over to you?" Rosie asked. "I'm thinking that if everyone knew how to make it, the restaurant might not sell as much of it themselves."

"First of all, I would bet that nobody in Ranchero will be taking business away from the steakhouse. Plus, it would be good advertising, since I'd give them full credit and include a personal testimonial. And even if it was shared online, that might end up being really good advertising and could up the restaurant's viability."

"I'm still skeptical," Rosie said, "but hey, like my mother always said, you'll never get what you don't ask for."

"I know, right?" Jordan turned to Alex. "Can you go with me after lunch?"

"Of course I can, but first I'll need to drop off my notes from yesterday's arrest to Norris, not that he needs them. My impression is that he's on top of things."

"We can do that on the way," Jordan said. "So, is that a *yes*?"

"It's hard to say *no* to you when you look at me with those puppy-dog eyes."

"Oh, criminy!" Victor said. "Those puppy-dog eyes have gotten me into more trouble than you'll ever know, Alex." He paused for a minute. "On second thought, you might have just hit on the perfect reason for all of us to stay in Amarillo. Your girl can sniff out trouble faster than an English hound chasing a red fox."

"Shut up!" Jordan said, playfully. "And who's always right there with me when I do?"

"Everyone knows who," Lola said. "If there's danger involved, you two are right in the middle of it."

"Okay, enough about me and Jordan. Is anyone interested in spending the afternoon with me at Palo Duro Canyon?" Victor asked.

"Why are you so pumped up about the place, Victor?" Ray asked.

"I'll tell you why. Did you know that it's the second largest canyon in the United States? Of course, we all know which canyon is number one, but I'll bet you didn't know that Palo Duro is nicknamed the Grand Canyon of Texas?" Victor's eyes lit up with excitement. "There's a lighthouse and a rock formation that Google says not to miss."

"Hope you brought your hiking boots, my friend." Danny walked into the room, still rubbing the sleep out of his eyes. "There's a lot of walking involved to really see everything there."

"We could all use a little exercise, especially after the way we've been eating this week, thanks to your mother," Michael said. "But I'm pretty sure that my adorable friend's idea of a cardio workout is lifting a forkful of dessert from the plate to his mouth and not hiking in a state park."

"Ha, ha! You're a funny guy," Victor retorted. "Just so you know, exercise might make you look good naked, but so does alcohol." He wiggled his eyebrows. "I'm going for the margaritas every time."

Danny laughed out loud. "Oh, my word! I'd forgotten how easily you can make me laugh, Victor, but you gotta stop. My ribs can't take it."

"Before you all start wondering if I'm introducing you to my athletic self, let me set the record straight. There's a Jeep tour that takes you all around the canyon," Victor said.

"I should have known," Michael said. "For a minute I thought you were celebrating your new healthy self."

"Darlin', I'm like a caterpillar. I eat a lot, sleep for a while, and then wake up beautiful." Victor narrowed his eyes. "And if you dare to disagree, I promise that life will not be pleasant."

Michael grinned and held up his hands. "Do I look that stupid to you?"

So, after the fun moment was over, it was decided that the five of them would go to Palo Duro Canyon with Victor, while Jordan and Alex paid a visit to Abby at the steakhouse.

After a fabulous lunch of ham and cheese sliders —Rosie style—the gang piled into Ray's Suburban, while Jordan and Alex went the other way in his Range Rover.

About ten minutes into the drive, Jordan turned to Alex. "I lied about the real reason I want to talk to Abby today." She paused. "Well, maybe it wasn't a total lie. I still would love to have that recipe."

"Don't tell me you've joined the 'let's get Danny and Abby together' club," Alex said. "Because it's been my experience that hookups never work."

"Heavens, no," she responded. "Danny's a big boy, and trust me when I say that my brother doesn't need my help finding women who will fall all over him." She grinned. "It must be those Irish blue eyes of his."

"So, are you gonna keep me in the dark about the real reason for this mission?"

She took a deep breath and blew it out slowly. "It may be nothing, but when Victor and I went back to the Lazy Days Motel to get my journalism stuff, there was a truck parked in front of one of the rooms. I noticed it because my ex drove one just like it, in the same burnt-orange and white UT school color scheme, when we were in college."

"One of these days, I'm hoping you'll tell me all about that time in your life."

"Nothing to tell, really. Stupid Me gave up on my dreams while he chased his. Stupid Me stood by him, even when I suspected that he was probably doing the weather girl. And Stupid Me fell apart when he dumped me with a 'Dear Jordan' email." She shook her head. "Smart Me got over him a long time ago. Smart Me found a guy who treats me like a queen. And Smart Me recently agreed to spend the rest of my life with him." She leaned over and kissed his cheek.

"Luckiest day of my life," he said.

"Honestly, I only mentioned him because his truck was just like the one I saw at the motel."

"So why do you think that was important?" Alex asked.

"Two reasons, really. As we were pulling away from the motel, I'm pretty sure I saw someone peeking out of the window in the room next to the office. Since Stevie had told us that was his room, I just assumed that the little twerp was hiding out so he wouldn't have to talk to us again. Now, I'm wondering if it was someone else in the room, and if so, could that someone have information about Stevie's death?"

Alex pulled into the parking lot at DEA Headquarters, turned off the ignition, and stared at her. "And the second reason a truck parked in a no-tell motel piqued your interest?"

"I noticed that same truck at the steakhouse. I wanted to ask Abby if she knew who the owner was."

"And you're thinking that person might have been a witness to Stevie's murder?"

"It crossed my mind. I'm also wondering if whoever owned the truck was the one peeking out the window and actually killed Stevie himself."

"Did you talk to Ray about any of this?"

Jordan shook her head. "I didn't think it was important since they said Stevie had overdosed and drowned."

Alex opened the door and grabbed the file he'd placed between the seats. "So let me run my report in there, and then we can sit down with Abby and see what she knows." He got out of the car, then turned back. "No matter what we find out, we should still talk to Ray tonight. If your theory about the person in Stevie's room is correct, then it's possible that whoever it was got a good look at you, as well. You're hard to miss with that curly red hair. I'd feel a whole lot better if both Ray and I shadowed you for the rest of our time in Amarillo, just in case that's what happened."

"Are you saying I might be in someone's cross hairs?"

"I don't want to get you all freaky about it, as it probably will turn out to be nothing but a coincidence, and—"

"You don't believe in coincidences," Jordan interrupted.

"You're right, so pacify me and Ray, and let us put on our cop hats and do what we do best." He gave her a half smile, then walked toward the building and disappeared inside, leaving Jordan alone to contemplate what he had just said.

Could she really be in danger?

THEY ARRIVED at the Yellow Rose Steakhouse just as the lunch crowd was thinning out. Like the night before, the *maître d'* led them to a table by the window. A young waitress, who looked to be in her early forties and introduced herself as Maggie, appeared almost immediately to take their drink order.

When she returned and set a margarita in front of Jordan, Alex gave her a slight grin. "So, I take it you're feeling a little adventurous this afternoon."

"You bet I am. I miss being alone with you so much that I'm about to die." She lowered her eyes, coyly. "And you know how frisky I get after one drink."

"I most definitely do." He glanced around to make sure no one was within hearing distance. "What do you say to us finding a nice secluded place to spend the rest of the afternoon after we leave here?"

"I like the way you think, Moreland, and I know just the place. Inspiration Point. It's where all the teenagers go to make out."

"And you know this place well?"

She tsked. "Have you met my brothers? They were the self-appointed guardians of my sex life. I may have gone to Inspiration Point one or two times, and when they found out, I thought they would kill the poor sap who took me there. Word traveled fast, and that was my last invitation to go back there."

Alex leaned over the table and whispered, "I think I'm liking your brothers more every day."

"Yeah, just wait till they start threatening your life if you ever do me wrong. They won't be so likable then."

"Are you kidding me? Sean pulled me aside the other night and literally thanked me for taking you off their hands."

She narrowed her eyes. "He did not, did he?"

Alex grinned. "Maybe those weren't his exact words, so if we do make it to Inspiration Point, we should probably agree not to mention it back at the house, just in case they're still wearing guardian armor."

"Deal!" She took a long sip of her margarita. "Why anyone would drink something other than this is beyond me. It goes down so smoothly."

"Just wait until you stand up."

Just then the waitress appeared and asked if they were ready to order.

"We're just gonna have dessert," Alex said. "Can you bring us one order of the Hot Fudge Cake and two spoons?"

"Bring us two orders. No way I'm sharing," Jordan said before looking up at Maggie. "Is Abby here today?" When the waitress nodded, Jordan continued, "Can you ask her to come by our table when she gets a free minute, please? Tell her that an old friend would like to talk to her."

"Okay. Let me get those desserts out first." Maggie turned and headed to the kitchen.

A few minutes later she reappeared with the rich chocolate desserts that were even better than the ones they'd had the night before, probably because they hadn't pigged out on appetizers and full-course meals beforehand.

When she had devoured all of her own dessert, Alex slid his half-eaten one over to her. "I'm trying to get on your good side before we get to Inspiration Point. I need you all hopped up on margaritas and chocolate."

"I knew you had an ulterior motive, Moreland, but I've got a little secret for you. Smart Me is looking forward to making out more than you are."

"Music to my ears," he said, just as Abby approached the table.

"Hey, guys, looks like you didn't get enough of the cake last night," she said as she greeted them.

"I could eat this every day," Jordan said. "That's not why we've come, although it's a fabulous bonus."

"I thought you said you were leaving today," Abby said, sitting down in one of the empty chairs.

"We were, but we decided to stay a few more days to help Danny."

"That's nice. Let me know if there's anything I can do." She looked at Jordan first, and then Alex. "So, what can I help you with?"

"I realize it's pretty cheeky of me to ask, but I would love to get the recipe for this dessert. Not sure you know this, but I'm the culinary editor at a small newspaper in Ranchero, and my readers will love it. They're mostly homebodies who will probably never make it to Amarillo and eat here. I feel sure you wouldn't lose revenue over this. Plus, I would give the restaurant credit and also write a testimonial. Might even bring you some business."

Abby pondered that for a minute before responding, "Consider it as my gift to an old friend. I'll run off a copy tonight, and you can stop by sometime tomorrow around this same time to pick it up." She started toward the kitchen then turned around and came back. "Be sure and say hello to your brother for me. I still have a soft spot in my heart for him."

"Will do. And thanks again. I'll see you tomorrow."

Jordan glanced toward Alex who was shaking his head just in case she decided this might be a good opportunity to try to spark a romance between Abby and her brother. The stern look on his face stopped her cold.

Jordan suddenly remembered the real reason for the visit to the restaurant. She called out to Abby, who had stopped to talk to one of her waitresses. "One more thing, if I may. Last night as we were leaving the restaurant, I noticed a burnt-orange Ford F-150 in the parking lot. I was wondering if you knew who owned the truck?"

Abby's smile faded as she walked back to the table. "Why would you want to know that? If you're interested in buying it, I can guarantee that it's not for sale. Jamie loves his truck."

"Jamie?"

"Jamie Hathaway. He was your waiter last night. He bought the truck about a year ago and spends most of his salary upgrading it. No way he'd let it go."

"Oh, we're not interested in buying it. I just wondered who owned it."

"Why would that interest you?" Abby asked.

Jordan glanced toward Alex and when he nodded, she turned back to Abby. "The other day when I went by Lazy Days Motel to retrieve something I'd left behind, I noticed that same truck parked by one of the rooms."

Abby laughed. "As you probably remember, Jamie's easy on the eyes. Every now and then he takes a pretty young thing over to the motel for an hour or so, if you get my drift."

"Oh, we get it, all right. That would certainly explain it," Alex said.

Abby stared at Jordan for second. "I'm still confused about why that truck was something you found interesting enough to drag you all the way down here to ask me about it."

"It was wishful thinking, I guess," Jordan said. "The day we saw the truck at the motel was the day the motel desk clerk was murdered. When I saw the same truck here last night, I hoped that whoever owned it might have seen something that could prove to be helpful in Danny's case."

"The clerk was murdered? I thought he overdosed."

"So did the cops," Alex said. "But new evidence surfaced that has them leaning toward homicide instead of accidental drowning."

"Oh my! Two murders at the same motel in less than a week is troubling." Abby stood up. "Well, I'm sure the cops will get it all figured out. In the meantime, I've got to get back to the kitchen, but I'll be sure and ask Jamie about it when he comes to work tonight. If he saw something, I'll have him call the police station and let them know."

"That would be terrific," Jordan said. "Anything that might help Danny's case would be appreciated."

"It's been good connecting with you, Jordan. I'll have that recipe ready for you tomorrow."

Jordan and Alex walked to the door, and as soon as they climbed into the car, she turned to him. "I find it a little hard to believe that a waiter who looks like Jamie would pay good money for a quickie at a dump like Lazy Days."

"If he's spending all his money on the truck, he probably still lives at home with his mother, and that may be his only option. A quickie is a quickie anywhere you are lucky enough to get one, you know."

"Maybe," she mused. "I'm still gonna run it by Ray and let him decide if he should tell his friend down at the police station or not."

"Great idea." Alex turned on the ignition. "Now, tell me how to get to Inspiration Point. I'm beginning to feel like a teenager with raging hormones."

She winked at him. "The wait will be worth it."

Halfway to their destination, his cell phone rang. He looked down at caller ID and then back at Jordan. "It's Norris."

"By all means, answer it," she said. "He might need clarification of the notes you left with him."

Alex nodded, then hit TALK. "What's up Phil?"

Jordan watched his facial expression change as he listened to the man on the other end. It was obvious that he was not getting good news.

"When did this happen?" After a few more minutes of conversation, he disconnected and turned to her. "Would you be terribly disappointed if we don't make it to Inspiration Point today?"

"Yes, I'll be disappointed, but we have an entire lifetime ahead of us for places like that. I can tell by the look on your face that something bad has happened. It's not about Danny, is it?"

He shook his head. "Do you remember me telling you about the veterinarian we arrested yesterday?"

"The one who was being blackmailed by Carlita?"

"Yes. His name is Dr. Barry Rollins. Phil just got word that the man had complained of having difficulty breathing in his cell, and even before the ambulance arrived, he lost consciousness and went into cardiac arrest. The EMTs tried unsuccessfully to resuscitate him, but he never regained consciousness and was dead when they arrived at the hospital."

"What? Did he have a heart attack or something?"

"We don't know," Alex responded. "The only information Phil has is that they were waiting on the DA to finalize a deal for him. DEA had high hopes that he'd give up the bigger fish in the drug operation in exchange for a leaner sentence and were waiting on the paperwork to come through before questioning him."

"What will happen now?"

"We're back to square one. No choice but to start over."

14

Jamie Hathaway finished up his shift at the steakhouse and headed to his truck. Before sliding into the driver's seat, he walked around his glossy F–150. She was a beauty, and he'd spent every extra dime he had making her look good. He remembered back to when he'd first seen a truck like this on the University of Texas El Paso campus. He vowed right then and there that one day he'd have one just like it. Maybe then all the kids who'd bullied him in high school would have to stand back and take notice.

He drove home with a contented smile on his face, and as he pulled into the lot at his building, he thought about how far he'd come. He walked up to his second floor apartment, still thinking about all the kids who had gotten off on slapping him around and calling him names like *retard* and *fat boy*. He thought when he moved to El Paso that he'd left all that ugliness behind.

But it hadn't taken long for new bullies to find him. He sometimes wondered if he just looked like the loser they made him out to be, or perhaps there was a LOSER sign on his back that would never go away.

Somehow, the bullies had always sensed his vulnerabilities and knew he wouldn't fight back.

When he'd gotten his degree, he'd thumbed his nose to all the jerks who had ever made him feel less than them, packed his bags, and moved to Amarillo. Once there, he'd joined a gym and lost forty pounds, then dyed his dark hair a medium blond shade, before snagging a job as a waiter at the Yellow Rose Steakhouse. He loved his job—loved that the people there accepted him for who he was and didn't resort to name-calling.

Once inside his apartment, he walked to the bathroom and stripped off his clothes before jumping into the shower, catching a glimpse of his body as he passed by the mirror. Not too bad for a kid who used to think of food as a security blanket and had been overweight all his life. Except for the scars on his upper chest, he looked pretty good. He looked away, not wanting to be reminded of the many cigarette burns at the hands of his abusive stepdad.

When the old man had dropped dead after a night of drugs and booze, Jamie had cried with joy.

But the elation had been short-lived. Apparently, his mother had learned a few tricks from her no-good husband along with a couple of new ones of her own, and the torture and humiliation continued. When he was a senior in high school, she was diagnosed with lung cancer that had metastasized throughout her body. He watched her wither away, sometimes in so much pain that the Hospice nurses had to give her massive doses of morphine, but to this day, he still felt no compassion for her.

On her death bed, she'd whispered something that would change his life forever. She'd lied to him before, too many times to count, so he didn't believe her. He'd assumed it was her way of taking one last, cruel jab at him before she went to meet her Maker. He felt sure that particular highway would take her south and not north.

After her death, he took what little money he could find stashed away in the house, again packed his bags, and drove the family Oldsmobile to El Paso, where he enrolled at the University. He'd always been a good student, seeing that as the one thing he was able to control in his life. He was accepted into the business program not long after he applied and offered a room on campus with two other roommates.

He'd loved living on campus. Loved the freedom of doing whatever he wanted, whenever he wanted, without having to worry about what would happen when he got back home and was greeted by two drunken parents. Parents who liked to take out their frustrations on him. He enjoyed El Paso so much, he'd even thought about making it his permanent home.

Until the bullies found him.

They could no longer tease him about his home life, but they used other ways to berate him. He'd retreated within himself and stayed away from most of the events on campus. Without friends, it had been a lonely two years, but somehow he'd managed to get through it. On the day he'd graduated, he'd thrown his cap in the air, hopped in his car—which had already been loaded with his luggage and all his personal belongings—and headed to Amarillo with an Associate Degree in Business Administration.

How pathetic was it that all his belongings didn't even fill two medium-sized boxes.

He'd been thinking about Amarillo ever since his mom had died, dreaming about the good life he'd find there, hoping to get the acceptance from people he cared about. He couldn't wait to get there and finally start living the life he'd only dreamed about.

But just like everything else in his life, Amarillo was a disappointment, and his arrival in the city was not met with the enthusiasm that he'd hoped for.

Still, a new place where nobody knew him was definitely appealing. He wandered around the city, doing odd jobs here and there for a little cash to get by. He finally realized that he would have to move on if he ever wanted to get his head on straight and bury the unpleasant memories of his childhood.

Having made that decision, he'd used the little bit of money he had left to treat himself to a really expensive steak at the Yellow Rose Steakhouse. His bags were already packed as he anticipated leaving the city after dinner and heading toward Lubbock to find a job and finish his education at Texas Tech. He was hoping that a BA in Business Administration would open up a lot of doors for him.

At the steakhouse he'd met Abby Rivera, the manager, who took an instant liking to him and offered him a job waiting tables. After chatting with several of the wait staff and hearing how they loved working there, he'd made a split-second decision to give it a try. Although it would take longer to get a degree, he put his plans for Tech on hold and decided he could wait tables at night while he attended West Texas A&M Canyon during the day. Since everyone at the steakhouse seemed so nice, he'd agreed to start working the next day.

This really could be the start of a great new life for him, he'd thought at the time.

In the year that he'd been working there, he'd made several friends and was especially close to his boss, Abby. There was nothing physical between them. She was older and didn't seem interested in him romantically. But he adored her, and if some day her feelings toward him changed, he wouldn't say *no* to a physical relationship.

Older or not, she was hot.

After taking a shower, he put on a pair of old, ratty sweatpants, his usual sleeping garb, then walked into his bedroom. The first thing he saw was his poster board with pictures of that other woman plastered all over it. He'd been obsessed with her and had followed her all over town, snapping pictures whenever he could get them.

He knew his actions could be classified as borderline stalking, but he didn't care.

He walked over to the board and stared at her for a few minutes before he pulled the knife out of one of the pictures.

She was dead. It was time to let it go.

He'd come to Amarillo on a mission. Now, he needed to get out of Texas and move to Florida. One of the waitresses who'd moved to Tallahassee a few months before to attend Florida State University had invited him down there, had even checked into the university's business administration program for him. She'd assured him that he wouldn't have to worry about finding a place to live, as he could stay in the house she'd rented with three other roommates, if he was interested.

He thought about her offer. He'd known for a while that she'd had a crush on him, and maybe it was time to just take things easy and see where a relationship with her would go.

He glanced one final time at the pictures on the corkboard before ripping them all off and tearing them into shreds.

That part of his life was over. It was definitely time to move on, especially after what he'd done.

~

THEY WERE all sitting around the dining room table enjoying their morning coffee after stuffing themselves with Sylvia's breakfast pizza. Tonight, the Ranchero gang was going to introduce both her and Danny to their game-night ritual. After she showered, Jordan planned to make a grocery run to pick up the items that Rosie would need to make Sylvia's recipe for dinner. Alex reminded her to pick up a couple bottles of tequila and one or two buckets of margarita mix to freeze for the gang, as well.

Nothing made game night more fun than frozen margaritas.

Alex left shortly after breakfast to spend the afternoon with his FBI friend, Phil Norris. Although the medical examiner hadn't officially declared the cause of death for Barry Rollins, the veterinarian they'd arrested two days before, given the rapid onset of his symptoms and death, the initial conclusion was that more than likely, the man had died of cyanide poisoning.

After carefully examining the camera footage of the jail cell once the veterinarian had been arrested, the only people who had access to the prisoner before his death had been two veteran cops who were on duty at the time, the caterer who brought lunch in to Rollins that afternoon, and Brianna Rollins, the dead man's wife.

They'd already checked out the caterer who had brought in the food. He'd delivered three bags, one for the prisoner and two for the cops on duty, and none of the bags had been specifically marked with their names. That meant that there was no way anyone could have known which bag with tainted food would be the one given to Rollins, if indeed that's how he'd been poisoned.

Norris had also looked into the two cops on duty that afternoon. Both had been on the force for many years, and camera footage didn't show either one of them opening any of the food bags prior to consumption. Furthermore, neither had walked back to the jail cell after delivering the random bag of food to Barry Rollins. He'd gotten warrants to look at their financial records, though, just in case.

That left Brianna Rollins. Since the case belonged to DEA, the local cops agreed to let them run with it. DEA, in turn, asked Norris to follow up with the wife since he'd been the arresting officer. Knowing that Alex would be in town a couple more days, he'd asked him to join him when he interrogated the dead man's wife. A background check of the Rollins suggested they were ordinary citizens who were both active in their church, and other than the fact that the vet had been supplying the deadly Xylazine to Carlita and possibly to the cartel, they both looked good on paper. Nothing was out of the ordinary with their bank statements, except the usual deposits and withdrawals one would expect to see.

Until you scrolled down to the previous day's transactions.

At exactly 9 a.m., the bank received a wire transfer from an offshore account, designated to the Rollins account in the amount of $50,000.

That got their attention.

They'd gone back to the video of the cellblock and watched it again, this time in slow motion from the minute Brianna had arrived, which was right before Rollins began to eat the burger and fries that she'd unwrapped and placed in front of him. That's also when they noticed that the woman first glanced up at the camera, then turned her back obscuring the view of her preparing her husband's food. Norris shared his suspicions that this was probably the moment she'd added cyanide to her husband's tea.

Although they were still waiting on toxicology reports to confirm that it was cyanide that killed the man, the crime scene technicians had reported that the tea definitely had the odor of almonds, a classic cyanide characteristic. But with no real proof of any of this and no glaring motive, Norris would have to somehow trick Brianna into confessing to the murder.

So, with the bank statement and a copy of the jailhouse video in hand, he and Alex set out to interrogate the woman.

In the car, he brought Alex up to speed about his suspicions and the medical examiner's initial cause of death.

"I seem to recall that people can be inadvertently poisoned with cyanide after inhaling smoke from a home fire," Alex said. "Most of those people get treated for it but usually don't die."

"That's true. Smoke inhalation is one of the most common causes, but cyanide can also be given by mouth and even through the skin with the liquid form," Norris answered.

"Yeah, now it's coming back to me. Wasn't cyanide the cause of all those Tylenol deaths in Chicago back in the eighties?" Alex asked.

Phil nodded. "That was tragic. A child woke up complaining of cold symptoms, and her mother gave her a Tylenol. The little girl was dead a few hours later. Seven deaths after that, they discovered that some sicko had been going into a pharmacy and injecting the capsules with the poison."

"And the minute amount that he could inject into a capsule was enough to kill?"

"Yes. Ever since the M.E. called with his initial cause of death, I've been doing a deep dive on the Internet. If hydrogen cyanide is inhaled, it can cause a coma with seizures and cardiac arrest, leading to death in a matter of seconds. Cherry-red skin color results because of increased hemoglobin oxygen saturation." He stopped. "That's a lot of medical jargon, but simply put, a single tablespoon of potassium cyanide can be potentially lethal."

"So, where can you get this liquid cyanide?"

Norris snorted. "On the internet."

"And was there proof that Brianna Rollins ordered it?"

"We couldn't find a record of any internet purchase. But that doesn't mean she didn't get it somewhere else and used it to kill her husband, although the motive for her doing him in is unclear. By all accounts, their marriage was good."

"Unless you factor in that he was sleeping with a hooker," Alex said.

"That could be a compelling motive, for sure. But back to the cyanide, in crystalline form it resembles table sugar and can be mixed with ordinary granulated sugar or placed in a packet of artificial sweetener. What I took away from everything I read is that even a small amount of cyanide, about the amount of salt most people put on their French fries, is toxic and enough to kill a person."

"Did Rollins have the red skin color like you mentioned earlier?"

"He did. That's what alerted the M.E. of the possibility of cyanide poisoning in the first place, but until the doc gets the toxicology results, he can't say for certain that it was the culprit."

"So you're thinking that the wife administered the poison to her husband in his jail cell?"

"Right now, it's the only thing that seems plausible. We know that she checked out the camera in the cell before turning her back and obscuring the view of his food. More than likely, this is when she slipped a little poison into his tea. She left soon after that, probably didn't want to be around when he crashed and died."

Norris took the Flamingo Street exit and turned down the road into a nice neighborhood, driving slowly to avoid all the kids playing in the streets.

"Do the Rollins have kids?" Alex asked

"No, it's my understanding that they were trying to adopt."

"Having sex with a stripper in a rundown motel is not the best recommendation for adoption," Alex said.

"You know what they say," Phil said. "Sometimes we guys don't think with the head above our shoulders."

"I wonder if his wife knew about the sex and the blackmail. The guy said he'd only done it once, but I'm not totally sure I believe that."

"Me neither."

They parked the car on the sidewalk in front of a nicely kept house, the kind you'd expect in a neighborhood like this. The yard was overflowing with several miniature magnolia trees, a boatload of lush green plants, and lots of colored geraniums and day lilies.

"Somebody's got a green thumb," Alex said, as they walked up to the front door.

After knocking several times with no response, they were about to leave when Alex glanced into a window at the side of the house.

"Hold on. There's a woman on the kitchen floor," he yelled to Norris.

He made it back to the front just as Norris kicked in the door. With guns out, they entered, being careful to make sure there was no one inside who also had a gun. When they were sure the house was secure, Alex searched for the woman's carotid pulse. Looking up at Norris, he shook his head.

"After watching the jail cell video," Norris said. "I'm almost certain this is Brianna Rollins."

Alex bent down for a closer look at her face before proclaiming. "Looks like she has cherry-red skin to go with that green thumb."

Norris pulled out his phone and made two calls, one to the medical examiner and the other to the crime scene technicians at the police station.

When he heard the sirens, Alex walked over to the window. Just as the crime scene van pulled into the driveway next to a silver SUV, he noticed the sign on the passenger door, and something clicked in his brain.

SPECIALTY CAKES, the same name as the one on the SUV that was seen in the gas station close to the motel on the night of the murder.

"Phil, come over here," he called out, pointing to the SUV. "I think this is the same vehicle that the police checked out the night of Carlita's murder."

"Is it somehow involved?"

Alex shrugged. "They didn't think so at the time. Said it was parked for a long time at the gas station around the corner from the crime scene. When they traced it back to the owner, he said he stopped at the gas station for a late-night snack and realized he'd lost a hubcap. According to him, he parked the van on the side and retraced his steps. About a mile down the road, he found it and walked back. The cops crossed it off their radar at the time, but I'm thinking it's too much of a coincidence to ignore."

"Did the police investigate the guy who claimed to have seen the SUV at the gas station?"

"They did," Alex said. "Not sure we can jump to any conclusion, but it does sound like a convenient coincidence that the SUV was parked right around the corner from the motel. Like my fiancée recently reminded me, I have never believed in coincidences." Alex paused. "Those all-night convenience stores usually have surveillance videos to protect the workers. Can we get a look at their Saturday night and early Sunday morning recordings?"

Phil punched in a number on his phone. "Calling right now. I know they probably already have it so, they can text it and we can get a look at it before we leave."

In the meantime, the crime scene techs had arrived, and while Phil and Alex watched them do their job, one of the men brought over a file and handed it to Phil. "We found this in a locked desk drawer in the office. You're gonna want to see it."

He grabbed the file, opened it, and studied it before handing it to Alex. "There are twelve photos here, some of them of our veterinarian in compromising positions with our murder victim, but the others of the happy couple laughing it up in bed—all date stamped on different nights."

Alex stared at the photos. "So much for Rollins's one-time-only-sex theory. Guess our veterinarian wasn't so innocent after all."

Just then Norris's phone dinged, and he glanced down at his messages. "The surveillance video from the gas station," he explained.

Alex moved closer so he could see while Norris played the video. Just like the police report indicated, a man parked the car on the side of the parking lot and then walked away.

"His baseball cap is pulled down over his face, almost as if he knew he was being filmed," Norris said. "Hold on." He fast-forwarded the video.

Together they watched as the owner of the car returned approximately thirty minutes later. When he turned to open the driver's side door, he made a fatal mistake.

He looked directly into the camera.

"Holy crap!" Alex said. "That's not a man. It's Brianna Rollins."

"I'm trying my best not to jump to conclusions after seeing this," Alex said.

Another tech walked over with the woman's purse. "You're definitely gonna want to see this, sir," he said, handing the expensive–looking leather purse and a pair of gloves to Norris. "Put these on before you open it."

Donning the crime-scene gloves, Norris carefully pulled open the zipper and looked inside. A distinct odor of almonds assailed his nostrils, and he noticed that everything in the purse was wet. Something caught his attention, and he dug to the bottom and pulled out one of those old-time motel keys with the number 21 stamped on the front.

"Look what we have here," he exclaimed, as he plunged the key into the evidence bag the technician was holding. "Bag the entire purse. If I'm as smart as I think I am, it's full of liquid cyanide that spilled out.

This may be just the proof we need that the dead woman killed her husband."

"I'd be willing to bet that the key belongs to the Lazy Days Motel. Room 21 is where Carlita brought all her johns."

"So, what are you thinking?" Norris asked.

"I'm thinking this is good news for my fiancée's brother. A car parked around the corner, photographs of a continuing sexual relationship between the victim and our vet, and the possible key to the murder scene in the wife's purse should give the police, at the very least, someone else to investigate besides Danny."

Norris grinned from ear to ear. "I think it's safe to jump to conclusions now."

15

As soon as the crime scene technicians had gone through the entire Rollins house and bagged everything that might later be used as evidence, they packed up and left. Alex and Phil Norris waited around until the tow truck left with the family SUV for processing before they headed toward the door themselves.

Phil turned to the young officer standing outside. "Nobody comes in or out of here until the HAZMAT guys arrive. Understood?"

The cop nodded. "Should I go through the house again to see if the techs missed anything?"

"No," Norris replied. "Why don't you sit in your cruiser and chill until the ambulance arrives to take the body to the morgue. You can talk to your supervisor after that to see if there are any further instructions for you."

"Okay." The young officer walked down the driveway toward his police vehicle, leaving Alex and Phil alone in the doorway.

Phil made a call and found out that the Hazardous Material Unit was five minutes away. The house would need to be completely checked out and sanitized to make sure that whatever was in Brianna's purse hadn't spilled anywhere. They'd have to wait on the lab to verify that the liquid was indeed cyanide, but they couldn't take any chances that someone might unwittingly walk in and touch some place where the liquid may have leaked out. Like Phil had said earlier, just a few drops of the poison was enough to kill a person.

Even though an earlier search of the house by the crime scene technicians hadn't turned up any other poisons or tranquilizers, Alex felt sure that Norris's theory about how Brianna had dosed her husband's jail-cell iced tea was more than likely the way it went down. He was just as sure that the liquid in her purse would turn out to be the murder weapon.

But where did the woman get the small bottle of the stuff? They'd already confiscated her laptop, as well as her husband's when they'd searched the house after Barry Rollins was arrested. If there had been any damning evidence on either computer—like a receipt for the poison—they would have already found it.

And why had Brianna Rollins killed her husband in the first place?

"I can see you're off in another world," Norris said, coming up behind Alex. "What's going on in that head of yours?"

"I'm wondering why Brianna would kill her husband. By all accounts, there was nothing to indicate that their marriage was strained or that—"

"Unless she knew about her husband's affair with Carlita," Phil interrupted.

"That would definitely be motive for divorce, but murder?" Alex responded. "Right now, the evidence is pointing to the possibility that Brianna Rollins may have killed Carlita before she killed her husband."

"Hmm. Maybe," Norris started, "she saw the pictures of her husband with the stripper and then followed Carlita from the bar."

"According to her husband's alibi, he was in his clinic operating on a German shepherd who'd been hit by a car around the same time Carlita was killed. Although he was working solo, the dog's owner verified that Rollins was in the operating room until a little after 2 a.m." Alex said. "It's possible he could have slipped out the back door, murdered Carlita, and then returned to finish the surgery, and if in fact Brianna was already suspicious that there was another woman, she may have staked out the clinic and saw him leave."

"Are you thinking that she followed him to the Lazy Days? That would explain her SUV parked so near the motel."

"It's possible," Alex responded. "But more than likely, Brianna Rollins knew her husband was preoccupied with the injured dog and may have seen it as the perfect opportunity to get Carlita out of the picture, simply because she was jealous."

"I'll have the guys down at the station take another look at the footage from the parking lot at the clinic to see if they missed anything. They were pretty thorough the first time they watched it, so I'm not holding out any hope that your theory might be valid."

"Me neither," Alex said. "But it's worth checking out."

"Makes sense, until you factor in the fentanyl around the rim of Carlita's glass at the motel. How would Brianna have managed that?"

"The only explanation I can think of is that she might have been able to somehow bribe the motel clerk to let her into Room 21 beforehand, knowing that Carlita's MO was to bring back men to that room to set them up for blackmail. From what my fiancée told me, the motel clerk was all about money and probably would have done just about anything to support his cocaine habit."

"If what you're saying is true, maybe our church-going Brianna Rollins wasn't so innocent after all." Norris paused. "So, what do you think our next move should be?"

Alex thought about that for a second. "Do you have Barry Rollins's mug shot?"

Norris nodded and patted his phone. "Right here."

"Then I say we head over to Spicy Salsa and talk to Destiny, the dancer that my friend and I questioned last night. She's probably not there this early, but I think her boss might be. We can ask him about his business arrangement with Carlita, and then get Destiny's home address and pay her a little visit."

"Why do you want to talk to the waitress again?"

"My guess is that when we show her the mug shot of Barry Rollins, she'll identify him as the man who Carlita had introduced as her boyfriend."

"And what would that prove?"

"Nothing, really," Alex said. "Except that it would support my conjecture that a jealous Doctor Rollins may have slipped away from the injured dog for a brief time and possibly killed Carlita himself, although I think that's the least likely scenario here."

"That still leaves us with the fentanyl-laced glass that killed Carlita before the steak knife was plunged into her chest."

"I know. We may never know how that happened." Alex opened the door to allow Norris to go out, then followed behind and got into the passenger side of his friend's car. "Let me call my fiancée and tell her not to expect me home for a couple of hours.

As they drove away from the Rollins's house and headed in the direction of the strip club, he couldn't help but think, *something didn't fit.*

JORDAN WAS in the kitchen washing the breakfast dishes when she heard her phone ring. Grabbing a towel, she quickly dried her hands and rushed into the living room to answer, but it had already gone to voicemail. Listening to the message, she heard Alex say that they had uncovered new information and that he and Phil Norris were on their way to Spicy Salsa to question Destiny again. He said he'd explain it all later, and ended with the promise to be back at Sylvia's house by dinnertime.

Although she hated that she wouldn't see Alex until much later that day, Jordan was relieved that he wouldn't be around to monitor her whereabouts on their last day in Amarillo. Despite all the warnings from everyone, she planned to run by the Yellow Rose Steakhouse to snoop around a little. She was going on the pretense of getting the recipe for the

Hot Fudge Cake—which really wasn't a pretense at all, since Abby had already offered to give it up for her column. And if the young man who'd waited on them the other night was there, she planned to have a little chat with him to find out why his truck was at the Lazy Days Motel the day Stevie was murdered.

She might even be talked into bringing back enough of the dessert to satisfy everyone's sweet tooth before the gang headed back to Ranchero the next day.

She finished the dishes, took a long, hot shower and dressed, and then walked toward the door.

"Where are you going, Jordan?" Danny asked from the couch.

"To the grocery store to pick up the stuff Rosie needs to make Mom's new casserole recipe tonight," she said. "Since when did you become so nosy?"

He grinned. "I can read you like a book, little Sis. I know that look on your face. You definitely have something up your sleeve."

She was about to respond with something sarcastic, then thought better of it. Instead, she walked into the living room and sat down beside him. "If you must know, I want to run by the steakhouse to get that recipe that Abby promised me."

"And?"

"And what?"

"Hello, it's me, the brother who plotted with you all our lives against our older siblings. Like I said, I know that look, so spill it."

She stared at him for a minute, then lowered her voice. "Okay, you win. I'm hoping to talk to Jamie while I'm at the steakhouse."

"Jamie?"

"He was our waiter from the other night. It was his orange truck that I saw at the motel the day Stevie was killed. I want to ask him a few questions about that."

"Are you crazy? What if he's the one who killed the motel clerk—and maybe even killed Carlita? Do you honestly think he's just gonna smile sweetly and confess all the gory details to you?" Danny narrowed his eyes. "Don't make me call Alex and tell him what you're planning to do."

Her eyes widened. "You really wouldn't do that, would you?"

"In a heartbeat. I love you too much to let you take a risk like that."

"I promise to be careful. My gut tells me that seeing the truck at the motel has something to do with your case—that maybe somehow it can cast doubts about you being the killer or possibly even exonerate you altogether." She pleaded with her eyes. "Please, Danny. Don't be a tattletale."

He stared at her for a few seconds while he thought about it. Then he nailed her with his eyes. "Okay, I won't tell Alex... yet. But you have to promise that you'll call me from the steakhouse every fifteen minutes to tell me you're okay. If you don't, then I'm placing the call to Alex."

"Deal. Now, let me get on the road before I run out of time and Alex gets back."

"Where is he, by the way? He said he'd be home by lunchtime." Danny glanced up at the big clock on the wall. "It's almost noon now."

"He called to say that he and his FBI buddy are following up another lead. He sounded excited. Said he'd see us around dinnertime."

"The fact that he will be out of pocket while you go on your little sleuthing adventure makes it even more important that you call me every fifteen minutes." He leaned over and kissed her cheek. "Be careful."

"Trust me. I will, especially after what I just went through at the casino last weekend." She stopped talking, silently cursing her big fat mouth when she noticed the way his eyes narrowed.

"What happened last weekend?"

"Now's not the time. The clock is ticking before Alex returns. I promise to tell you everything before we head back to Ranchero tomorrow. For now, I have to get going. Time's a-wasting."

She stood up and headed for the door, grabbing her notebook and pencil case on the way out. Maybe she could use her journalism talents and get Abby to sit down with her to give her a little history about the steakhouse. It would be a nice touch when she printed the recipe. She might even get a few pictures of the inside of the restaurant to go with it.

Once outside, she hopped into her mother's car and drove off in the direction of the steakhouse. The groceries could wait until after she left the restaurant.

She used the twenty-minute ride to the Yellow Rose Steakhouse to listen to soft music on the radio to help calm her nerves. She kept thinking about what Danny had said when she'd mentioned Jamie. What if her brother was right and the waiter *did* know something about Stevie's murder—or worse, he'd actually been the one who'd killed him? She'd have to be really careful how she approached him with questions, glad there would be a lot of people at the restaurant, just in case. The last thing she needed was for Jamie to get suspicious about why she was questioning him in the first place.

As soon as she turned into the parking lot at the restaurant, she noticed the burnt orange truck parked on the side of the building.

Good! Jamie Hathaway was there.

She waved off the valet and drove around to the back to park the car herself. Then she took a deep breath for courage and walked around to the front, where the big guy manning the door—otherwise known as the tuxedo dude—greeted her with a huge smile that was hard not to return. After telling him she was looking for a quiet table off to the side, he led her to a two-person booth in the corner and left her with a menu.

The lunch crowd looked to be in full swing with two-thirds of the tables occupied, and although she'd just devoured a huge breakfast, she decided to order an appetizer and Texas sweet tea so her intentions to question Jamie wouldn't cause attention. She was disappointed when a young girl approached and announced that she would be her waitress.

"Where's Jamie today?" Jordan asked, hoping she wasn't too obvious.

The young waitress, who introduced herself as Charlotte, seemed confused for a minute, before she gave Jordan a knowing smile, probably assuming that Jordan was just another female who had the hots for the good-looking waiter.

"Jamie's downstairs in Abby's office right now. He isn't scheduled to work until four today, although he told one of the other waitresses earlier that the reason for the meeting with the boss was because he's resigning and moving to Florida." She paused. "I promise, I'll treat you as good as he does."

"I'm sure you will. I just have something that I need to talk about with him." She glanced down at the menu, not willing to divulge any more information. "Can I just have an order of potato skins and a glass of sweet tea, please?"

"Absolutely. Give me a second to put in your order, and I'll be back with your tea."

She started to turn when Jordan stopped her.

"You said Abby's office is downstairs?"

"Yes. I saw Jamie go down there about fifteen minutes ago." Charlotte pointed to a door adjacent to the bar, then walked toward the kitchen to place the order.

Twenty minutes passed without any sign of either Abby or Jamie. Jordan made her first reassuring call to her brother before finishing off the potato skins. She was about to go looking for Abby's office when she saw Jamie come through the door by the bar with Abby right behind him.

She got up, left enough money on the table for the food and the tip, and then headed toward the bar where Abby had stopped to talk with her brother. As Jordan rounded the corner, she noticed that Abby and Marco were in what appeared to be a heated discussion about something, and she took a few steps back so that it wouldn't look like she was trying to eavesdrop.

At one point, Abby poked her brother in the chest hard enough to push him back a step. She wished she *could* eavesdrop to see what that was all about. Knowing how she and her brothers had always managed to find every little thing to fight over, she chalked it up as nothing important. Perhaps Marco had screwed up with the liquor order or something.

When Abby walked away from the bar, Jordan stepped forward and waved. The surprised look on the manager's face changed to a smile. "Jordan, what are you doing here today? Isn't this your last day in town?"

Jordan nodded. "Yes, but you promised to share the awesome cake recipe for my readers back in Ranchero. Remember?"

Abby slapped her forehead. "I did forget that. This has been an absolutely crazy day, and it doesn't look like it's gonna get better anytime soon."

"I promise I won't take up too much of your time," Jordan said. "If you'll just hand me the recipe, I'll be on my way, although I was hoping to have a little sit-down with you so that I could add a brief history of the steakhouse to go with the recipe."

Abby's face colored slightly. "I'm so sorry. I've been so busy I haven't had time to print it out for you."

Jordan held up her notebook. "No problem. I came prepared. I can just copy it if you want."

"That's crazy. It will just take me a minute to print it out for you." Abby looked around the restaurant and pointed to the door by the bar. "Go down to my office and wait for me there. I have a couple of fires that I need to put out, and then I'll join you and pull up that recipe on my computer." She motioned to Marco, who was standing at the bar staring at them. "If you want a drink while you wait, Marco can get whatever you want."

Jordan shook her head. "No thanks. I just had two glasses of tea to go with an order of potato skins, which were delicious, by the way."

Abby grinned. "Potato skins are my favorite, and our chef makes them better than anyone in town." Again she pointed to the door. "I won't be long."

Jordan watched her walk away before she sauntered over to the door leading to the office. When she noticed Marco staring at her, she nodded, but he quickly looked away.

She couldn't help wondering if he'd really quit high school to take care of his sick mother. With a personality like that, he'd probably gotten into trouble and been suspended.

Mentally, she scolded herself for being so snarky.

She opened the door and walked down the steps to a large area with what looked like the liquor supply room on one side and a large steel door in the middle of the room with a temperature gauge set at 65 degrees Fahrenheit beside it. She assumed this was the meat locker. In the other corner she spotted a small office with filing cabinets and a large desk covered with files and facing the stairs.

She walked over and sat down in the chair opposite the desk to wait. She hoped it wouldn't take too long, as she wanted to catch Jamie before he left. No way she'd be able to sneak back to the restaurant at four, when he began his shift.

She opened her notebook and then unzipped her pencil case for something to write with. She reached in for a pen, then froze as she noticed a red-and-black zip drive.

When in the heck did I put that in there? This wasn't one of the drives she used for recipes with the *Globes* logo. How long had it been in there? Before she had time to think about it, she heard the door open and close at the top of the steps and assumed it was Abby.

Her pulse raced, her respirations quickened, and her eyes widened when she realized that her assumption was wrong. Walking toward her was Jamie Hathaway, and from the look on his face, he wasn't a happy camper.

He stopped directly in front of her and nailed her with a steely gaze. "I heard you were looking for me."

16

Alex walked into Spicy Salsa with Phil Norris following close behind. The place was empty except for a man behind the bar and what appeared to be a three-person cleaning crew, busy mopping the floor. Alex had no idea what Jonathan Harris looked like, but he was pretty sure he wasn't one of the four people in the main room.

"Hard to believe those poles bring countless thrills to so many men who crowd around the stage and cat-whistle all night," Phil commented, pointing to the stage. "As for me, I see them as the kind of poles used by firemen to slide down when the bell goes off. You know, like in all the old movies."

"Trust me when I tell you that although I am happily engaged to a beautiful woman, last night was an adventure, watching the girls—all of them young and pretty—gyrating on those things. The drunker the men got, the more dollar bills they threw at the dancers like confetti at a ticker tape parade."

"I'll bet you didn't share that little tidbit about the pretty girls with your fiancée," Phil mused, mischievously.

"Oh, hell no. Do I look like I have a death wish?"

The two agents headed toward the bar, where a burly gentleman with an ugly scar across his cheek looked up.

"We're not open yet," the man said, as he continued to stack the bar glasses behind the counter.

"We know," Phil said. "We just need to talk to the owner." He looked toward Alex. "What was the guy's name?"

"Jonathan Harris. Is he around?"

"Who's asking?" The bartender slipped his hand discreetly under the counter but quickly withdrew it when Alex and Phil flashed their badges.

"Hold on. I'll see if he's available." Scar-face scurried off to the back, then returned in a few minutes. "Follow me," he instructed.

They walked down a long hallway behind the big guy and pushed past him as soon as he opened the door to the office.

Jonathan Harris looked up from where he was sitting at a small desk covered in a mountain of paperwork. The man was probably in his early forties, with a full head of dark hair and a body that said he had a gym membership somewhere. "So what can I do for two FBI agents today? Before we even get started, though, I need you to know that all our licenses are up to date, and we just passed our annual fire inspection last week with flying colors."

Alex stepped closer. "Mind if we sit down?"

Harris waved his hand toward the two chairs around the desk. When the agents were seated, he asked, "How can I help you gentlemen?"

"We've received what we believe to be credible information about a business deal between you and one of your former employees, Carlita Fontaine," Alex began.

Harris paled for a second, before he recovered and nodded. "That's right. Carlita used to dance here. More recently, she ran the entire club for me."

"We've heard she made a ton of money," Norris said, sarcastically. "She must have been really valuable to you."

Again, the color drained from the club owner's face. "That would be an understatement," he said, finally. "Carlita was a marketing guru and brought in lots of new business every week. She definitely will be missed."

"Rumor has it she made more money for you than all the other girls combined." Alex watched for the man's initial reaction, which was always very telling.

As expected, Harris's face froze momentarily, before he exhaled slowly and addressed the agents. "So what? She was good at what she did, and I compensated her well for that."

"You wouldn't have had a reason to want her out of the picture now, would you?" Phil asked. "Maybe you were one of the johns paying her blackmail money every month."

This time Harris stood up. "I have no idea where you're going with this line of questioning, but as you can see, I'm very busy. So, unless you have a warrant, I'll have to ask that big guy at the bar to show you out." He smiled, but his eyes remained hard. "And if you decide to come back, let me know ahead of time. I'll make sure to have my lawyer present."

Alex shrugged. "Your choice, but frankly, I'm beginning to wonder why you think you need a lawyer. All we're doing is asking questions."

"And as of right now, I'm done answering them. So please leave before I have to file a harassment charge."

"No need for that. We've got most of the answers

we need." Alex stood up. "Just one more thing though, and we'll be out of your hair. We need Destiny's address."

Harris looked confused. "Why does the FBI want to talk to her?"

"We know she was friends with the dead woman, and we've just got a few questions for her."

Harris narrowed his eyes. "She lives in the Riverdale Apartments over on Seneca Street, apartment 201B. She worked late last night, and she's not going to be real happy when you wake her up." A slight smile crossed his face. "She can be a raging witch when she doesn't get her beauty sleep."

Norris stood and nudged Alex toward the door. "We'll take our chances."

With that, they walked out of Jonathan Harris's office, past the bar, and out the front door.

Once outside, Alex turned to Norris. "He was lying right through his teeth."

"I know."

JORDAN MET Jamie Hathaway's eyes straight on, hoping that her own eyes wouldn't show how terrified she was. "You waited on me the other night, remember?" When he nodded, she continued, "I was admiring your truck, and I wanted to ask you a few questions about it."

The hard look on Jamie's face softened. "She is a beauty. That's for sure."

"The burnt-orange paint job makes me think you graduated from UT. So did I."

"Why do you want to know about my truck? I don't plan on selling it anytime soon." He glanced down at his watch. "Sorry, I have to be back here for my shift in a few hours, and I was hoping to run a few errands before then."

Jordan decided it was now or never, since she'd effectively gotten him out of defensive mode with talk about his truck. She swallowed hard and plunged ahead. "I first noticed your truck parked outside the Lazy Days Motel on Monday night. I couldn't stop staring at it."

His eyes turned defiant. "Who are you, really? Are you a reporter? If you are, let me assure you that the cops have already questioned me about that day."

She shook her head. "Actually, I write a culinary column back home in Ranchero, Texas. So, no, I'm not a reporter looking for a story." She sighed. "What did you tell the cops when they questioned you?"

"I don't think that's any of your business, but if you must know, someone borrowed my truck that day. I was here working in the supply room all afternoon."

How convenient, Jordan thought.

"And the police verified that?"

"Look, lady, I don't know who you are, but like I said, my life is none of your business."

Jordan bit her lip, knowing she was about to enter into dangerous territory if she pressed him further, but this was her last chance to help her brother. She decided to be honest with Jamie. "Okay. My name is Jordan McAllister, and my brother is being charged with the murder of a stripper at the Lazy Days Motel on Saturday night. My friend and I were there to talk to the clerk on Monday to see if we could get any information that might help Danny's case. Coincidentally, we saw your truck parked outside one of the rooms at the motel around the same time he was murdered."

His eyes widened. "And you think I did it?"

She shrugged. "I don't know. That's why I'm asking. Were you at the motel for a quickie, maybe? If so, I'm wondering if you saw anything that might help my brother."

Jamie sat down in the chair next to her. "You say you're Danny McAllister's sister?" He waited for her response before he continued. "I know your brother. He comes to the restaurant a lot. I think he even dated my manager a few times."

"He did," Jordan agreed. "So, if you remember him, you've got to know that he's a decent guy. Is there anything that you might have seen that day that could possibly help his case?"

Jamie stared at her intensely. "I wasn't at the motel that day."

"I saw your truck parked there with my own eyes."

"I'll tell you exactly what I told the cops," Jamie said. "That day, I was restocking the meat locker, and someone borrowed my truck."

"Someone?" Jordan leaned closer to him. "Come on, Jamie, I'm really trying to help my brother out. Who borrowed your truck that day?"

He stared at her for a few seconds, probably trying to decide whether or not he should say anything else. Finally, he lowered his voice. "Marco Rivera."

~

ALEX AND PHIL NORRIS walked down the long hallway at the Riverside Apartments, stopped in front of room 201B, and then knocked on the door. After several minutes, Alex was about to knock again when the door opened, and Destiny peeked out from behind the chain lock. Before she could react, he held up his badge. He watched as her eyes left his badge and moved up to his face.

"Hey, I remember you from the club last night. You never mentioned you were a Fed. Weren't you there with an older man?"

He nodded. "You are correct. We appreciated your cooperation then, but my partner and I have a few more questions we need to ask."

"About Carlita?"

"Yes. Can we come in?"

She opened the door and waved her hand in the direction of the living room. "What can I help you with this time?"

Alex decided that in the light of day, dressed in a long white robe that he suspected was stolen from a hotel somewhere, with bags under her eyes and no makeup, Destiny would never be mistaken for an exotic dancer.

Then he chastised himself for going there. The woman had just been awakened from a much-needed sleep after working late the night before. He needed to cut her some slack. No one looked good in the mornings, at least not until they've had a cup or two of coffee.

Well, that's a lie. Jordan was gorgeous no matter what time of day it was. He glanced down at his watch, thinking it wouldn't be much longer before he went back to her mother's house and could be with her.

When they were all seated, Norris pulled out his phone and scrolled down to the picture of Barry Rollins. He passed the phone to Destiny.

She stared at it for a few minutes before responding. "Is this a mug shot? Is this man in jail?"

"Not anymore," Norris said. "He was killed yesterday."

Her eyes widened. "Holy hell! Who killed him?"

Alex shook his head. "It's still under investigation, but that's not why we're here right now. We need to know if you recognize him."

"Of course, I do. He's the big spender that Carlita paraded around as her boyfriend."

So there it was.

Hearing Destiny confirm that Rollins was definitely more to Carlita than just one of her tricks got Alex thinking that maybe the veterinarian wasn't being blackmailed at all. Maybe he was just as involved in the whole fentanyl/Xylazine drug dealing as Carlita was. It was beginning to look more and more like Barry Rollins had played them for suckers, making them believe he was an innocent man being extorted by a calculating woman.

The DEA believed that one of the Mexican cartels was behind the drug ring that was using the Xylazine to cut with the fentanyl. That possibility, coupled with this new implication about just how involved the veterinarian had actually been, would add another layer to Danny's reasonable doubt defense.

And what if Carlita had gotten greedy and threatened to withhold the supply of Xylazine, or worse, to expose the cartel if they didn't give her a bigger piece of the profits? Knowing how the cartel dealt with people who didn't play by their rules, Alex knew they would never tolerate being threatened, especially by a woman.

Another good reasonable-doubt theory. Who wouldn't believe that a vicious cartel had killed Carlita with a knife through the heart? They'd been known to kill like that before.

"What can you tell us about Carlita's boyfriend?" Alex asked.

"I told you everything I know," Destiny said. "The man was always flashing hundred-dollar bills around, and just between you and me, he never missed an opportunity to flirt with all the young girls behind Carlita's back."

Alex stole a glance toward Norris, who nodded and then stood up. "Thank you for cooperating with us, Miss. You've been very helpful. Call me if you think of anything else about the boyfriend." He handed her one of his cards as he and Alex walked out the door.

Once outside, Alex turned to Phil. "I can't prove it, but now I definitely suspect cartel involvement here."

"No kidding," Norris said, as he slid into the driver's seat of the FBI Escalade.

Alex's phone rang before they even left the parking lot. Glancing down at caller ID, he said to Phil, "This is my friend, the ex-cop I told you about. I need to talk to him." Alex held the phone up to his ear. "Ray, what's going on?"

"We may have an emergency here," Ray said.

"What kind of emergency?"

"I just got a call from my buddy down at the police station. He's the one I called after Jordan told us about seeing the orange pickup at the motel the day of the clerk's murder."

"Yeah, what about it? Jordan said the truck belonged to one of the waiters at Yellow Rose Steak House."

"It does," Ray said. "The guy's name is Jamie Hathaway. Anyway, the cops thought it was important enough to check him out and executed a search warrant at his apartment a little while ago."

"Did they find anything useful to the investigation?"

"You bet they did," Ray said, excitement evident in

his voice. "There were several pictures of Carlita, torn up and tossed in the trash can. Apparently, Hathaway had been stalking her for a while."

Alex stiffened. "Do they know why he was following her?"

"No," Ray responded. "But get this. They discovered a slit in one of the pictures in the vicinity of Carlita's heart. And they found a knife in the kitchen that looked like it could have make the slash."

"That certainly adds a new dimension to the investigation," Alex said. "So, what's the emergency?"

"When I told Danny about all this, he confessed to me that Jordan was going to stop by the steakhouse today to have a chat with Hathaway."

The hairs on Alex's neck stood at attention. "Oh, my God!" He turned to Norris. "Light us up and get to the Yellow Rose Steakhouse as fast as you can. My fiancée might be facing down the killer."

Norris did as instructed. "The restaurant is about thirty minutes away."

"Too long," Alex said, unable to stop the fear from creeping up his spine. "I'm gonna call the Amarillo PD and have them send a couple of black-and-whites over there now."

"Alex," Ray said, still on the line. "I'm on my way to the restaurant now. I think I can get there before you do."

"Go, my friend. I don't care how many traffic laws you have to break, just get there quickly."

Alex closed his eyes and said a silent prayer. Surely the powers-that-be wouldn't have saved him from the cruelty he'd endured in the jungles of Mexico, only to punish him again by taking away the only woman he'd ever loved.

17

Jordan stared at Jamie Hathaway, not sure whether to believe him or not. She didn't know him well enough to read his face. "Are you telling me that Abby's brother borrowed your truck the day I saw it parked at the Lazy Days Motel?"

Jamie nodded. "I distinctly remember that he came to me on Monday and asked if he could use the truck for a few hours, right after he told me to help the two security guards unload the meat delivery from the Hereford Company."

Jordan squinted her eyes in disbelief. "Do you really expect me to believe that story, especially about the security guards? Last time I checked, the only guy who might even slightly resemble a security guard is the dude in the tuxedo who controls the front door from—oh, I don't know—maybe from drunken customers who get a little too rowdy."

Jamie's eyes flashed anger. "You can believe me or not. It doesn't matter much, since I don't think the cops believed me, either. All I know is that I offloaded the meat packages from the Hereford truck with two scary-looking dudes who didn't talk much and carried automatic weapons."

Jordan snorted. "Do you think maybe you've been watching too many movies? Two scary dudes with weapons who didn't talk much?" She giggled. "I've seen that sci-fi movie a few times myself." She realized as soon as the words left her mouth that she'd come off more sarcastic than she'd meant to.

He shrugged. "So, if you're done making fun of me, was there anything else you needed to talk to me about? Like I mentioned earlier, I have a shift in four hours."

Jordan forced herself to wipe the smile off her face, realizing how condescending she'd just sounded. "I'm sorry, but your story just doesn't seen credible to me. For now, though, let's go back to the part about Marco borrowing your truck. Doesn't he have his own car?"

"He does, but he said it was in the shop." Jamie glanced behind him before speaking again, as if he was making sure that nobody would hear him. "I can tell you this, though. He's not gonna be too happy when he finds out that I told the cops exactly what I just told you."

"Why would he care if they know that he borrowed your truck? That's certainly not a crime."

Jordan opened her pencil case to grab a pen so she could write this all down. It might only be something trivial and have absolutely nothing to do with Danny's case, but at this point, she was desperate to figure things out for her brother's sake.

Grabbing the pen, she noticed the zip drive, and once again, wondered why she would have brought that with her. She opened her notebook and began writing down what Jamie had just told her.

Then her phone rang, and she glanced at caller ID.

"It's my fiancé. I'll only be a few minutes. Please

don't leave until I have a chance to talk to you again. I still have a couple of things that I think you can clear up for me."

"I'll give you five more minutes. No more." He sat down in the chair next to hers and pulled his phone from his pocket.

"I can live with that," she said, before answering her phone. "Hey, Alex, are you back at my mom's house?"

"Jordan, where are you?"

She wondered why Alex seemed a little distressed. "I'm at the Yellow Rose Steakhouse. Why?"

"Are you sitting at one of the tables?"

"I was. I had the best potato skins I've ever eaten. Now I'm in Abby's office waiting for her to finish up and come down here to give me the recipe she promised." She glanced at her watch. "I should be home in about an hour or so after I stop at the grocery store."

"Where's Abby's office?"

"Downstairs." She was beginning to get a little nervous. "Why is that important to you, Alex?"

"Are you alone?"

Now she was beginning to get concerned. "No."

There was a slight pause before Alex spoke again. "Is Jamie Hathaway with you?"

Now he was freaking her out. "Yes, why?"

"First of all, I need you to know that Phil and I are on our way there, but unfortunately, we're about twenty minutes out. Ray is also on the way, but I'm not sure when he'll get there. And the Amarillo police have been notified and should be en route as we speak."

"Alex?"

"Jordan, don't talk," he interrupted her. "I don't

want you to alert Hathaway to the fact that something might be wrong."

Jordan stole a glance at Jamie and was relieved to see him playing on his phone and not really paying attention to her conversation with Alex.

"Jamie, I'll be with you in just a sec. Keep playing your games while I say goodbye to my fiancé," she said, hoping to send the message to Alex that everything was okay.

"It doesn't sound like he's getting suspicious. That's good."

"So, why are you making a big deal about it?" she asked.

Alex exhaled noisily. "We think Hathaway might be the one who killed Carlita."

"Why would you think that?" Jordan was definitely getting uneasy now.

"The police found multiple pictures of the stripper in the trash when they searched Hathaway's apartment. One of them looked like it had been slashed with a knife. He wouldn't tell the cops why he'd been stalking Carlita, though, and since they had no other evidence linking him to the murder, they had to let him go."

"Oh my gosh!" Jordan exclaimed.

"Jordan, you can't let him see you react," Alex said quickly. "Say something that will make him think this conversation isn't about him."

Jordan racked her brain and finally came up with what she thought might work. Before she spoke again, she forced herself to slow her breathing and stay calm. "Oh, Alex, I'd love to have a romantic dinner with just you and me tonight. Make a reservation for eight o'clock, and I'll see you at home soon."

"Good girl. Now hang up and try to find a way to

get back upstairs where there are lots of people milling around. I'll be there as soon as I can," he said, before adding, "Please be careful. I love you."

"Me too," she said, as she hung up and turned to Jamie, who was still scrolling through the pictures on his phone.

When she was sure that Jamie wasn't staring at her, she studied his face. He didn't look like a killer, but then again, neither did Ted Bundy. So, why would he stalk Carlita and then kill her?

She shoved the pen back into the case and zipped it up. Then she stood up. "Well, it looks like I have a date with my fiancé tonight, so I'll have to get the recipe for the Hot Fudge Cake another time."

"That's why you're here today? To get a recipe?" When she nodded, Jamie pushed a few buttons on his phone before looking up at her. "Every now and then Abby asks me to help out in the kitchen when the chef is under the weather. My specialty is desserts." He handed her the phone. "Here's what you're looking for."

She glanced down and smiled when she saw that he indeed had the recipe she'd come here to get. She knew she should hightail it out of there like Alex had instructed, but she didn't think a few more minutes would hurt. She was pretty sure that Jamie didn't suspect her of anything.

She pulled out her own phone and took a picture of the recipe, then had just started toward the door when it opened. Seconds later, she froze when she came face-to-face with Marco Rivera, who was glaring at her, his face flushed with anger. In his hand was a gun which was pointed directly at Jordan's head.

"Where you going in such a hurry, Jordan?"

RAY VARGA HUNG up the phone, grabbed his car keys, and raced out of the kitchen. He didn't bother to stop and explain where he was going. Not to Danny or to any of the gang, who were sitting around the TV and were now looking at him like he was a crazy man.

"I'll call you when I can," he said.

Danny jumped up from the couch. "Oh, no, you don't, Ray. You'll tell me right now what's going on."

Ray stared at him before realizing that Jordan's brother had a right to know that his sister was in danger. "Jordan's in trouble at the Yellow Rose Steakhouse."

"What do you mean she's in trouble?"

"I don't have time to explain, Danny. You just have to trust me on this. I'll call you once I'm on the road heading in that direction."

"Dammit! I knew I shouldn't have let her go there by herself." He stared Ray down. "You can't keep me from going with you after you just told me that my sister's in trouble. No point arguing about this. I'm going with you."

"No, Danny, you're not. It will violate your house arrest. Have you forgotten that you're wearing an ankle monitor? If you get out of range for any reason, all bets are off, and you go back to jail."

"You think I give a crap about that? This is Jordan we're talking about. I'd like to see you try and stop me from going with you."

Ray took a deep breath, then nodded. "Then come on. I'll call my friend's son from the road, and maybe when they lock you up for violating your house arrest rules, they won't throw away the key."

Danny fell in step behind the ex-cop.

"Better hurry," Ray said over his shoulder. "Time's not on our side."

❧

"WHAT'S WITH THE GUN, MARCO?" Jamie asked, moving over to stand in front of Jordan. "Abby sent this woman down here to get a recipe. Nothing more, man."

Marcus turned his attention from Jordan and focused on Jamie. "Why did you rat me out to the cops?"

"Rat you out? I only told them the truth—that you borrowed my truck on Monday. Why would that be a problem for you?"

"Because he might have been the one who killed Stevie, the motel clerk," Jordan blurted.

For the first time since she'd arrived at the restaurant, she realized how much trouble she'd gotten herself into. And the fact that she'd just accused Marco of killing Stevie definitely wouldn't help her cause. Here she was, in a secluded basement with one man who may have killed the stripper and another who more than likely had killed the motel clerk.

Either way you looked at it, she was screwed.

"I knew you saw me that day," Marco said, his eyes defiant as he screamed at Jordan.

Jamie turned to face her. "You didn't mention that you saw him at the motel with my truck. All this time you've been suggesting that I might be the one you saw there when all along, you knew it was him?"

Jordan shook her head. "Honestly, this is news to me. I saw someone peeking out of the curtains in Stevie's room, but I didn't know who it was. Actually, I thought it might have been Stevie trying to avoid me." She made eye contact with Marco. Somehow, she had to get his finger off the trigger of the gun still pointed in her direction. "Come on, Marco, even if you did kill the clerk. I'm sure you had a good reason. The guy was a coke-head, and you were probably acting in self-defense. I'll tell the cops that I witnessed Stevie coming at you with a knife."

She hoped she sounded convincing. No way the cops would ever believe that story, knowing that Stevie had been drugged with fentanyl and then dragged over to the pool and shoved in. She hoped Marco was dumb enough to buy it, though. What happened in the next two minutes depended on him believing her.

"You think the cops will fall for that?" Marco asked, a ray of hope lighting up his eyes.

"Sure they will," Jamie said. "I'll even say that you told me what happened that day when you returned my truck. That way there will be two of us backing up your story."

"How can I believe either of you?" Marco stepped further into the room. "You both probably already know about the meat locker, and you're just trying to trick me so I'll let you go and tell the cops."

Jordan noticed that his hand had begun to shake —the one holding the gun. She had to convince him quickly, or she and Jamie might not make it out of there alive. "We didn't go anywhere near that room," Jordan assured him. "Whatever is in there is your secret, and we have no intentions of talking to the police about it. Like Jamie said, I'm only here for the recipe, and now that I have it, I'll be on my merry way." She patted her phone and stepped away from Jamie, but quickly slid back behind him again when Marco took a step closer.

"How do I know you're not lying about the stuff in

there?" He pointed to the door to the refrigerated supply room. "I'm not sure I can trust either of you."

Just then the door opened, and Abby appeared at the top of the steps, shock registering on her face when she saw the gun in her brother's hand.

Jordan was never so glad to see Marco's sister than at that moment. Hopefully, she could talk him down and get the gun away from him.

"What in the hell do you think you're doing?" she asked him.

Marco turned to her. "I'm sorry, Abby, but they both know that it was me who killed that lowlife motel clerk and—"

Abby cut him off. "Shut up, Marco. You're already in enough trouble without adding more with your big mouth."

"It's all gonna be okay, Abby. Both of them are gonna say that I killed the clerk when he came at me with a knife."

Abby grunted. "Sometimes I think you were born without a brain, like Scarecrow in the Wizard of Oz. Do you really think the cops will believe you acted in self-defense, when I'm sure they already know that the man you killed was drugged and then tossed into the pool?"

"They'll believe it, Abby. These two will make sure they do." Marco's face scrunched up, and tears threatened to overflow. "And I'll pay back every penny I took from the bar receipts, I promise. Rolando doesn't even have to know about it."

"What part of *shut up* didn't you get?" Abby said, walking over to her desk and pulling out a box of tissues from one of the drawers. "Give me the gun and go back upstairs and wait on me," she commanded. "I'll deal with Rolando and smooth things over for you, just like I always do."

Marco's shoulders dropped as he lowered his eyes, almost as if he were afraid to look at her when he handed her the gun. She grabbed it with a tissue-covered hand.

Jordan breathed a sigh of relief and knew that Jamie was probably feeling relieved as well.

But that feeling didn't last long.

As soon as Abby had control of the gun, she turned to Marco and said, "I love you."

Then she aimed the weapon at his head and pulled the trigger.

18

"Oh, my God!" Jordan screamed, as she ran toward Marco, who was now face down on the floor, blood seeping onto the rug from his head wound.

"Stop!" Abby commanded. "He's gone. I was afraid he was going to kill both of you. I had to do it," she said, her voice calm and without emotion.

"No, you didn't," Jamie said, his face still showing shock over what had just happened. "He gave you the gun. Why would you kill him if he no longer presented a threat to us?"

A cynical smile spread across Abby's face. "He'd already admitted that he'd killed the clerk at the motel, and he was high on meth. I couldn't take the chance that he would kill all three of us in the paranoid haze he was in." She turned to Jamie. "I think there are other things you need to worry about, besides this. I've heard that the cops are closing in on you for killing the stripper last Saturday night. When I tell them how you and Marco got into a screaming match, and that Marco pulled the gun and shot you, it will be quite the believable story, since they already think you're a killer."

She turned her focus back to Jordan. "Unfortunately, Jordan, you died trying to grab the gun from my drug-crazed brother. Your fiancé will be heartbroken to know that you took a bullet as well, but he'll be comforted, knowing that you died a hero."

"Do you really think the police will believe that fictitious story?" Jordan asked. "Because I sure as heck don't. It has more holes than a slice of Swiss cheese." Jordan stared at her, and for the first time, she was gripped with real fear for her life.

"Oh, they'll believe me, all right, especially after I show them proof that my brother killed the motel clerk."

"The police will want to know why you didn't call them immediately after you found out your brother was a killer—why you protected him instead. I'm not a cop, but I've been around a few of them. I know that makes you an accessory after the fact and just as guilty as if you murdered the clerk yourself."

Abby tsked. "Sometimes you can be so naive, Jordan, just like your stupid brother."

"Are you referring to Danny?" When Abby nodded, Jordan tried not to react, but she couldn't stop herself. "What did my brother ever do to you to make you say something like that about him? I thought you two were friends."

"We are, or at least we were, until he went and stuck his nose into my business. It's not what he said, but what he was about to do. He had no idea how his next move would have changed everything for me."

Jordan was confused. "What could he have possibly done that would have changed your life?"

"That's not important now, and since both you and Jamie are about to join my brother on the floor momentarily, you really don't need to know. Suffice it to say that Danny was threatening my livelihood."

"So, what did you do about it, Abby? Did you set Danny up in that motel room so that he'd take the fall for Carlita's murder?"

Jordan had no clue where that idea had come from, but it was worth a shot. As long as Abby was talking, she wasn't shooting, and that had to be a good thing.

Abby narrowed her eyes. "You might be surprised to know that as of this morning, the cops believe that Jamie here is suspect number one in Carlita's murder? Somehow, they'll connect him to your brother and say they collaborated to kill her."

"That's crap, and you know it. I'm not sure my brother even knows Jamie. Besides, what motive would they have? Danny was drunk and picked Carlita up at the bar that night. He can't remember anything after feeling dizzy and leaving with her, and the police are checking to see if he was drugged." She took a deep breath, knowing that was a lie. The police had already checked and Danny's tox screen was negative for anything that might have caused the memory loss he claimed to have had.

Abby snickered. "I happen to know that the cops didn't find any drugs in your brother's blood that night. Matter of fact, they didn't even check it out until the next day at the hospital."

"And to further discredit that ridiculous story about me and Danny, I can tell you that the police will find nothing that connects me to either him or to that woman," Jamie chimed in, moving farther in front of Jordan to protect her.

"They already have," Abby said with a smirk.

"You're lying," Jamie protested.

"She's not," Jordan blurted. "The police raided your apartment about an hour ago and found pictures of Carlita Fontaine torn up in the trash can. One of the pictures looked like someone had slashed it with a knife."

"How do you know that?" Abby asked, nailing Jordan with an icy stare. "My guy on the inside downtown only called me with that news less than an hour ago. He said they've issued a warrant for Jamie's arrest."

Jordan ignored Abby and made eye contact with Jamie. "Why were you stalking Carlita?"

Jamie lowered his head. "I have my reasons, but I swear, I didn't kill her."

"Then why follow her all over town and take pictures, only to desecrate them back at your apartment? It must have taken a lot of rage to do something like that," Jordan said, her voice soft as if she were soothing a small child.

"Like I said, I had—"

"Jamie, I want to believe you," Jordan interrupted. "But you're making it really hard. Did you kill Carlita and then for some reason help Marco kill the motel clerk, too?"

"Hell, no!" Jamie shouted. "Sure, I was angry with the woman. She was the reason I came to Amarillo in the first place."

"And what was that reason?" Abby asked, still pointing the gun at them.

Jamie took a deep breath and blew it out slowly. "Before my mother died, she told me that I had been adopted—that she was my great aunt." He paused as a tear slid down his cheek. "She also told me that a woman named Mary Alice Winters—stage name Carlita Fontaine—was really my mother."

Jordan's eyes widened. "Carlita Fontaine was your biological mother?"

Jamie sighed. "I just wanted to talk to her. I wanted her to know that the people she handed me over to were cruel, sadistic drunks who made my entire life a living hell. I needed to know why she gave me up in the first place." He swiped at several more tears escaping down his cheeks. "All I really wanted was for her to say that everything would be okay, that we could be a family now that I'd finally found her."

"The knife through the picture suggests that it didn't happen that way." Jordan couldn't help herself and put her hand on Jamie's shoulder. "Is that why you killed her?"

"No. She told me she had no idea what I was talking about and warned me that if I ever approached her again, she'd get a restraining order against me. Despite the fact that I did want to kill her right then, I'm telling you, I didn't," Jamie said. "Yes, she rejected me, and yes, I was really angry at her, but after I found out that she was dead, I knew I had to get past that anger if I was ever going to be whole again." He looked up at Abby. "The only reason I came into work early today was to give you my two weeks' notice and to tell you that I've decided to go to Florida and get on with my life in the Sunshine State."

Jordan thought for a moment, trying to piece it all together. "So, if you didn't kill Carlita, then who did?" She turned to Abby. "Marco?"

"For being a big-time college graduate, Jordan, you definitely aren't the sharpest knife in the drawer, pun intended," Abby said with a chuckle, as she turned back to Jamie. "I had no idea that Carlita was your mother. I remember back in high school when she was sixteen and found herself knocked up by one of the many boys she'd seduced, trying to find the love she didn't get at home. The rumor mill said she'd gone off to stay with her aunt for a little R and R, when we all knew the real reason. I didn't know what happened to her after that until she showed up in Amarillo about five years ago."

"So, no one even knew she had a kid?" Jamie asked. "You'd think she would have welcomed me with open arms."

This time Abby laughed out loud. "Let me tell you a little something about your mother, Jamie. She was a real piece of work. The woman didn't have one drop of maternal blood running through her veins. When you showed up and confronted her, she must have panicked, seeing you as a possible snag in the life she'd grown accustomed to." She paused, and her voice softened for a minute. "Your mother had her hands in so many illegal ventures that I'm surprised someone didn't kill her a long time ago. I'm pretty sure that her rejection of you was not personal, although I know that's hard to believe when you're hurting."

"What kind of illegal ventures was Carlita involved in?" Jordan asked, thinking that was one more bit of information that might help Danny's case.

"Too many to talk about now. Enough talk. I need to get this over with before the police arrive. I will tell you this, Jamie. Your mother would have definitely seen you as a threat to her new way of life and would have done whatever was necessary to keep everyone from knowing what a fraud she was. You showing up and calling her *mom* must have scared the bejesus out of her. She might have even suspected that you were after her money, which I'm here to tell you was nothing to shake a stick at. She was rich and used that cash to bully people. She paraded around Spicy Salsa like she owned the place, telling everyone how she'd been a big-time casino dancer in Las Vegas."

"You seem to have known her well," Jordan said.

"We were friends in high school. After she moved back to Amarillo, I saw her every now and then, occasionally had lunch with her." Abby looked at Jamie. "I had no idea she had a kid, though."

Jordan pressed on. "So you knew that she was blackmailing men out of that motel room?"

"Of course I did. Actually, she and that raunchy-looking boyfriend of hers worked for me." Abby shook her head in disgust. "And the woman lied like a rug, but I kept her secrets. The only casino she ever danced in was one of those small gas station-slash-casino dives in New Mexico. Hell, I doubt that she'd even been to Las Vegas." Abby waved the gun at them. "Now, let's get on with the business at hand."

"I wasn't looking for money," Jamie said, unable to hide the sadness in his voice, "I only wanted her to know about me."

"Some women should never have children, Jamie," Jordan said, before glancing at her watch, wondering when Alex and Ray would show up. She had to keep Abby talking. As long as she did, she and Jamie had a better chance of surviving. "So, did Marco kill Carlita?"

Abby shook her head.

"Then who did?"

"Me."

Jordan gasped. "Why?"

"She was collateral damage. I needed to get Danny out of the picture before he ruined everything I'd worked so hard to accomplish up to this point." Abby took a step closer to them. "Unfortunately, the time has come for me to say goodbye to the two of you. But first, I have to make it look like I fought with Marco over the gun before I shot him." She turned the gun toward her body and fired a single shot into her upper arm at close range.

At that moment Jordan realized just how deranged the woman screaming in pain and bleeding from her self-inflicted wound really was. She knew that in the next two minutes, she and Jamie would be on the floor beside Marco, and Abby would be rushed to the hospital as the hero who had stopped her crazed, killer brother.

Jordan tried one more thing, doubtful that it would work, but she couldn't give up. "You don't have to do this, Abby. Jamie and I will verify your story about how all this went down."

Abby tried to laugh through the pain. "How dumb do you think I am?" She looked at Jordan. "It's too bad, really. I think you and I could have been good friends. We think alike, and—"

"Don't even go there," Jordan fired back. "I'm nothing like you and never will be."

With Abby's attention focused on Jordan, Jamie threw himself at her, knocking the gun away. It clattered to the floor, and Jordan dove for it.

The gun felt as heavy as a cannon in her hand as she pointed it directly at Abby, who was being restrained on the floor by Jamie's knee pressing into her back. "To answer your earlier question, yes, I *do* think you might be pretty dumb," Jordan said sarcastically. "I'm standing here with your gun, and you're on the floor with your face pushed into the rug. Who do you think looks like the smart one now?"

"Seriously, Jordan, do you really think the cops are going to believe anything you tell them about me? I made sure there was nothing—and I do mean nothing—that could connect me to any of this, not to mention that I have friends in high places who know that it's in their best interest to keep me out of jail."

"Don't count on it. I can be very convincing." Jordan turned to Jamie. "My phone's back at the desk. Where's yours?" When he pointed to his back pocket, she bent down and retrieved it, then called 911.

Just as she hung up, the door opened, and Ray and Danny charged down the steps.

Danny spied the gun in her hand and slowly walked toward her. "Are you okay, Jordan?" When she nodded, he reached out and took the gun from her with the hand in a cast, then held her trembling hands tightly with the other.

He nodded toward the body on the floor, face down. "Marco, I presume?"

"Abby killed him. He admitted to killing Stevie."

"Was Stevie the one who killed Carlita then?" Ray asked, reaching down to see if Marco was still alive. He shook his head before he called the police station and requested back-up and two ambulances, one for Abby and the other for her brother.

"I don't know how Stevie fits into all this, but Abby was the one who killed Carlita," Jordan said, finally calming down a little.

"That's a filthy lie," Abby, who up to this point had been unusually quiet, said from the floor.

Danny stared at her, but she wouldn't meet his gaze.

He looked at his sister. "And why would Abby do that? Was Carlita blackmailing her, too?"

Jordan shook her head. "No."

"Then why?"

Jordan wrapped her arms around her brother's neck and hugged him.

When she pulled away, she looked directly into his eyes. "Abby had Carlita killed to frame you."

19

"Carlita was murdered to frame me?" Danny looked stunned.

He glared at Abby, who was now on her feet while an Amarillo police officer cuffed her. They'd arrived on the scene shortly after Danny had. "What reason could you possibly have for doing that?"

Abby's eyes bored into him as he waited for an explanation. "Lawyer," she said with a smirk.

"Oh, no you don't. I deserve to know why I've just been through hell the past week. Is it something I said when we decided that we were better friends than lovers?"

"You men always think everything is about sex." A slight smile spread across her face. "When my lawyer gets here, you'll see that I had nothing to do with any of this. I'm exercising my right to remain silent until then."

"There are two witnesses who contradict your story, Abby," Ray said. "You should have exercised that right long before you opened your mouth and talked to them."

"Really? Any good cop would already know that it's my word against a former employee who I recently fired and a woman who will do anything to keep her brother out of jail."

"You're lying," Jamie said. "You never fired me. The cops will see right through your story."

Again, Abby smirked. "I wouldn't bet money on that, Jamie." She turned to the police officer who had handcuffed her. "Did you know that Carlita Fontaine was this man's biological mother? He murdered her for the money he thought he would inherit."

Jamie started toward her, anger lighting up his face, before one of the police officers stepped in and stopped him. "The courts will sort this all out. Right now, I'm going to have to cuff you, sir, since there's still an outstanding warrant for your arrest."

"No," Jordan protested. "Jamie didn't kill Carlita." She pointed to Abby. "That woman did, and I've already told you why."

Just then Alex and Phil Norris pushed open the door and practically flew down the steps.

Immediately, Alex walked over to Jordan and hugged her. "Oh, thank the Lord! I thought I might be too late." He held her out in front of him, pleading with his eyes. "Tell me you're not hurt."

She shook her head and tried to smile. "Ray and Danny made sure of that," she said, not wanting to let on exactly how close she'd come to... She couldn't even finish that sentence in her head, let alone say it out loud.

Before long, the room was filled with several more cops and the medical examiner, who had arrived on the scene moments before.

Ray moved toward Jordan. "Did Marco give you any indication of why he tried to kill you both?"

"Marco was a meth addict," Jamie replied, before Jordan could answer. "Everyone at the restaurant knew that. He came down here with his gun, all para-noid about Jordan seeing him at the motel the day the clerk was murdered." He turned to one of the officers. "That was the day you all believed I had gone there and killed the clerk myself. It was actually Marco in my truck, just like I tried to tell you."

"He's telling the truth about the truck. I saw it at the motel myself," Jordan said. "And I heard Marco admit that he'd peeked out of Stev... the clerk's motel room and saw Victor and me that day. It had to have been him."

Alex took a step toward Abby. "Why would your brother want to kill the clerk? Did he see him the night Carlita was killed?"

"Lawyer," Abby repeated.

Alex turned back to Jordan for an answer to his question. "And Marco gave you no reason for killing the clerk?"

"No. Like Jamie said, Marco was suspicious and accused us of knowing all about what he had done. He was so paranoid that at one point, he accused us of looking into the meat locker—" Jordan stopped talking mid-sentence. "What's in that meat locker, Abby? Another dead body?"

Abby glared at her before looking away.

"Phil, can you get a warrant for the contents of the freezer to see what Marco might have been talking about?" Alex asked.

"On it," Phil responded, as he pulled out his cell phone and dialed.

By the time an FBI agent arrived with the warrant, the ME had already finished the preliminary inspec-tion of Marco's body and had given the okay for it to be taken to the morgue.

Jordan glanced toward Abby and noticed that the

smugness she'd displayed since everyone had arrived
had been replaced by what looked like fear—maybe
even panic—when Phil opened the freezer door and
he and Alex stepped inside.

Nobody said a word while they waited to see if the
two agents would find anything in there that might
have caused Marco to think he needed to kill to protect himself.

The freezer door finally opened, and Alex
emerged with a large bag of multi-colored tablets. He
looked directly at Abby. "I'm willing to bet the lab will
find out that these are fentanyl. I'm anxious to hear
how you're going to explain how these tablets ended
up in one of the boxes of frozen ribeyes in there."
When Abby didn't respond, he continued, "And by the
way, before you give us some lame-ass answer for that,
let me advise you that we stopped opening boxes after
we found at least twenty-five bags of these pills in
there, enough to put you away for a very long time."

"I don't know anything about the pills," Abby said,
her voice softer than before. "My brother's in charge of
ordering and processing the supplies every week. I
had nothing to do with it. I don't even go in the freezer
unless I absolutely have to."

"Do you really expect us to believe that Marco was
the brains behind the drug trafficking that you were
apparently running right out of this steakhouse?"
Jordan asked. "Jamie and I can both attest to the fact
that Marco wasn't smart enough to run an operation
like this. You even said it yourself that Marco was like
the scarecrow in the Wizard of Oz with no brain."

"Good luck proving that," Abby said, changing her
attitude back to defiant again.

"Get her out of here and lock her up," Norris said
to one of the Amarillo cops.

"One more thing," Jordan said. "She mentioned having cops on the inside who tipped her off about Jamie's arrest warrant. Someone may want to look into that."

"I'll definitely pass that info along to the Amarillo chief of police and get DEA to take over this crime scene and to interrogate her back at the station." Norris turned to Alex. "In the meantime, take your girl home and try to enjoy your last night in Amarillo with her family. I promise I'll call if there are any updates."

"Thanks, Phil, it's been a pleasure working with you."

Phil nodded. "Mine, as well. And if you ever decide to settle down in this part of Texas, I can promise there will be a job waiting for you."

Alex nodded and reached for Jordan's arms. She pulled away and walked over to Jamie, now in handcuffs and waiting to be carted off to jail. "I'm so sorry that things didn't work out between you and your mother, but I'm glad you've made peace with it. I promise I'll do everything in my power to clear this up. I'm sure we can convince Danny's lawyer to take a look at the evidence the police have against you."

He gave her a weak smile. "I've seen you in action, Jordan. I have no doubt you'll have me out of jail in no time."

Jordan watched as they led him up the stairs, then she took a deep breath. "I'm ready to go home now," she said to Alex.

They drove to the police station with Danny and Ray to pick up Alex's vehicle. Other than small talk, not much was said throughout the entire drive.

Once they were by themselves in the car, Jordan turned to face Alex. "Is Danny off the hook for Carlita's murder now?"

He didn't say anything for a minute then reached over and patted her hand. "I'm sorry, love, but the police have found no evidence that implicates anyone other than your brother. Like Abby said, it's your word against hers, and even you have to admit that you have a pretty good reason to lie about it."

"You don't think Abby will walk away from all this, do you? I'm one-hundred percent sure that she was the brains behind everything."

"Yeah, you're probably right, but like I said, there's no proof. She blamed the drug stuff on her brother, who she conveniently silenced before the cops arrived. Despite her explanation that she killed him before he shot you and Jamie, we both know that wasn't the real reason. More than likely, she knew her brother was using drugs and that he was getting more paranoid by the day. My guess would be that she believed he had loose lips, and she was afraid of what he might say to the cops." Alex sighed. "At this point, the evidence points to Abby getting duped by her brother, who was trafficking right under her nose. The police really have nothing to hold her on."

"I know she was angry at Danny for some reason, and I suspect she killed Carlita just so she could frame him."

"Wow! How'd you come up with that theory?"

"Abby admitted it." Jordan stopped to think about it. "Well, not exactly. But she did say that Danny was about to do something that would—what were her exact words? Oh, yeah, threaten her livelihood."

"Any idea what that's all about?"

"Not a clue, but my gut tells me that when we find out what she was talking about, it'll be the one thing that'll break Danny's case wide open."

Alex parked the car in Sylvia's driveway and took

both of Jordan's hands into his. "Even if we do find out what that was, it would still not prove that Abby murdered Carlita."

"So, Abby will walk while Danny has to fight for his life in court?"

"Unfortunately, that's the way it looks right now. We just have to trust that your brother's lawyer is as good as they say he is and can convince at least one juror that there's enough reasonable doubt after all this."

Jordan swiped at a tear. "Let's not tell Danny any of this. Even though nothing's changed in his case, it won't hurt to let him think there's hope. I want our last night here to be cheerful and not all doom and gloom."

"I think I know the perfect way to keep things light." Alex grinned. "Since you never got a chance to pick up the groceries for tonight's dinner, what do you say to my ordering take-out for all of us—a feast of sorts."

"That's the best idea I've heard today. That way nobody has to work hard, and we can all relax and enjoy my family. So, what did you have in mind?"

"With all the Mexican food we've eaten, I've missed my own Italian cooking. When I close my eyes, I can envision spaghetti and meatballs, chicken Parmesan, and lobster ravioli."

Jordan's eyes lit up. "I know the perfect place." She looked up the restaurant on her phone and dialed, then handed the phone to Alex so he could order.

When he finished, he opened the car door and stepped out. He stuck his head back in and said, "Put that beautiful smile on your face before we walk in, unless you plan on being a Debbie Downer in there."

"That's gonna be hard to do, but I'll try. No Debbie

Downer for me." She walked with him to the door.
"You know you're about to become Victor's best friend
when he takes one look at that tiramisu you ordered."

AFTER THEY DEVOURED the Italian feast, they all sat
around the table with a cup of fresh coffee and a
plateful of dessert.

"Jordan, are you ready to tell us what happened?"
Sylvia asked. "You've been quiet all night, and even
Danny, who usually tells me everything, has remained
tight-lipped."

Jordan glanced first at her mother and then at
Danny and her friends. "I'm sorry, Mom. I didn't want
to ruin this fantastic meal." She took the final bite of
her dessert before continuing.

No one said a word as she related everything that
had happened that day—well, mostly everything.
She'd purposely left out the part about the probability
of Abby Rivera walking away scot-free while Danny
still had the fight of his life ahead of him.

"Holy cow! Our waiter from the other night is really Carlita's kid?" Rosie asked. "After what you told us
about the police finding all those pictures of the
stripper in his apartment, I'd say he had a pretty good
motive for killing her."

"He didn't do it," Jordan said. "We're still not sure
who did, but my money's on Abby's brother. According to Jamie, Marco was always strung out on
something or another, and he admitted to killing Stevie." She shrugged. "I still can't put two and two together about that, but I know there has to be a
connection."

"So, will Danny be cleared of Carlita's murder?" Sylvia asked.

"No, they can't find any evidence that points to anyone else," Alex said, sadly.

"Don't worry, Mom. I'll be cleared," Danny said. "Abby implied to Jordan that she went after me for something I said or did. For the life of me I can't figure out what that might be, but I know sooner or later, the truth will come out."

"Hope so, honey," Sylvia said. "Maybe when your father gets home on Tuesday, we can get Patrick to make a trip to Amarillo to explain everything to all of us."

"Sounds like a plan. For right now, though, that's enough talk about what happened today. It's my last night with Jordan and all her friends." Danny pointed to the table with all the paper plates and disposable silverware. "The good thing about takeout—other than the fact that it was delicious and on Alex's dime — is that there are no dishes. Let's clear the table and sit around the TV and relax. Maybe watch a movie on Netflix."

"Good idea," Jordan said. "But first I need to get this Hot Fudge Cake recipe off to my editor. I'm already two days behind schedule, and if I want to keep my job when I get home, I'd better get this to him ASAP."

"You go ahead, honey," Sylvia said. "We'll get everything ready and be waiting in the living room for you." She grinned. "Rosie and I went out earlier and bought three bottles of Bailey's Irish Cream. So far, we've had Mexican to celebrate Victor's heritage, and tonight was Italian for Alex. I thought it was time we paid homage to our own McAllister heritage. We're going to drink BBCs while we watch TV. Hopefully, Danny can find a funny movie for us to watch."

"BBCs?" Alex asked.

"Just wait until you taste them," Jordan said. "You know how much I love Bailey's, and what could be better than my favorite liquor with bananas and coconut?" She got up and started for her mother's bedroom before calling over her shoulder. "Danny, go help Mom make those. I'll be right back."

Once there, she sat down on the bed and opened up her laptop. After scrolling down on her phone to the picture of the recipe Jamie had given her, she typed it on the computer. Satisfied that her job would be safe after her boss got a look at the recipe, she hit SEND and was about to join everyone in the living room when she remembered the thumb drive in her pencil case. She was curious about what she'd thought had been important enough to bring to Amarillo with her.

She dug it out of the case, plugged it into the USB port on the laptop, and waited for the content to appear, fully expecting to see some vacation photos she'd taken ages ago, or maybe some crazy recipes she'd never gotten around to using. As a picture emerged, she gasped, mesmerized by what was playing out on the screen.

Then she saw it, and she screamed. Within seconds everyone came running into the bedroom.

Alex rushed to her side. "What's the matter, Jordan?"

Tears streamed down her face as she pointed to the computer. "I just found the smoking gun."

20

D anny plopped down beside Jordan on the bed while she rewound the video from the thumb drive back to the beginning. "What smoking gun?"

Everyone gathered around as she pushed PLAY. You could've heard a pin drop as they collectively held their breath.

For the first few minutes, all you could see was what appeared to be the inside of a motel room.

"Is that what I think it is?" Danny asked.

"Yes. Watch closely," Jordan said, as the door to the room opened and Danny and Carlita entered.

"Oh my!" Sylvia cried out. "Please tell me you're not going to make me watch Danny murder that woman?"

"Of course not, Mom, but you *will* see someone else do it. I'll tell you when to close your eyes."

The scene played out exactly as Danny had said. Carlita helped him to the bed and then took off his clothes, smiling up at the camera in the process. When she had him naked and under the covers, she ran her fingers across his chest, causing angry red scratches. Then she walked over to the dresser where there was a bottle of liquor.

"That's why the cops found Danny's DNA under her fingernails. Probably so she could insinuate that they'd had rough sex when she blackmailed him," Ray commented. "That's the Scotch the police found," he added, as Carlita reached for the lone glass and poured herself a drink.

Then she threw back her head and chugged it.

"Is that the glass that had the fentanyl on the rim?" Rosie asked.

"I think so. Just watch it all play out," Jordan said.

After finishing the Scotch, Carlita walked back to the bed, and with her back to the camera, peeled off her clothes, then climbed under the covers. All of a sudden, she sat up and gasped before collapsing back onto the pillow.

Sylvia began to cry. "Anyone who looks at this video has to know immediately that Danny had nothing to do with that woman's murder."

"I know, Mom, but let's keep watching. There are a few interesting things yet to come and one really big surprise."

Everyone quit talking, and once again, they stared at the computer screen. Approximately five minutes later, the motel door opened, and a man walked in.

"Is that Marco?" Danny asked.

"Yes. He picks up your jeans and puts a small bottle in the pocket. Probably the fentanyl the police found."

"You gotta be kidding me," Danny said. "They went to a lot of trouble to frame me."

"I know, but keep watching. Surprise number two coming up."

All eyes were once again on the computer screen, as the motel door opened and another person walked in.

"Wait for it. The best part is coming."

Nobody spoke a word as they stared at Abby Rivera, carrying a towel. With gloved hands, she unwrapped it, pulled out what looked like a steak knife, then sauntered over to Danny's side of the bed and looked down. Then she reached for Danny's right hand and curled his fingers around the knife handle before walking back to stand beside Carlita.

Jordan hit STOP and turned to her mother. "This is the part that you don't want to see, Mom."

With Sylvia's back to the computer screen, Jordan restarted the video. At that moment Abby looked up at the camera in the ceiling and smiled before plunging the knife into Carlita's chest.

"Holy crap! So she was the one who killed Carlita," Rosie said.

"Technically, Carlita was already dead, and stabbing a dead woman is not a major crime," Alex said as Jordan again stopped the video for a moment. "The actual killer is the one who laced the rim of her glass with fentanyl. Unfortunately, with both Stevie and Marco also dead, we may never know who that was. Hell, Carlita may have even done it herself, hoping to get high before she left Danny to sleep it off." Alex turned to Danny. "At the very least, this proves that you had absolutely nothing to do with her death. It's obvious you'd been drugged before you arrived in the room."

"So even if I hadn't pulled the knife out of Carlita's chest, my fingerprints would have still been all over it, right?" When Alex nodded, Danny continued, "I've been beating myself up, thinking this might not have been blamed on me if I had just left the knife in her chest."

"Getting your fingerprints on the knife was key to

Abby framing you, so, no, it wouldn't have mattered. You can turn around now, Mom." Jordan hit PLAY. "You won't want to miss Abby incriminating herself big time."

All eyes were glued to the laptop as they watched Abby take off her shoes, jump up on the bed, and smile up at the camera before ejecting the tape.

"Holy cow!" Lola exclaimed. "How's she gonna explain that to the cops?"

Alex narrowed his eyes. "This video clearly shows Abby taking the recording that night and probably destroying it. So how did you get it, Jordan?"

Jordan shrugged. "I don't know. I just found it in my—" She slapped her forehead. "It was in my pencil case. Remember, I admitted that when Victor and I first visited the motel to check out the crime scene, I left the case on the counter in the office. When we went back the next day—the same day Stevie was murdered—the office was empty. Although we never got to talk to Stevie, I discovered my pencil case in the Lost and Found container on top of one of the filing cabinets. It wasn't until later that I noticed the zip drive and just assumed I had left it in there the last time I interviewed someone back in Ranchero for a story to go with a recipe."

"Hundred bucks says that's the reason Stevie was killed," Victor said. "Someone had to turn the camera on before Carlita and Danny entered the room. It had to have been either him or maybe Marco."

"But how would Stevie have gotten his hands on the tape?" Lola asked. "Surely, Abby wasn't stupid enough to leave it lying around."

"You can use a lot of adjectives to describe Abby Rivera, but *stupid* isn't one of them. She was as sly as a fox," Jordan said. "And to answer your question, Lola, the only reason I can think of is that Stevie was using a laptop when we were there. I'm not sure if the hotel computer was broken or if that's just the way they did business. I'm betting he was in cahoots with Carlita in the blackmailing scheme and was the one who set up the camera when she brought johns back to the motel. Although he was usually strung out on drugs, like every other kid his age, he was probably very proficient on the computer and somehow set it up to record not only on the ceiling camera, but also onto his own laptop. That would certainly be a way of making sure that Carlita didn't screw him out of his cut."

"I can understand that," Alex said. "But why would he put the zip drive in your case?"

Danny laughed out loud. "Have you looked at that thing lately? I'm sure he assumed that if Marco and Abby ever found out that he had a copy from that night, they would never look in that ratty old thing to find it, especially if it was in Lost and Found."

"You think that's what got him killed?' Ray asked "If he was as sleazy as Victor and Jordan say he was, you wouldn't have a hard time convincing me that maybe he tried to blackmail them. He did have a habit to feed, you know."

"And he probably thought Jordan would never come back for her pencil case." Danny took a deep breath and closed his eyes. When he reopened them, they were brimming with tears. He leaned over and hugged his sister. "For once, your snooping paid off in spades. I believe you just saved my life."

By this time, everyone else had tears in their eyes, especially Jordan. She'd come to Amarillo to see if she could help Danny out. The video was proof positive that she had done just that.

"Jordan, send a copy of that recording to me, and I'll get it to Bobby Sanders at the police station right away," Ray said. "They can use it when they interrogate Abby. Because Carlita was already dead when Abby put the knife in her chest, they can't charge her with murder one. Hopefully, they'll be able to lock her up for killing her brother, although it will be her word against yours."

"No way she killed Marco in self-defense," Jordan said. "She implied that he was skinning money off the top of the bar profits and she would have to pacify a guy named Rolando, who I'm guessing was high up on the drug trafficking chain. I think she was worried that her brother might be willing to give up a bigger fish once he was indicted, maybe even implicate her to save his own sorry self. She killed him for one reason only—to silence him."

"You're probably right, Jordan," Alex said. "But like Ray mentioned, *proving* that is an entirely different story."

"So she'll get away with all this?"

"Hopefully not. The cops will dig deep into her beef invoices to try to connect her to the fentanyl. But we all know how smart she is, so no guarantees that she'll spend any time in prison."

"That sucks," Jordan said, making a face.

"I know. We can only hope she's not as smart as we're giving her credit for." Alex paused. "Can you send me a copy of the video as well so that I can get it to Phil? Now that they've found the fentanyl and know where the Xylazine supply was coming from, maybe they can find something from the vet's office to pin on Abby and pressure her into possibly giving up her bosses. It's always been my suspicion that this case had drug cartel written all over it. Maybe DEA can get her to give up this Rolando guy you mentioned."

He paused as his brows wrinkled in deep thought. "Cartel involvement might also explain why Brianna Rollins, the vet's wife, killed him before he had a chance to squeal on anyone else. Her bank account showed a fifty-grand deposit the day she poisoned him. I'm guessing the cartel threatened her and offered her the cash. Given the fact that she had recently discovered that her husband was cheating, it must have sealed the deal for her."

"Cartel involvement makes sense," Jordan said. "That would explain the two armed guards on the truck when the shipment arrived at the restaurant."

Danny's head jerked up. "What did you just say?"

"Jamie told me that the day Marco borrowed his truck, he stayed behind to help unload the meat order that had just arrived. He said it was uncomfortable working with two guys carrying automatic weapons and watching him like a hawk."

"That's it!" Danny exclaimed, jumping up from the bed. "That's why Abby needed to frame me."

"Because of two guys on a meat truck?" Rosie asked. "That's a little far-fetched, don't you think?"

"No, it makes perfect sense now. About a week before the murder, I was with Abby in her office when a delivery truck arrived. She whisked me out of there and up the steps in a hurry, but not before I noticed the same thing Jamie had—two heavily armed guards on the truck. When I asked her about it, she said that several of their trucks had been hijacked on the highway from Hereford to Amarillo and that the guards had just recently been hired to prevent any further theft."

"Why would she need to frame you for that?" Jordan asked.

Danny blew out a breath. "I mentioned to her that I was going to check into it and find out if any other trucks had been hijacked on that highway. Knowing what we now know, they were probably transporting the fentanyl on their trucks. I can see where she might not want me sticking my nose into it. She would also know that as an officer of TSCRA—Texas and Southwestern Cattle Raisers Association, for those of you who might not know what the initials stand for—it was my job to report any theft like that and to start an immediate investigation." He turned to Jordan. "Didn't Abby tell you that I had become a threat to her livelihood?"

"She did. I didn't understand it at the time, but it's becoming crystal clear to me. She needed you out of the picture, and what better way to do it than to have you in prison."

"We parted ways—at her suggestion, I might add —a few days after that. She must've been so worried about me finding out about her drug operation that she was willing to sacrifice Carlita, who was one of her friends, in order to accomplish that."

"The more I hear about Abby Rivera, the more I believe that she's a psychopath," Lola said. "And to think we were all trying to find a way to hook you up with her, Danny."

"The sad part of this whole thing is that I would have still been interested. She's the one who kicked me to the curb with the friend card." He laughed. "That aside, Abby timed her defensive move perfectly. Before I even had time to look into the hijackings, I found myself in a jail cell for a crime I didn't commit. Hell, I wouldn't put it past her to have hired Tucker and his son to get themselves arrested and thrown into the cell to finish me off, once and for all."

"The woman was definitely covering all her bases. Hopefully, she'll get what's coming to her for causing you so much grief, honey," Sylvia said. "Right now, I need to call your dad with the news. It's 9 a.m. in Abu Dhabi, and I know he'll be up. You know how he likes an early breakfast."

After Ray and Alex sent the video from Jordan's computer to the Amarillo Police Department and the FBI, they gathered in the living room. Although no longer interested in watching a funny movie, they spent the next two hours rehashing everything until they finally headed to bed.

Jordan thought she'd never be able to fall asleep after the night they'd just had, but she did, and when she woke up at ten the next morning, she felt refreshed. Today they would leave for Ranchero, but now, it would be a much more pleasant drive, knowing that Danny was going to be okay.

She grabbed a cup of coffee and sat down at the table, noticing that not everyone was there. "Are Alex and Victor still sleeping?" she asked, planning to razz Alex about being a sleepyhead.

"Victor went with Alex to the FBI office to finish things up with Norris," Rosie said. "I think they're going to stop and pick up snacks for the drive home. They also mentioned bringing back lunch for all of us."

"Good," Jordan said. "That way we only have to stop when nature calls. Truth be told, I'm ready to get back to some form of normality again. And believe it or not, I'm even looking forward to talking to my boss to see how he liked the recipes."

"For heaven sakes, woman. Who are you and what

you done with my friend Jordan?" Rosie asked with a grin. "Everyone knows Egan is a jerk and will never give you credit for all those great recipes."

"You got me there. Maybe I did exaggerate a little when I said I was looking forward to seeing him."

"You definitely did," Rosie said as she poured Jordan another cup of coffee. "So, I'm all packed. What are we going to do until we leave?"

"You're way ahead of me," Jordan said, grabbing her coffee. "It will only take me about thirty minutes or so to pack. By then the guys should be back with food. I'm starving."

"Lola and I need to pack, too." Ray got up from the table and turned back. "Oh, I forgot to tell you. Jack said that his son looked into the idea of a dirty cop at the station. He thinks he knows who Abby's inside guy is, an older cop whose wife has Alzheimer's, and we all know how expensive that can be."

"Good to know," Jordan said. "Sorry for the cop, but glad he won't be spying for the cartel any longer. Hopefully, they'll go easy on him, knowing his motive for doing that." She headed back to the bedroom.

Around 12 o'clock, everyone was seated back at the dining room table waiting for Alex and Victor to return. Jordan reached for her phone to call and find out how much longer they'd be, when the guys came in with several bags of food and groceries.

"Burgers and fries for everyone," Victor said. "After that, we need to get on the road."

The room was eerily quiet while they consumed their last meal in Amarillo. Nothing stops chatter like food in everyone's mouths.

When they were finished, Alex shoved all the trash into a bag and headed for the kitchen.

When he came back, he said, "Phil called. Apparently, the DEA was finally able to get some straight answers from Abby after they discovered a second set of records that clearly pointed to money laundering at the restaurant and two offshore bank accounts with over a million dollars in each. Although she denied being involved in killing both Carlita and the motel clerk, she's too terrified of the cartel to give up any of them. Having seen the cartel in action up close and personal, I can't say that I blame her. So they won't be able to close the investigation into the fentanyl deaths, but at least now, the supply chain has been disrupted. I'm sure the cartel will eventually find another way to bring the drugs into Amarillo, but for now, the Xylazine snake head was cut off when they arrested the veterinarian."

"Not giving up the cartel is not a wise move for Abby," Ray commented. "There's no way the cartel can let her live with the fear hanging over them that one day she'll get sick of prison life and make a deal."

"You're right," Alex said. "If she dealt them the cartel now, she'd be put into witness protection, and although they might eventually find her, her chances would be much better than being in prison with people who are loyal to the cartel."

"And what about Danny?" Jordan asked.

"I spoke with Danny's lawyer while Victor and I were out," Alex said. "The DA looked at the zip drive, and coupled with Abby's confessions, all charges are being dropped. Final paperwork should be filed shortly if it hasn't already."

"Oh, thank the Lord!" Sylvia exclaimed. "I can't even begin to express how grateful I am to all of you for taking time out of your busy schedules to come with Jordan to help her brother." She faced her daughter. "I love you so much and can't wait until I can call your wonderful fiancé my son."

"On that note, let's make that a little more official. Hopefully, I'll be able to call you Mom sooner rather than later." Alex walked over to stand in front of Jordan's chair and bent down on one knee.

She smiled at him "Didn't you already do this?"

He grinned back. "I did, but not with this." He pulled out a jewelry case from his pocket and opened it. "Now you can't back out."

Jordan stared down at the emerald-cut diamond. "Is this—"

"Yes, it is," Victor interrupted. "After I told Alex how much you loved this ring, he knew he had to get it for you."

Jordan stared at Alex. "Although I love it, there's no way I want you to spend that much money on a ring. I would be happy with a much smaller one."

He reached for her hand and slipped the ring on her finger. "Nothing but the best for you, love," he said, before a mischievous grin covered his face. "Besides, I got one heckuva discount."

"He sure did," Victor said, enthusiastically. "The jewelry store didn't open until noon today, so Alex called the owner and asked him to meet us there earlier. He—"

"I can't believe the owner would do that," Jordan interrupted. "You'd think he would have suggested that you come back at noon."

"I might have mentioned that I was an FBI agent." Alex winked at her. "I wish you all could have seen Victor in action. I'm convinced he was a lawyer in another life. I'm still in awe at the way he manhandled the guy."

"That's my BFF," Jordan said. "But Alex, I know

how much this ring cost. There's no way I need one like this."

"Hear me out, please," Alex said. "When Victor asked the jeweler about the ring Carlita had ordered, the guy's face turned beet red, and he admitted that he'd already sold it. That's when Victor went in for the kill, pretty sure the guy got the full price for it and also got to keep Carlita's twenty grand down payment."

"You should have seen his reaction when I mentioned that Carlita's heir might be interested in the ring that legally would be part of her estate." Victor grinned from ear to ear.

"No, you did not," Jordan said, trying to maintain a stern look on her face, but failing miserably. Almost everything Victor did made her laugh, and this was no exception.

"Yes, he definitely did. After that, the price of your gorgeous diamond ring amazingly dropped another thirty percent. But don't feel sorry for the guy. I'm pretty sure that even with the discount, he still made a decent profit, especially with Carlita's down payment," Alex said.

"What if Carlita's heir really wants that big ring?" Lola asked.

"First of all, the deal is done. No going back. Second of all, Phil informed me that when Carlita's will was read, they discovered that Jamie Hathaway was the sole heir to all her fortunes. Carlita may have rejected Jamie as her son, but she must've had at least one maternal bone in her body." He paused. "After we left the jewelry store, Victor and I made a stop at the police station just as they were releasing Jamie. After we told him about Carlita's will and how we leveraged the ring that legally belonged to his mother and now him, he said he wanted no part of it. Said to consider the discount that I got on your ring as his gift to you for all you did for him."

"He also wondered if we thought it would be okay with you if he kept in touch after he gets to Florida," Victor added.

Jordan's eyes misted over. "I would love that. I hope you told him yes." After Victor nodded, she turned to Alex. "So now, Moreland, you'd better set a date before my mother goes on a mission and calls us six times a day to ask when you plan to make an honest woman out of me."

"You got that right," Sylvia said. "Do you have any idea how much work I have to do to plan this wedding? You are my only daughter, and it has to be perfect."

Jordan looked at her husband-to-be and raised her eyebrows. "You don't know my mother like I do. All her life she's stood by and watched as my dad and brothers turned me into a tomboy. Now is her one big chance to bring out my girly side."

"She's right, Alex," Danny said. "My mother probably already has names picked out for all your kids."

"Kids? How many do you want, Jordan?"

"I can't answer that. Right now, I'm more interested in how much fun we'll have working on it."

"Oh, dear! That's way too much information for me, young lady," Sylvia said. "Maybe I do like you better as a tomboy."

RECIPES

A note to my readers. Over the years, I've included at least ten or more of my recipes in the back of each of my cozies. I'm running out of originals, so I scoured the internet for some really delicious dishes. Rest assured, with the exception of the *Semla*, I have personally tried each one of them. You will not be disappointed. I included most of the recipes mentioned in the story. Credit was given to each site used. Enjoy!

JALAPEÑO CHEDDAR CHEESE BEER BREAD

Adapted from: https://www.aforkstale.com/easy-cheesy-jalapeno-beer-bread-recipe/

- 3 cups all-purpose flour
- 1 Tablespoon baking powder
- 1 teaspoon salt
- 3 Tablespoon sugar
- 1 cup sliced pickled jalapeño peppers
- 1½ cup sharp cheddar cheese
- 12 ounces beer (see note below)

Preheat oven to 350°F. In a large mixing bowl, mix 3 cups flour, 1 Tablespoon baking powder, 1 teaspoon salt, and 3 Tablespoons of sugar.

Fold in 1 cup of cheddar cheese and 1 cup pickled jalapeño peppers, reserving a few jalapeños to add to the top of bread.

Create a well in the center of flour mixture and pour the beer into the center.

Mix with spoon until the flour absorbs the beer, being careful not to over mix. Dough will be sticky. Place dough into a large greased loaf pan.

Top dough with the remaining jalapeños and sprinkle on the remaining ½ cup of cheese.

Bake for 60-65 minutes until bread is done. Remove from oven and allow to rest in pan for 5 minutes. Remove bread from loaf pan and cool bread on wire rack until completely cooled, to retain moisture.

Notes

Use a lighter tasting beer. Lighter beers, such as **lagers, ales and pilsners,** will give your bread a lighter color, and mild taste that just about everyone loves. Darker beers like stouts and porters make a darker-colored loaf and have a stronger beer flavor. Hoppy beers like IPAs, will give your bread a more bitter taste. The reviews say that light beer works great in a pinch. You want to be able to taste the sweetness of the bread, blended with the salty cheddar and jalapeños. Toast leftovers.

SYLVIA'S EASY BEEF STEW

BOEUF BOURGUIGNON

1½ lbs. beef stew meat, with all the fat removed and cut into small pieces

½ cup flour mixed with 2 Tablespoons Lawry's Seasoned Salt

3 Tablespoons vegetable oil

1 (6 ounce) can tomato paste

¼ cup ketchup

Salt and pepper to taste

2 packages Lawry's or McCormick (or similar) beef stew mix

6 cups water

5-6 potatoes cut into bite-size pieces

1 bag baby carrots

Dredge beef stew meat in seasoned flour. (Easiest way to do this is to put the ½ cup flour with the Lawry's into a brown paper sack. Put the meat into the bag, several pieces at a time and shake.) Brown on both sides in hot oil in a Dutch oven. Add water, tomato paste, ketchup, 2 packages of beef stew mix, and salt and pepper. You can add more ketchup if necessary.

Bring to boil. Reduce heat. Cover and simmer for 1 hour. Add vegetables and again bring it to a boil. Cover and simmer this until vegetables are tender. (Approximately 30-45 minutes).

CHOCOLATE KAHLUA CAKE

Adapted   from: https://www.allrecipes.com/recipe/256531/chocolate-kahlua-cake/

Ingredients

Cooking spray with flour (I use Baker's Joy)

1 (16.5 ounce) package devil's food cake mix

1 (8 ounce) container sour cream

4 large eggs

½ cup Kahlua

½ cup vegetable oil

1 (3.9 ounce) package instant chocolate pudding mix

2 Tablespoons grated orange zest

1 teaspoon ground cinnamon

1 (12 ounce) package mini chocolate chips

1 Tablespoon confectioners' sugar, or to taste

Directions

Preheat the oven to 350°F. Grease a fluted tube pan (such as Bundt) with floured cooking spray.

Combine cake mix, sour cream, eggs, Kahlua, oil, pudding mix, orange zest, and cinnamon in a large bowl; beat with an electric mixer on medium speed until very smooth, about 4 minutes.

Fold in chocolate chips. Pour batter into the prepared tube pan.

Bake in the preheated oven until a toothpick inserted into the center comes out clean, 50 to 60 minutes.

Remove from the oven and cool in the pan for 10 minutes. Invert cake onto a plate and remove from pan; let cool completely, about 30 minutes.

Dust with confectioners' sugar to serve.

GERMAN CHOCOLATE POKE CAKE

Adapted from: https://12tomatoes.com
Cake
1 box Dark Chocolate Fudge Cake Mix
1 (3.4 ounce) box Chocolate Fudge Instant Pudding
4 large eggs
1 cup sour cream
¾ cup vegetable oil
½ cup whole milk
1 Tablespoon vanilla
¼ teaspoon salt
1½ cups mini chocolate chips

Filling
14 ounces sweetened condensed milk

Ganache
4 ounces German chocolate, chopped (can substitute regular chocolate)
4 ounces heavy whipping cream

Frosting
1 can Coconut Pecan Frosting (or make your own)

Instructions

Preheat oven to 350° F. Spray a 9x13-inch baking pan with cooking spray and set aside.

In a large bowl or stand mixer, combine all of the cake ingredients above until fully mixed, then pour into the prepared pan. (Use cake ingredients above and not the ingredients on the box.)

Bake for 30-40 minutes or until toothpick comes out clean from center of the cake. Remove from oven and poke holes in the cake with the handle of a wooden spoon.

Pour the sweetened condensed milk over the top of the cake and allow it to soak in while the cake cools.

Once the cake has cooled, prepare the ganache by placing the chopped chocolate in a medium bowl and then heating the heavy cream in a small saucepan just until the edges begin to boil. Pour the heavy cream over the chocolate and allow to set for 4 minutes. Do not stir.

After 4 minutes have passed, whisk together the chocolate and heavy cream until rich chocolate ganache forms. Allow the ganache to sit and thicken for 5 to 10 minutes before spreading evenly over the top of the cake.

Next, spread the Coconut Pecan icing over the top of the ganache covered cake. Enjoy immediately or store in the fridge.

SYLVIA'S SMEAR FACES (AKA SEMLA)

Adapted from: https://www.196flavors.com
  For the dough
  2¼ lb. all-purpose flour
  2¼ Tablespoons active dry yeast
  1½ cup milk
  6 Tablespoons butter, soft
  1 teaspoon salt
  ⅓ cup sugar
  3 eggs
  2 Tablespoons freshly ground cardamom
  2 egg yolks

For the whipped cream
  2 cups heavy cream
  1 cup powdered sugar
  1 egg white

For the almond paste
  2 cups almond meal flour
  ¾ cup powdered sugar
  ⅓ cup sugar
  1 teaspoon almond extract

½ teaspoon freshly ground cardamom

Dough

Heat milk until warm. Do not overheat.

Dissolve yeast in warm milk. Add sugar, butter, eggs, and cardamom, and mix well.

Pour the flour gradually until you obtain a smooth dough (you may not have to use all the flour). Incorporate the salt.

Cover and let rise for 1 hour, in a warm place, away from drafts.

Place the dough on a floured work surface and divide it into 25 equal pieces (about 1 oz), and form balls.

Line a baking sheet with parchment paper and place each ball, making sure you leave enough space between them.

Cover and let rise for another 30 minutes.

Preheat oven to 350° F.

Brush the rolls with the beaten egg yolk and bake for 15 to 20 minutes, or until they turn golden.

Take them out of the oven, and place each of them on a rack.

Whipped cream

Pour the heavy cream and the powdered sugar in the bowl of a stand-in mixer, and whisk for a few minutes until it becomes airy and not too dense. Transfer to a pastry bag with a tip.

Almond paste

Mix the powdered sugar, the sugar, and the almond meal until obtaining a fine powder. Then sieve the powder. Beat the egg white for 1 minute.

Pour the almond powder into the egg white, add the almond extract, then knead by hand to obtain a homogeneous and firm dough. Transfer the almond paste into a pastry bag with a tip.

Smear Face Assembly

Cut out a small piece at top of each roll and take out a little bit of the inside to make space to fill.

Using the pastry bags, fill each roll with a third of almond paste and two thirds of whipped cream, then cover with the small top. Dust a little powdered sugar on top of each *semla* before serving.

Disclosure: I have never made these, but they looked similar to the Smear Faces that I grew up with and still love to this day.

Anyone in the Columbus, Ohio, area can actually get Smear Faces from http://www.thedkdiner.com/donuts/ They call them Long Boys. I've eaten these. YUM!

And in the Bellaire, Ohio, area, check out https://www.facebook.com/UniqueTreatsByJacquie/

Multiple Ohio locations of Riesbeck's Food Market https://www.riesbeckfoods.com/shop/bakery/sweet

s_and_desserts/donuts_and_pastries/riesbeck_s_s
mear_face_donuts/p/8018455

I've eaten these as well. No wonder I'm cute and
chubby!

LOADED BAKED POTATO CASSEROLE

Adapted from: *https://www.allrecipes.com/recipe/231699/easy-loaded-baked-potato-casserole/*

- 10 Yukon Gold potatoes, peeled and halved
- 6 slices bacon
- 2 cups shredded Cheddar cheese, divided
- 1 cup evaporated milk
- 1 cup sliced green onions, divided
- ½ cup sour cream
- 1 teaspoon salt
- ½ teaspoon ground black pepper

Preheat the oven to 350°F. Lightly grease a 9x13-inch baking dish.

Place potatoes into a large pot and cover with salted water; bring to a boil. Reduce heat to medium-low and simmer until tender, about 20 minutes. Drain and return potatoes to pot to dry.

Meanwhile, arrange bacon in a large skillet and cook over medium-high heat, turning occasionally, until evenly browned, about 10 minutes. Drain bacon on a paper towel-lined plate; crumble and set aside.

Combine 1½ cups Cheddar cheese, evaporated milk, ½ cup green onions, sour cream, ½ of the crumbled bacon, salt, and black pepper in the pot with potatoes. Mash with a potato masher until creamy. Spread mixture into the prepared baking dish.

Bake in the preheated oven for 25 minutes. Sprinkle with remaining Cheddar cheese, green onions, and bacon. Return to the oven and continue baking until cheese is melted, about 5 minutes more.

Roth Family's Beer Battered Pork Steaks

6-8 pork steaks
    1 full bottle any regular beer
    2 large bottles hickory flavored BBQ sauce
    Salt and pepper to taste

Barbecue pork steaks until cooked clear through. As they are cooking, simmer two large bottles of hickory-flavored barbecue sauce with one full bottle of beer in a Dutch oven. Salt and pepper to taste. When pork steaks are done, take off grill and put into sauce on the stove. Continue to simmer for 4-5 hours or until meat falls off the bone. Stir periodically to avoid burning the sauce. This is a favorite family recipe growing up.

LAYERED LEMON DELIGHT

This is one of my old recipes. When the FDA decided that raw eggs might carry the salmonella bacteria, I altered this to cook the eggs in the second layer instead of leaving them raw. Try it. I never fail to get compliments when I bake this.

Pecan Crust

1½ cups flour
1½ cup finely chopped pecan
1½ sticks of butter, melted

First Lemon Layer

2 cans (14 ounces each) sweetened condensed milk
2/3 cup lemon juice
6 egg yolks
½ teaspoon of grated lemon rind

Cream Cheese Layer

1½ blocks of cream cheese (12 oz. total)
1½ cups of powdered sugar
1½ cups Cool Whip

1½ teaspoons of vanilla

Lemon Pudding Layer

1 small (3.ounce) package vanilla instant pudding
1 small (3.4 ounce) package instant lemon pudding
2 cups whole milk
1 teaspoon lemon juice

Cool Whip Layer

1 container (16 ounce) Cool Whip
½ cup chopped pecans (optional)

Instructions for Layered Lemon Delight

Crust

Combine flour, chopped pecans, and melted butter.

Stir together until well blended and crumbly.

Press into a 9x13 baking dish.

Bake at 350° F for 10 minutes.

First Lemon Layer

Mix all the ingredients and spread evenly over the baked crust. Bake for another 15 minutes at 350° F. Let cool completely before going to the next layer. (See note at the top about the eggs.)

Cream Cheese Layer:

With electric beaters, mix the cream cheese and powdered sugar until smooth and creamy.

Fold in Cool Whip and vanilla. Then spread this mixture over the completely cooled lemon layer.

Lemon Pudding Layer:

Whisk together the pudding packets and milk.
Add lemon juice and continue to stir until thick.
Spread pudding mixture over cream cheese layer.

Cool Whip Layer

Spoon entire Cool Whip over the pudding layer (or however much you want)
   Sprinkle with finely chopped pecans if desired.

Refrigerate for 4 hours before serving. Store any leftovers in the refrigerator.

BAKED MOSTACCIOLI

Adapted from: https://www.smalltownwoman.com/baked-mostaccioli/

Ingredients

1 lb box (16 ounces) Mostaccioli

1 lb bulk Italian sausage (I used mild)

1 large green pepper, seeded, veined, and chopped (I like this better without peppers)

1 medium onion, chopped

4 garlic cloves, minced

4–5 cups marinara sauce or tomato sauce (I used the 67 ounce jar of Prego Traditional Spaghetti Sauce and saved the rest to add to the individual servings when reheated.)

1½ cups provel ropes or provolone shredded (Couldn't find this-used sliced provolone cheese)

1½ cups mozzarella shredded

½ cup parmesan cheese (Use the shredded cheese from a bag)

Kosher salt and fresh ground black pepper

Instructions

1. Bring a large pot of salted water to a boil. Cook the Mostaccioli noodles *al dente*

    according to package instructions and
    drain well.
2. Brown sausage in a skillet on medium heat.
    Remove sausage to plate; cover and keep
    warm.
3. Add peppers and onions to the same skillet
    over medium-high heat. Cook for 3-5
    minutes or until the edges of the onions
    start to brown. Add garlic and cook for 1
    additional minute. Remove from heat.
4. Combine the cooked sausage mixture,
    cooked Mostaccioli, and marinara in a
    large baking dish sprayed with non-stick
    cooking spray. Season with kosher salt and
    fresh-ground black pepper to taste.
5. Sprinkle with provolone (**I laid three slices
    of provolone down the middle of the
    casserole and broke up another slice for
    the sides**), mozzarella, and parmesan.
6. Bake at 350° F for 25-30 minutes or until
    cheese is melted and started to brown just a
    touch. If desired garnish with chopped
    fresh parsley.

Store leftovers in an airtight container in the fridge
for up to 3 days. Reheat in the microwave at reduced
power.

To freeze, cool completely and cover with two
layers of plastic. Place in the freezer on a level surface
for up to 2 months. Thaw in the fridge overnight and
reheat in the microwave.

Overnight Blueberry French Toast
Adapted from: https://www.tasteofhome.com

For Casserole

12 slices day-old bread, cut into 1 inch cubes

2 (8 ounce) packages cream cheese, cut into 1 inch cubes

1 cup fresh or frozen blueberries (if using frozen blueberries, do not thaw.)

12 eggs, beaten

2 cups milk

1 teaspoon vanilla extract

1/3 cup maple syrup

For Sauce

1 cup granulated sugar

2 Tablespoons cornstarch

1 cup water

1 cup fresh or frozen blueberries (if using frozen blueberries, do not thaw.)

1 Tablespoon butter

Directions

Lightly grease a 9x13 inch baking dish. Arrange half the bread cubes in the dish, and top with cream cheese cubes. Sprinkle 1 cup blueberries over the cream cheese, and top with remaining bread cubes.

In a large bowl, mix the eggs, milk, vanilla extract, and syrup. Pour over the bread cubes. Cover, and refrigerate overnight.

Remove casserole from the refrigerator about 30 minutes before baking. Preheat the oven to 350° F.

Cover, and bake 30 minutes. Uncover, and continue baking 25 to 30 minutes, until center is firm and surface is lightly browned.

In a medium saucepan, mix the sugar, cornstarch, and water. Bring to a boil. Stirring constantly, cook 3 to

4 minutes. Mix in the remaining 1 cup blueberries. Reduce heat, and simmer 10 minutes, until the blueberries burst.

Remove from heat and stir in the butter.

Serve with the baked French toast

HOT FUDGE CAKE

Adapted from: https://saltandbaker.com/hot-fudge-cake/
Servings: 9 (½ cup)

1¼ cup granulated sugar - divided
1 cup all-purpose flour
2/3 cup natural cocoa powder - divided
2 teaspoons baking powder
¼ teaspoon salt
½ cup milk
1/3 cup unsalted butter - melted
1½ teaspoons vanilla extract
¼ cup brown sugar - packed
1¼ cups **HOT** water (One recipe I saw said to make this boiling water. See note below.)

Preheat oven to 350° F. Spray a 9-inch square baking dish with cooking spray. Set aside.

In a large bowl combine ¾ cup granulated sugar, flour, ¼ cup cocoa powder, baking powder, and salt. Stir in the milk, melted butter, and vanilla. Using hand mixer, beat mixture until smooth.

Pour the batter into the 9-inch baking dish.

In a small bowl, combine the remaining ½ cup granulated sugar, remaining cocoa powder, and the brown sugar. Sprinkle this mixture evenly over the batter.

Carefully, pour the hot water over the chocolate/sugar mixture. You don't want to pour with such force that you create a hole or dip in the sugar mixture or cake batter underneath. I like to pour the water slowly and move my hand around the pan so the water isn't just pouring into one spot **Do not stir!**

Bake 32-35 minutes or until center is almost set. Remember, this cake has the chocolate sauce in the bottom, so don't be alarmed by thinking the cake is under-baked if you fit a toothpick in it and it comes out saucy. You know it's perfect when the hot chocolate cake on top is set and the fudge sauce pools when you serve it.

Remove from oven. Let stand for 10 minutes.

Serve in individual dishes. Top with ice cream or fresh whipped topping.

Notes

Making this hot fudge cake recipe ahead of time is kind of hard because you want to eat it warm, after you remove it from the oven to get that self-saucing chocolate pudding effect.

Store any leftovers covered in the fridge for 1-3 days. Warm leftovers in the microwave. I don't recommend freezing this cake due to the fudge sauce that forms on the bottom.

My Sister Lilly's Fabulous Churro Dip

Churro Chips

8 pack flour tortilla (taco size)
 1½ sticks of butter
 1 cup sugar
 1 Tablespoon cinnamon

Dip

8 ounce cream cheese, softened
 ½ cup and 2 Tbsp. sugar
 ½ cup French Vanilla coffee creamer
 ¾ cup heavy whipping cream
 2 teaspoons cinnamon

For Cinnamon Crumble

1 Tablespoon butter, melted
 3 Tablespoons sugar
 1 Tablespoon cinnamon

For Chips

Preheat oven to 425° F. Line a baking dish with parchment paper.

Using a sharp knife, cut flour tortillas into 8 triangles (cut whole stack at once)

In a bowl, mix together the sugar and cinnamon.

In another bowl, melt butter in microwave (about 1-1 ½ minutes)

Toss the triangles in butter, then in sugar/cinnamon mix.

Place on baking dish with parchment paper. Do not overlap.

Bake for 8-10 minute.

Let cool. (Tortillas will still be tender but will turn crunchy when they cool.)

Store in an air-tight container.

MY SISTER LILLY'S FABULOUS CHURRO DIP

My Sister Lilly's Fabulous Churro Dip

Churro Chips

8 pack flour tortilla (taco size)
  1½ sticks of butter
  1 cup sugar
  1 Tablespoon cinnamon

Dip

8 ounce cream cheese, softened
  ½ cup and 2 Tbsp. sugar
  ½ cup French Vanilla coffee creamer
  ¾ cup heavy whipping cream
  2 teaspoons cinnamon

For Cinnamon Crumble

1 Tablespoon butter, melted
  3 Tablespoons sugar
  1 Tablespoon cinnamon

For Chips

Preheat oven to 425° F. Line a baking dish with parchment paper.

Using a sharp knife, cut flour tortillas into 8 triangles (cut whole stack at once)

In a bowl, mix together the sugar and cinnamon.

In another bowl, melt butter in microwave (about 1-1 ½ minutes)

Toss the triangles in butter, then in sugar/cinnamon mix.

Place on baking dish with parchment paper. Do not overlap.

Bake for 8-10 minute.

Let cool. (Tortillas will still be tender but will turn crunchy when they cool.)

Store in an air-tight container.

For Dip

In a small bowl, whisk together cinnamon, sugar, French Vanilla Coffee Creamer, and heavy whipping cream and beat on medium-high speed until smooth, about 3-5 minutes

In a medium bowl, whip the cream cheese on medium-high until fluffy, about another 3-5 minutes.

Add cinnamon cream back to the bowl and use a spatula to fold the cream and whipped cream
   cheese together until thoroughly combined and smooth.

Mix all ingredients until creamy.

For Cinnamon Crumble

In a small bowl, use a fork to mix together butter, granulated sugar, and cinnamon until mixture is dark and crumbly. Sprinkle on top of dip.

Place in refrigerator for an hour to set.

Serve at room temperature.

BBC

1½ cups Baileys Irish Cream
1 cup pineapple juice
1½ cups cream of coconut (I use Coco López)
12 bananas (not green ones)
Ice (the amount depends on you)

Place all the ingredients except ice in a blender and blend well.

Add ice cubes, several at a time, and blend until you get the consistency of a smoothie.

You can add whipped cream or toasted coconut on top of each drink, but really, there's no need. This drink is fabulous without it. Enjoy.

BREAKFAST PIZZA

    pizza dough (homemade or store bought)
    2 tablespoons olive oil
    8 large eggs
    2 Tablespoons cool water
    1½ tablespoons butter
    1¼ cups shredded provolone
    1 cup shredded Pepper Jack cheese
    6 slices bacon, cooked crispy and coarsely chopped
    ½ pound bulk pork breakfast sausage, browned
    ½ red pepper, finely diced
    3 green onions chopped
    salsa (optional)

Preheat oven to 425° F. Oil a 10×15-inch rimmed baking sheet.

Work your pizza dough around the baking sheet by pressing gently with your fingers and hands. It may take a little time to work the pizza dough out as it tends to pull back from the sides. Once it seems to stay put, use your hands to tuck and push a little of the dough up against the side of the baking sheet, creating a crust. Bake in the oven for 7-8 minutes.

Beat the eggs and water together. Melt butter in a large nonstick skillet over low heat. Add egg mixture and cook slowly, rotating them gently with a spatula. Be sure to slightly undercook the eggs as they are cooked again in the oven. Spoon the eggs onto the pizza dough.

Top the eggs with both kinds of cheese, cooked bacon, cooked sausage, red pepper, and scallions.

Place back in the oven for 10-12 minutes, turning on the broiler for the last 1-2 minutes. Rotate the baking sheet several times during the broiling process and stay close by.

Notes

Undercook your scrambled eggs by cooking on low and cutting off the heat early. The idea is to have them set enough to hold up on the pizza dough.

The pizza can be customized with various veggies like mushrooms, zucchini, jalapenos, or potatoes.

For a change of pace, add a layer of White Gravy right under the eggs like you would pizza sauce.

STRAWBERRY SANGRIA

Adapted from: https://www.acouplecooks.com/strawberry-sangria/

Yields 6

Ingredients

4 cups whole fresh strawberries

2 Tablespoons granulated sugar

1 bottle dry rosé wine, chilled

½ cup triple sec, Cointreau or Grand Marnier

1 handful mint leaves

1 orange, sliced into rounds

1 lemon, sliced into rounds

Soda water, for serving (optional)

For the garnish: Fresh mint, cocktail skewers

Instructions

Reserve 6 strawberries and set aside. Slice the remaining strawberries and place them in a blender. Sprinkle them with the sugar and stir.

Let the strawberries stand for 20 minutes at room temperature. Then add ½ cup of the wine to the blender and blend until strawberries are fully pureed. Pour this through a fine mesh strainer/sieve into a large pitcher and use a spatula to press the strawberry puree through. Discard the seeds.

Add the remaining wine and triple sec to the pitcher. Then add the fresh mint, orange and lemon rounds. Slice the 6 reserved strawberries and add them to pitcher.

Stir and refrigerate the pitcher for at least 1 hour, or up to 4 hours. (Don't go beyond 4 hours or the fruit texture starts to degrade.)

To serve, pour the sangria into ice-filled glasses, and top with a splash of soda water (if desired). Add fruit to each glass, preferably on long skewers for easy snacking.

ACKNOWLEDGMENTS

For the several years, I have been dealing with family health issues. Life has a funny way of bringing you to your knees at times. Writing about Jordan and her wonderful friends helped take my mind off my own problems and concentrate on just how much fun I could have with the Empire Apartment gang once again.

As always, Of course, I have to give credit to my siblings Don Roth, Dorothy Bennett, and Lillian Magistro. I know the other five are cheering me on from heaven. Without them, I might never have known how to love unconditionally.

Next comes my husband, kids, and grandkids who make every day worth getting out of bed. Thanks, Dan, Brody and Abby, Nicole and Dennis, Grayson, Caden, Ellie, and Alice. I love you all so much.

And the Bunko Babes, who have been my sisters from other mothers for over thirty years and who keep me supplied with humorous wisecracks, all of which go directly into my books.

My biggest supporter is my agent, Christine Witthohn, who has made this journey way easier than it should have been, both as my voice to the editors as well as my friend. I love this woman.

And then there's my critique partner, Joni Sauer-Folger, who never fails to ask, "WTF?" when I get a little crazy. Without her, heaven only knows what you might be reading.

For this book, I had Chris Keniston, author of her own wonderful romances, beta read for me. She kept me honest and reminded me when I wasn't clear enough. Check out her books. For the first time, my fabulous daughter-in-law also beta read for me. Abby Lipperman used her eagle eye to find all the bad grammar, etc. And thanks to the wonderful woman who edited this book for my publisher. She was so complimentary and made me smile on a day that was definitely a tough one.

And lastly to my publisher, Tanya Anne Crosby, as well as all the people at Oliver Heber Books, who go out of their way to make this process so painless. I am so grateful to have found them.

ALSO BY LIZ LIPPERMAN

As Liz Lipperman

Jordan McAllister Mysteries
Liver Let Die
Beef Stolen-Off
Murder for the Halibut
Chicken Caccia-Killer
Smothered, Covered & Dead
Enchi Lotta Bodies
Steak Through the Heart

Romantic Suspense
Can't Buy Me Love

As Lizbeth Lipperman

Garcia girls Mysteries
Heard it Through the Grapevine
Jailhouse Glock
Mission to Kill
Rock Around the Corpse

Stand-alone Romantic Mysteries
Shattered
Mortal Deception

Sweepers Inc. Romantic Thriller

SWEEPERS: A Kiss to Die For

SWEEPERS: Die Once More

ABOUT THE AUTHOR

Liz Lipperman started writing many years ago, even before she retired from the medical field. Wasting many years thinking she was a romance writer but always having to deal with the pesky villains who kept popping up in all her stories, she finally gave up and decided since she read mysteries and obviously wrote them, why fight it? She has two mystery series--the Jordan McAllister Mysteries (formerly the Clueless Cook Series) and The Garcia Girls Mysteries (formerly A Dead Sister Talking Series)which are available in all formats. You might also want to check out her romantic thrillers, Mortal Deception and Shattered and a romantic short titled Can't Buy Me Love. Also, be watching for the debut of a new romantic suspense series titled SWEEPERS coming sometime next year. She wants readers to know that her G rated cozies are written as Liz Lipperman and her R rated, grittier mysteries as Lizbeth Lipperman. Check out her web page for a more detailed listing of her books along with reviews and trailers. www.lizlipperman.com

She lives north of Dallas with her HS sweetheart hubby. When she's not writing she spends her time doting on her four wonderful grandchildren.